WHACK JOB

Also by Pete O'Brien

Ignorance, USA

WHACK JOB

Pete O'Brien

Impolitic Press
2023

Copyright 2023 by Impolitic Press

All rights reserved. No part of this book may be reproduced or used in any manner without the prior written permission of the publisher, except for the use of brief quotations in a print or online review.

This book is a work of fiction. All the characters in this book are fictitious and any resemblance to actual persons living or dead is purely coincidental.

ISBN: 979-8-9880507-5-9

Printed in the U.S.A.

Published by
IMPOLITIC PRESS

For Susan and Linas

BOOK ONE

The Prototypes

Pete O'Brien

ONE

It took a while for Jeff Land to start recognizing them, but the disadvantages of being born a privileged white male in post-postmodern America were now starting to manifest themselves in painful abundance. His problems had all likely started the moment after his birth when his parents, both staunch Libertarians, had placed on his birth certificate the name of a former U.S President and slaveowner notorious for having had an exploitative sexual relationship with an odalisque in his possession. In that one move, he was anointed a patrician in all likelihood doomed to socio-gender associations of the wrong sort as well as being a sort of pariah in the realms of ever-evolving politically correct social discourse, most notably in regards to New Age feminism's rage against the patriarchy and how his own generation of women were choosing to react aggressively to its inherent and persistent injustices.

In his early education, administered in large part by middle-class white men and women who had never heard of Howard Zinn let alone read his progressive treatise on a somewhat more accurate history of the United States and not the one that an older privileged white class seemed intent on shoving down his throat, Jeff was fed what can only be recognized now as a typical serving of miscues, since largely debunked in higher intellectual circles. For a young boy, as sensitive and good-natured as he was, these misstated "facts" were not helpful to his overall early development. Not specifically told so in so many words, he'd been persuaded to believe by implication that men made better presidents and corporate chief executives than women, only white people fought against the British in the American Revolutionary War, The Civil War was fought to free Negro slaves, Thomas Edison invented the light bulb, Andrew Carnegie was a benevolent philanthropist, World War Two was fought to free Europe's Jews from concentration camps and to punish Hirohito for bombing Pearl Harbor, Socialism was an evil and Godless plot to take over America perpetrated by shady immigrant foreigners, the Vietnam War was fought to halt the infectious spread of Communism, and the only Black men who'd ever done anything notable in American history were Booker T. Washington, Martin Luther King, and maybe Jackie Robinson. At the same time, in his Saturday morning catechism classes at St. John the Evangelist Catholic Church in his hometown of Pawling, New York, he was taught to regurgitate the words of an absurdly improbable Apostle's Creed, crafted by Christian theologians seized by a mind-control fervor in late 6th Century France, a period also commonly referred to as Europe's Dark Ages. This was the education of Jeff Land up until he was providentially delivered into an entire other realm of human discourse, in this case made manifest by his acceptance to the Parsons School of Design on lower Fifth Avenue in the heart of New York City's Greenwich Village. Situated just an hour and a half from Pawling by commuter train and no more than two hours by car, it might just as well have been located on the dark side of the moon for all its intellectual and social proximity.

It should be noted here that Jeff is twenty-one years old when this story opens, an age where all young men regardless of race, creed or country of origin operate for the most part in a fever-pitch frenzy of sexual obsession. By the time they reach that age, visual image stimulation of the amygdalae region of the male brain's limbic system is hitting on all cylinders, testosterone production is at its peak, and the post-teenage male is in a near-perpetual state of horniness. For a young man released from the chains of parental supervision and turned loose in the wilds of lower Manhattan with a freedom limited only by the funds at his disposal, the reality that Jeff had been introduced to upon his arrival in the city was akin to a pig being introduced to a very large wallow of sloppy mud. In practically no time he'd gotten himself a Billy Idol haircut, an earring, a couple square feet of gaudy ink, and taken to wandering the Village in denim work shirts with dabs of paint on them and stove-pipe skinny jeans as one of a legion of kids who believed themselves terminally hip. Once he'd gotten his bearings he'd joined a band—he played decent drums and could sing on key—that had evolved to playing regular gigs at venues like the Bowery Ballroom and Arlene's Grocery.

With a vivid imagination, a knack for drawing, some better-than-decent carpentry skills, and a broad knowledge of tools developed while spending his childhood and teenage years in his father's

Whack Job

commercial cabinetry shop, Jeff had decided to major in furniture design, figuring that it might not be as likely a venue for meeting a wide variety of free-thinking, promiscuous young women as fashion or interior design but that it would at least be a means of getting his dick in that door. When he'd arrived at Parsons, it turned out he could already draw better than anyone at the school and that his impressive portfolio full of furniture ideas, rendered in great detail, had tended to intimidate a majority of the design faculty. In the three years since, he'd managed to turn several of those ideas into actual pieces of furniture, one of which had recently won a national design competition.

It was on a mid-week afternoon late in the first semester of his junior year when Jeff received a call from a third-year MFA graduate student, asking his advice on a chair she was building for her final project. He knew very few of the grad students other than those who worked as TA's in the undergraduate design program and the woman's name wasn't familiar to him. All the same, he agreed to meet her in the school's big production shop later that evening.

Amy Brock turned out to be a ballsy Amazon of a woman not much shorter than Jeff's own six-foot-two, her entire demeanor aimed to suggest that she owned any space that she occupied. How the hell had he never heard of this person he wondered as he stopped to observe her from a distance, taking in the pile of straight, jet-black hair tied up in a red bandana and the distressed leather shop apron worn over a ratty rock concert t-shirt and black leggings. She appeared to be the process of fashioning an uncomfortable looking rocking chair out of molded Plexiglas and strips of walnut bent and laminated to form a supporting frame. As he then approached her, he caught the scents of Frankincense, Patchouli and Clove with maybe a hint of Orange Peel.

"I like the contrast of the clear Plexi and the walnut," he said

The scowl of disdain she fed him would likely melt dry ice, but the eyes that threw it were the greenest he'd ever seen, set in a face that had some East Asian somewhere in her recent ancestry. Predictably, he was more than a little taken aback by the overall impact of this gal.

"What?" she asked. "I'd think that somebody who just won a

national design award would at least have some taste. This is a piece of shit."

Jeff moved to view the chair from a different angle and shrugged. "Not totally. It's just that the place where a butt would go doesn't work. You could sit on it, sure, just like all that furniture Frank Lloyd Wright designed. It looks really cool, but ouch."

Her project involved a two-foot-wide sheet of 3/8-inch Plexiglas, bent and curled like the front-end of Santa's sleigh and mounted nose-down on the walnut frame. Nothing was working there and she was clearly struggling to figure out just what that was.

"At this stage, it's pretty much garbage," she grumbled. "But I'm sure that somebody who just won a national design award can come up with a solution," she said.

"If I were you, I'd think about vacuum-forming your plastic to soften those lines and give it some actual human contour," he said.

Her scowl became a deep frown as she turned to contemplate her creation more directly. "Oh, sure. Like that's never been done before."

Several loose wisps of jet-black hair had escaped the confines of her bandana to frame her face, further forcing Jeff's focus onto her eyes. They gleamed like a pair of backlit emeralds, recalling that famous *National Geographic* cover photo of a beautiful young Afghani woman staring directly at the camera's lens.

"So, if you don't want to be at least slightly redundant, just what is it that you're trying to accomplish here?" he asked.

"To create a humanized chair for both home and office," she replied. "Every piece of really comfortable furniture being manufactured these days looks so tech-y, like it was designed for the Starship Enterprise, not somebody's living space, which is where more than half of today's workforce works. A chair that looks like a friend instead of something that always seems to be demanding you sit your ass down and be productive. It's something that I've been thinking about for a long time but still have no idea how to accomplish."

"I suppose it needs to be gender neutral, right?" he said. "A they/their chair, not a his or hers."

She frowned. "Isn't all furniture?"

"Up 'til now? Pretty much," he said. "But why does yours have to be? Men generally have skinnier butts and wider shoulders. Women mostly have bigger butts and narrower torsos. That's not sexist. It's just a physical fact. So, why not embrace those anatomical differences and make two chairs?" He paused to gesture in the air with his hands. "You know, like two different famous marble statues. The Venus de Milo and Michelangelo's David chairs. With a decent mold, vacuum-forming could probably capture enough of the right two human bodies to make them pretty realistic."

As off-the-wall as the idea might have sounded, it seemed to give her pause. She considered the idea for a long moment while staring at her own failed creation, then waved a hand in the air between them, a gesture that was asking for more information. "Just how much do you know about vacuum forming? You sound like you've had experience."

"Not me. A friend of mine works for a custom kayak builder. His boss has this dope-ass set-up where he plays with a lot of new forms. Mostly in polypropylene, but I'm pretty sure Plexi would work, too. But if I was going to make chairs like that, I'd use white plex instead of clear."

"And why is that?" she asked.

"So they would actually look like marble; that those two statues had just been sitting in them and then stood up." These ideas were coming to him on the fly, but he sort of liked the mental images forming in his mind's eye.

"I couldn't exactly use those Venus and David statues for my molds," she said. "Whose bodies would you suggest instead? Yours and mine? You look like you're in decent shape and I work out like a maniac. My lovers generally tend to remark on just how much it shows."

If her aim was to shock him, she likely got satisfaction in watching how he nervously shifted on his feet and quickly averted his eyes.

"Anybody's you want," he said. "They're your chairs."

"I assume we'd need to make plaster casts first, correct?" The look of challenge she was projecting had grown bolder.

He nodded.

"Take your shirt off," she ordered.

"Right here?" he asked.

"As good a place as any," she said. "I want to see what your back and shoulders look like."

Suddenly self-conscious beneath that intense green-eyed gaze, he glanced around to see who might be hiding in the shadows there. The shop was mausoleum quiet. Hoping to Christ he was in the clear, he pulled his t-shirt up over his head to stand bare-chested before her, wondering at how quickly she'd gotten him to go there.

"Turn around and undo your belt. I need to see your butt, too."

"Really?" Suddenly he wasn't feeling quite so cocky confident as he had on first arriving for this so-called consultation.

"What? You know you've got nothing to be ashamed of. Grow a pair, Prodigy-boy."

Having spent much of his childhood hiking the Appalachian Trail near his home in Pawling and helping neighboring farmers throw hay and split mountains of winter firewood, Jeff was lanky while also muscular. He met her challenge with some defiance of his own, turning to loosen his belt and ease his jeans down over his naked ass.

His new acquaintance stepped closer, lightly touching his back, fingers tracing the contours of it while slowly drifting down until they cupped one of his butt cheeks. When she spoke, her breath was hot in his left ear, the scent of patchouli, frankincense and clove now heavy in his nose.

"You just might do," she growled.

"Just might? I haven't even said I want the job."

Her lips came even closer as her hand tightened its grip. "Of course you want the job, Prodigy-boy. Every male in this fucking program wants the job. Ask around."

TWO

"Holy shit, dude! Amy Brock? That bitch is hot!"

DeShawn Lewis, Jeff's roommate in an apartment owned by Parsons and located around the corner from the school on West 12th Street, was a dreadlocked Brother from Louisville who fancied himself a sculptor. He, too, was in his third year. Jeff had just asked him what he knew about making large-scale plaster castings.

"I really couldn't tell," he admitted. "She was wearing a shop apron. All I know? She's really tall and has these amazing eyes."

DeShawn seemed mystified that Jeff had never heard of the woman. "Where you been hiding, Homes?" he asked. "Everybody knows she's also rich as fuck. Her daddy's like a billionaire or some shit. And she wants you to help her do what?"

Jeff had somehow managed to miss the Amy Brock memo but then again he wasn't as socially involved at Parsons as Dee and most of his peers at the school all seemed to be. If he wasn't in his room working on some new furniture design, most of his social life revolved around his band, practice sessions in Brooklyn, and playing gigs.

"Make two anatomically correct, vacuum-formed Plexiglas chairs like the negatives of marble statues, one male and one female," he replied. "It was my stupid idea and now she wants to use me for one of them. To do that, we have to make a mold of my back and butt."

DeShawn looked at him now with even more disbelief. "Now you're yanking my dick, Homes. Ain't no fucking way."

"Are you saying it can't be done? Because I know it can."

"Course it can. Take a shit-ton of plaster, but that stuff's cheap, especially if your daddy's rich. But what I ain't believing is, why you?"

Jeff had asked himself the same question at least a dozen times while heading home from the shop that past night. The most reasonable answer he'd managed to come up with was that he'd just won a national design award. "I guess you'll have to ask her that yourself, Dee. Maybe because I've got some actual design sense? Just tell me what you know about plaster casting."

Still having trouble pushing his disbelief out of the current equation, DeShawn wasn't about to be distracted by Jeff's attempt to steer him back on track. "Every grad student in the school has tried to get up with that bitch, Bro. They all convinced she's a dyke."

Considering how his roomie had just minutes ago described the woman's hotness factor with so much apparent awe, Jeff, a card-carrying red-blooded male with an abiding interest in getting up with as many hot chicks as he could, didn't know why he suddenly felt like he needed to get defensive there. "I didn't ask for your advice on how to get into her pants," he complained. "I just asked how we can make some big plaster molds."

"You serious about this shit."

"Why else would I ask?"

"I dunno. I thought maybe you was needing somebody to laugh in your face. Only reason I could think of." DeShawn then paused to think. "You gonna need someone knows how to mix big batches of plaster up quick. That shit goes off fast. I know this one chick in my program did a project doing casts of dudes' erect johnsons, had all kinda problems. They complained about how hot it got, going off. Everybody took Viagra, went in rock hard, and them molds all came out limp noodles. Maybe you should ask her."

The next afternoon, Jeff invited Amy Brock to meet with him in the Parson's sculpture studio along with DeShawn and Monica Lopez, she of penis-casting repute. This time Amy had her hair contained in a yellow bandana instead of a red one, with Timberland boots working in interesting contrast to some black fishnet tights with gaping holes in them and an over-size Boy Pablo Leave Me Alone t-shirt, knotted at her waist. It left her midriff exposed enough get her slut-shamed by the radical feminist element on campus but otherwise, DeShawn's assessment was pretty much spot-on. Amy Brock, Amazon extraordinaire, was a definite smoke show.

She and Monica Lopez had apparently already met. In contrast to Amy's Amazonian dynamic, Monica was pint-size and eating-disorder thin, with short, spikey chartreuse hair, arms covered in bright ink, ear gauges, and one of those u-shaped gizmos hanging through her Columella that always left Jeff thinking of silver snot.

Whack Job

The idea that the woman's MFA project had involved casting a wide variety of male penises with failed erections had seemed somewhat intriguing until he actually met the woman, at which point any such curiosity took immediate flight. Where she'd had managed to find enough willing subjects was the first question he'd asked himself, and then guessed you probably had to get to know her.

At that moment, the would-be sculptress was speaking. "So, if I got this right, you want to make negative molds of his naked ass and yours in plaster, then pour positives from them to take to some industrial vacuum-form company to make your chair seats."

"That's the plan," Amy replied. "If you think you could help me with that, I can pay you."

Monica lifted her chin toward Jeff. "Why him?"

"It was his idea. Besides that, he's evenly proportioned and in excellent shape. I want my chair to be a celebration of the human form, Michelangelo style, not Lucien Freud."

Jeff glanced nervously at Monica. "How do you see this going down?" he asked.

"I think we should invite the whole Art Department, make it a party, just like we do when we pour hot metal," Monica replied. She turned to Amy. "You buy the plaster and the beer and let me have access to those molds once you're done with them, you don't have to pay me nothing. I'm thinking of how good a video of this will look in my portfolio."

"Whoa! Wait a minute," Jeff blurted. "A party and a fucking video?"

Monica stared right back at him, unflinching. "You privileged white dudes been exploiting women on film ever since Louis Le Prince invented motion pictures. You owe us a little Post-Modern quid pro quo, dude. It's time you get to know what it feels like to have a whole bunch of bitches objectifying your fine white ass."

Later, as Jeff was leaving that meeting feeling a lot like he'd just been ambushed, Amy hailed him from down the corridor.

"Prodigy-boy. Wait up."

He turned to see her hustling toward him.

"How's it feel to have the privileged white male tables turned on you like that?" she asked. "Sucks the big one, right?"

He knew that at twenty-four or five or whatever she was and coming from the kind of undoubtedly well-travelled background that having a billionaire daddy most likely provided for, she was undoubtedly a lot more worldly than he was. Still, the stubborn upstate rural rube living at his core was determined to find and establish some sort of equal footing there. "You think that's the first time?" he asked. "They're calling it Third Wave feminism now, not the first or even the second. And you're talking to the wrong white male if you think I've enjoyed much privilege. My dad's a cabinet maker. I'm here on a combo of scholarships, a Pell Grant, and student loans. Any spending money I have I earned working ever since I was twelve. Fuck you. Find some other whipping boy to help you make your shitty chairs." And that said, he turned and strode away while she called out to him, asking him to stop. Instead, he lifted a hand to flip her the bird.

THREE

DeShawn was off somewhere, probably partying with his sculpture homies as he was so often prone to do, while Jeff, still licking his wounds from his earlier humiliation, was in no mood to go out. Happy to have the apartment to himself, he was seated on the sofa with a sketch-pad in his lap, toying with an idea for a simple straight-backed dining chair, when a soft knock came at his front door. It was a Thursday with end-of-term approaching fast. Anyone home in his building that night was most likely eating Adderall by the handful and working frantically on final projects. He wasn't expecting anyone as he drained his near-empty beer, set the sketch-pad aside, and stood to cross to see who'd come calling.

"Who is it?" he asked through the door.

When his question met with silence, he leaned to peer through the peep and saw a woman he didn't recognize at first. Long black hair hung to gently frame a somewhat familiar face. Jade green turtleneck sweater and a single strand of pearls, sleek, green-framed European-style glasses to match the sweater and…the eyes. His tongue then stuck in his mouth, mid-swallow. How the fuck did Amy Brock known where to find him?

She spoke before he could when he opened the door,.

"I can read your mind, Prodigy-boy. You want to know how I found you."

"I guess that's the first question that came to it," he said.

She held up a hand to discourage further interruption. "And your second question is what the hell am I doing here."

"Yeah, pretty much."

"Your buddy DeShawn gave me your address. And I'm here to apologize." She pointed past him into the living room to indicate the empty beer bottle on his coffee table. "You in the mood for a few more of those? I'm buying."

In contrast to how she'd dressed earlier, the rest of her was as conservatively turned out as the hair, the pearls and the sweater. Tailored black slacks. Simple black mid-ankle boots. The arms of a black hoodie were pulled around her hips and knotted at her waist.

That art student arrogance she'd worn earlier like a suit of armor had been left propped in a corner somewhere.

"Where you got in mind?" he asked.

She shrugged. "Somewhere non-studenty. Considering the fact that NYU and the New School are practically on top of each other down here that's a tall order in this neighborhood. I say we grab a cab and go north."

"Do I need to change?" He was barefoot, in jeans and a long-sleeve Carhart t-shirt.

"Shoes might be good. And maybe a jacket. It's a little chilly out but not really cold yet."

Five minutes later, Jeff found himself standing next to Amy Brock in the elevator, headed for the lobby and street. "That's a radically different look from the one I saw at school the other day," he said. "You lead two lives?"

She took a deep breath and sighed as she nodded. "Sort of. I just had dinner with my dad. I learned a long time ago that it doesn't pay to be confrontational when I'm asking him for money."

Jeff guessed it was none of his business but couldn't resist asking anyway. "Money for what?"

She turned to pat his arm and smile. "Down, boy. That's part of the reason I just knocked on your door. We'll talk about it over drinks."

They ended up at the Black Sheep on Third Avenue in Murray Hill, where both of them ordered Guinness with Green Spot Irish whiskey chasers. Amy suggested they take a booth in the back where they could talk. Seated across from Jeff, she lifted her glass to click it with his.

"Cheers, Prodigy-boy. I'm sorry about how Monica and I got up your ass today. I shouldn't have said those things about your presumed privilege. You were the one doing me the solid. My bad."

Jeff looked at her in surprise. Where was the ballsy, I-could-give-a-shit woman he'd seen the other two times they'd met? An about-face this radical could only mean one thing. She wanted something from him and he couldn't imagine what that might be. She said she'd just had dinner with her dad to ask him for money.

Whack Job

What, he wondered, could he have to do with that?

"Not that I don't appreciate free beer, but I think this is the point where you tell me what the fuck this is all about," he said. "I should be home working on my portfolio."

"When I heard it was some third-year who'd won that big award and that you draw like Leonardo DiVinci, I asked Jen Rumson what she thought of you," she said.

Jen was a professor teaching one of Jeff's design classes that semester.

"She told me that you're probably the best that any of the current faculty at Parsons has ever seen. That you've got that special eye that no one can teach."

Jeff was surprised to hear it. Jennifer Rumson was a flamboyantly arrogant gay woman who rarely made a positive comment to any male in his class. He'd always wondered about people like her. The ones who seemed to think giving out positive strokes might somehow detract from their own sense of self-worth.

"Interesting. My impression is that she pretty much hates it that I breathe the same air as her."

"Jen can be a bitch sometimes. But I trust her opinion."

"What's that got to do with why I'm sitting here right now?"

She lifted her glass to take a sip of her beer while those remarkable green eyes maintained direct contact. "For the past three years, ever since I started grad school here, I've been looking for a collaborative partner. One with a better eye than mine but one still compatible. Up until two days ago, I'd about given up. Then your cocky-confident ass not only tells me what's wrong with my latest design, but actually has a much better idea that I can use, to build off what I already have."

Jeff was a little mortified to hear her put it quite like that. When he started to speak in response, she hurried to interrupt him yet again. It seemed to be a habit of hers.

"Don't. You were right. After I talked to Jen, I asked our program director if I could see some of your other work. And, honestly? I was pretty blown away. They may not have admitted as much to you, but Jen tells me that she and the rest of them are all a little intimidated. She also said you know the woodshop and production end of these things better than any of them do."

No instructor at Parsons had ever given Jeff an indicator of their being intimidated. In fact, to that point, it felt to him like his various professors had been nothing but hyper-critical with their questions. Why would he do it like that? Why that detail? It's superfluous. How many times do you think that's been done before? Etc. He couldn't count how many times he'd told one or another of them to fuck off, at least in his mind.

"I spent my whole childhood in a production woodshop," he said. "My dad and uncles had me running tools by myself by the time I was twelve. I could read shop drawings before I graduated middle school."

She played with the edge of the damp coaster beneath her beer, picking at it with a fingernail painted a bright jade. Green was definitely her color.

"If I want this thing I'm proposing to my father to actually work, I need someone like you," she said.

He had to admit he was intrigued. This same woman who'd looked like a rip-off version of Siouxsie Sioux that afternoon in the sculpture studio and now looked more like a recruiting poster for the Junior League sounded like she was getting ready to offer him a job.

"What thing?"

"I got into this program because I want to start an American haute couture furniture line accessible to the middle class. One that rivals anything anyone is doing right now in Chicago, Miami, or Milan. From Ray and Charles Eames to Florence Knoll to Edward Wormley to Sam Maloof and Gustav Stickley, America has this fabulous tradition of producing quality furniture that people actually used. And that seems to have gotten lost, buried by mountains of throw-away crap sold by companies like Ikea and mostly manufactured on the cheap in China. I want to celebrate that old tradition. Bring it back."

"What about guys like Jonathan Nesci?" Jeff asked. "He's American and super hip and happening right now."

"And surviving because art galleries and their rich clientele fucking love him. I want to build a company where I can mass produce award winning designs so middle-class people can have access to them."

"And that's what this dinner with your dad was about?"

She nodded. "He thinks I'm out of my mind. He owns a heavy equipment rental empire. Construction cranes, giant earthmovers and excavators. You want to build a skyscraper in Dubai or a dam in Nairobi, he's your guy. Forget about aesthetics. A chair is something you sit in to get work done, not to fucking look at when you're not sitting in it."

"So, considering that mindset, how did your dinner go?"

"I played off his guilt."

Jeff knew nothing about her upbringing or personal life and wondered what that might mean. "His guilt," he said.

"Yep. Right after I was born my mom sank into a serious post-partum depression. So serious that he shipped her to a clinic in L.A. near her French-Vietnamese family for almost a year. I and a wet-nurse were passed around between two aunts and my grandmother, who was born in Saigon and barely spoke English."

So that was the hint of Asia he saw in her eyes.

"Daddy was too busy screwing this conniving bitch who worked in his company's finance department and who got pregnant a month before mom was released from that clinic. He filed for divorce and the conniving bitch is now my step-mother."

Jeff felt himself blink. "Cold," he said. "Where's your mom now?"

"Re-married and living in Scarsdale."

"And your dad lives here in the city?"

"Sometimes, but mostly in East Hampton when he isn't traveling. In addition to getting a huge settlement when they split, my mom fought him for primary custody of me and won. Ever since, for the past twenty-five years, he's been trying to buy his way back into my life."

Jeff shot his Green Spot, replaced the glass on the table and sat back against the banquette. "Hence the guilt."

She smiled. "It comes in handy sometimes. Mostly though,

he's just a hypocritical pain in my ass."

"I assume this dalliance of his and the resulting pregnancy produced a half-brother or sister, correct?"

That got him an exaggerated eye-roll. "Oh, yeah. And she's a whole other nightmare. My step-mother miscarried right after they were married and then had Katya, her own personal mini-me. Both of them are total bitches."

"Katya. Interesting name. Is the step-mother Eastern European?"

"Bulgarian."

Jeff was still attempting to get a handle on the dynamics there and trying to imagine the way people must have treated this woman growing up. It had to have been super-strange to live in a bubble like that.

"And this step-mother is how old now?" he asked.

"Forty-six. Dad is sixty-eight."

"And attractive I assume?"

"If you like them hard as flint, she might be your dream girl. Five inches shorter than me but smoking-hot. Works out even harder than I do to maintain that shit." She drained the remainder of her Guinness. "Another round?"

When he nodded, she pushed her glass toward him and followed it with a twenty pulled from a front pocket of her slacks. "I buy, you fly."

It took a few minutes for the barman to properly pour two glasses of Guinness and so while Jeff waited he had plenty of time to digest most of what he'd just been fed. This woman who was definitely way out of his economic league had just asked if he wanted to collaborate with her on something even his wildest ambitions had never imagined. Even design students who won national awards were generally forced into harness at one big manufacturer or another. Either that, or to labor in obscurity creating one-off works of furniture art for thirty years while eating canned beans and teeny-weenies before anyone started to recognize them. He knew that if she controlled the purse strings of the venture she'd just described, she would also have the ultimate power in any partnership they formed. How much did that idea bother him? And if he did accept her proposal, how did he protect himself over the long haul? From the chair he'd seen her trying to build, it seemed obvious that she needed someone like him in her corner, but how much equity would she be willing to surrender to his side of that equation?

She was on her phone when he got back to their booth and he had to sit a moment waiting for her to conclude her conversation. From what little he was able to gather, it had irritated her.

"Boyfriend," she growled. She reached around to shove her phone into a back pocket. "The more he gets on my nerves, the more I ask myself why I need one of those."

"He live here in the city?"

"Brooklyn. He's a chef. Brazilian, and prone to deep jealousy. I told him I was having drinks with you and he wanted to know who you are and insisted he come join us. I told him no. He's mad."

"I wouldn't care if he did," Jeff said.

"But I would. We're talking business here. Besides, I don't need to feed that kind of insecurity. It creeps me out." She paused to sip the foam off her new beer and then focused on him more directly. "So, where were we?" This was followed quickly by a raised index finger, the brightness of her gaze intensifying to match the shade of that fingernail. "That's right. I was reading your mind again. You're wondering what kind of equity you might have in a partnership where I and my dad control all the money. That, and how you can protect the time and ideas you'll need to invest."

It was so uncanny that Jeff felt himself blink. What was she, some sort of witch? "Let me ask you," he said. "Do you get this same kind of interstellar message every time your Brazilian boyfriend grabs some server's ass at his restaurant? Because you know he does, right?"

She was in the middle of taking another sip of her beer and almost choked on it. Finally recovered from her coughing fit, she gasped, "Don't do that!" And then, "Of course I know he does. And don't you worry your pretty head about Rey. You spend much time around me, you'll learn that none of them really lasts all that long."

Ray?"

"Reynaldo. Right now, it feels like he's just about run his course. For me, jealousy is a dealbreaker."

As attractive as he found her, Jeff wondered just how much more information he wanted to hear on that particular subject. It was time to push this conversation back onto its tracks.

"Let's say your father decides to back you in this. What are my protections?" he asked.

Apparently, she'd already worked through all that. "A contractual fifty-fifty split of half our net profits. My dad will want the other half of our net for putting up the cash, but he'll have no say in how the actual business is run. You'll have absolute veto power over any proposed design project, and so will I. In other words, both of us have to agree. That protects your personal artistic integrity, but here's the kicker. At least in the public eye, this won't be an actual partnership."

"How so?" he asked.

"I intend to be the face of the business and if you'll hear me out, I'll explain why."

Jeff blinked. "How do you figure I'd want to be a part of something like that?"

"Because it's almost guaranteed to be successful. Right now, our society is starving for smart and ambitious young women of color to champion in business. I intend to take advantage of that fact. Call our company Brocking Chair and put my name on all of our designs, just like Alexander Graham Bell did on the telephone."

Once again, Jeff was confused. "Wasn't that because he invented it?"

"No. A black man working for him named Lewis Latimer invented it. Same dude credited with helping Edison make a lightbulb that actually burned for more than ten minutes. The problem for Latimer back then was, if you hoped to see an invention make it to market, you needed a white male to front it for you."

All of a sudden Jeff realized exactly where she was going with all this. "And today, because of the shitty history of how white males have treated minorities and women in business, a lot of that is being flipped on its head."

She fed him a smug smile. "Jen said you were smart. Me? I did a dual major in design and marketing as an undergrad. And I've been thinking about nothing but this for the past seven years. To make this work we can't be Charles and Ray Eames. It's got to be a young, ambitious, solo Eurasian woman entrepreneur. I need you to design the furniture and let me be the front bitch."

"With a fifty-fifty split on our end, even though it's your name up in lights?"

She nodded. "In five years, there'll be a buy-out clause where we can seek other financing and take my dad out of the equation if that's what we want to do."

Again, this was a lot to digest. Jeff had to sit a minute trying to wrap his brain around everything he'd just been told. At least on the surface it sounded like a pretty good deal, in spite of the fact that he would be confined to working in her shadow. If he had ambitions of any of his designs ever seeing the light of day and him owning major equity in them, it seemed like an awesome opportunity. "I'm gonna need a little time to think about all this," he said. "If I go this route with you, it'll mean me dropping out of school and not getting my degree."

She'd clearly thought about that, too, and didn't even hesitate. "Think of yours as a Bill Gates and Harvard-type situation. He showed up there already knowing more about writing code than anyone on their faculty could teach him. From what I've seen of your portfolio, I think you're in pretty much that same boat."

"I guess I'll need to meet your dad, too. Just so I know who I'm signing my life over to."

"Again, I've pre-read your mind on that one, too. Tonight, when I told him about you, he said he wants to meet you. We're invited to dinner at their place Saturday night."

"Reynaldo invited, too?"

"He works Saturdays."

"And their place is where?"

"East Hampton. You're gonna love my half-sister, Katya. On the conniving bitch spectrum, she and my step-mom are almost a matched pair."

Jeff was still digesting her recently recounted family history and now sought to work the math. Amy's father had gotten this step-mother pregnant before divorcing her mother. Then she'd miscarried and eventually gotten pregnant again. "How old is she?" he asked.

"Same age as you. Pack a toothbrush by the way. We'll likely be staying the night."

"How do we get out there? Train?" East Hampton was 90 miles away, located in the most extreme reaches of Long Island and a place where mega-moguls and movie stars were reported to frolic. Jeff had never been there.

"No, lucky us. He's sending the helicopter."

FOUR

After their cab dropped Jeff back at his building he entered the lobby feeling a little unsteady on his pins and knew it owed to more than the three beers and Irish whiskies he'd imbibed. For a kid from the sticks, this was way too much all at once. An Amazon Eurasian grad student—who also just happened to be a billionaire's daughter—had just asked him to quit school and join her in a furniture design and manufacturing venture, albeit with some fairly curious strings attached. But what an opportunity. Even if a designer won a few awards right out of the chute, he or she generally had to labor in obscurity for years before this kind of break ever came their way. And here his was practically being dumped in his lap. Because she was a woman and a Parsons alum with a mega-rich father, news of her new enterprise would be guaranteed to create a splash in the business press.

For a kid who hailed from far outside the New York world of big money, those realizations, once chewed, swallowed, and at least partially digested, created more dread than euphoria. Jeff started to ask himself how many ways he might be able to screw this up. From fiction and movie plots he knew that the last thing he wanted to do was get involved with his partner, no matter how strong that temptation might sooner or later become. He'd never been that attracted to women almost as tall as he was, but that probably owed to the fact that six-foot females were generally as rare as eighty-degree days in January. It seemed fortunate that this particular one seemed to see him more as a gifted toddler than a peer, in spite of that naked butt grab.

He also knew that, while he was good at saving money, he didn't have a well-developed business sense and probably shouldn't try to get involved in the financial side of Amy Brock's proposed enterprise. Sure, he would be interested to know what the numbers were inasmuch as they were the health indicators of any business. They would also be his only means of keeping track of whether he was, at any point, being ripped off. The fact was that he knew neither Amy Brock nor her billionaire father from Adam. And from what little he did know of their world he knew that billionaires didn't generally tend to play fair unless doing so bought them something even bigger in return.

His own creative stubbornness was another issue he would need to address. Amy hadn't seen that side of him yet. He'd felt his sphincter tighten when she'd talked about putting her name on his work. There wasn't a single design in his portfolio that he hadn't slaved over for dozens of hours to get perfect before anyone ever got a look at it. And once he brought one of his designs to that point, his faith in it was pretty much cast in brass. In his studio classes he'd workshopped designs and seen any number of his so-called peers make mostly laughable suggestions as to how he might improve on them. The heat of their ignorance could generally be counted on to bring him to a rolling boil because most of the people making them weren't capable of designing folding lawn chairs. The few who had just a modicum of design acumen were usually smart enough to keep their mouths shut. So, how would Amy Brock perform under similar circumstances? She'd already asserted that she, too, would have veto power over any proposed project, his only comfort being that he would contractually also have that same power over her.

He pushed past the front door of his apartment to find DeShawn and two of his sculpture-program buddies in the living room clustered around the resident bong.

"Yo, Homes," his roomie greeted him. "We just scored some bomb-ass shit from this chick in fashion design." He held out a Bic lighter. "You up?"

Jeff waved it away. "Gonna pass, Bro. I know it's late but I've still got work to do."

"Suit yourself, Homes. Brewskies in the box, courtesy of my man Oliver here. Help yourself."

In all matters domestic, DeShawn was a major-weight slob. But if nothing else, he was almost too generous with his possessions. You like these kicks? Take them m'man. I got a hook-up. Coke, weed, Molly, the password to his Brazzers porn account, you name it. Jeff had yet to embrace the mindless inanity of the rave scene and had little use for the drugs. And for him the novelty of porn had pretty much worn off late in junior high. DeShawn lived on a steady diet of all those things plus Wendy's Baconator burgers, French fries and Dr. Pepper by day, and any beer he could get his hands on by night. Rail skinny, he gave Jeff cause to wonder where the hell he put it all, but being something of a food slut himself, he couldn't well throw rocks at glass houses.

It was a Thursday night. Amy's proposed dinner in East Hampton was scheduled for Saturday. She'd suggested that he work up some sketches of those two chairs she was proposing they make and turn them into 3-D CAD drawings as well as cull out a half-dozen favorite designs from his portfolio that he believed were commercially viable, then deliver them to her tomorrow so she could incorporate them into a PowerPoint presentation she wanted to show her father. Even after two-and-a-half years at Parsons, he'd developed no better than modest 3-D CAD skills and figured he'd be up most of the night. Like everything else, if he did this, he was going to make those renderings perfect.

☉☉☉

Katya Brock was pissed off. Many of her acquaintances believed she'd come out of the womb that way and didn't think there was any time when she wasn't angry about one thing or another. Today, the objects of her ire were two girlfriends from high school who'd cancelled on a trip that weekend to Stratton for some mid-November skiing. A junior at Stony Brook University on the North Shore of Long Island, Katya had matriculated there ostensibly to major in Business & Finance because it was the closest big college to where she and her East Hampton party animal friends had grown up. Heaven forbid that any of them drift too far from the comforts of their childhood nests.

In spite of the fact that most of the people in Katya's world saw her as a spoiled brat with an explosive temper, her mother saw her as a near-spitting image of herself and therefore not only almost as beautiful, but also someone who could do no wrong. And when you were an over-indulged profligate with a prodigious appetite for mischief, the blessings of a mother so blinded by her own narcissistic self-love was a big plus-mark on your side of life's ledger.

Seated on a kitchen stool while watching her mother construct a smoothie from kale, wheatgrass, ginger, plain yogurt and a banana, Katya was looking for sympathy. "I bought three new outfits for this trip and now I don't have anywhere to wear them. Maybe I'll invite some people over for a party Saturday. I just met these two dudes who are really cute. Daddy's out of town. You can have your pick."

Her mother, fresh returned in tights and a thong leotard from a spin class at the country club, used a tea towel draped across one shoulder to wipe the sides of the Vitamix while shaking her head. "He's cancelled that trip and your sister is coming for dinner. You're welcome to join, but so far as parties go, yours can't happen. Not that night."

Katya bristled. "I'll use the guest cottage."

Again, her mother shook her head. "Occupied. This is business, Baby Girl, though I can't imagine what kind. Amy is bringing a partner of some sort. I've got my eye on an emerald and diamond bracelet I saw at Harry Winston, so be nice. A hundred and eighty grand. Christmas is coming and I don't want you rocking my domestic boat right now."

For Katya, her half-sister Amy had always been a sore spot. Throughout her childhood, Amy hadn't been around much more than the occasional weekend, but even those small doses had always seemed like way too much. For some reason, her father had doted on her in a totally revolting way ever since Katya could remember. Lavish gifts every birthday, Christmas, and even Valentine's Day. A new Porsche 911 Cabriolet for her sixteenth in spite of the fact that she and her mother lived in Manhattan and she had few reasons to drive it anywhere. New clothes by the truckload. A townhouse on the Near North Side of Chicago while she was matriculated as an undergrad in college there. A co-op loft in SoHo now while she attended grad school at the Parsons School of Design. Katya's mother had always made sure that she got plenty of gifts, too, but never stuff like that. She'd even heard her mother arguing with her father over it and more than likely threatening less sex if he didn't capitulate—the vaginal wrench was the one tool that usually worked best on him—and yet she'd never been able to get that particular nut to budge. Not the

Amy nut. That sucker was frozen in place.

"So, this partner. Her latest conquest?"

"It doesn't sound like that," her mother replied. He's is some design genius she thinks is going to help her become the next big thing. A boy the same age as you, in his third-year at Parsons."

"Is he cute?"

Her mother scowled. "How do I know this? I think he is probably a nerd. If you wish to see, I guess you will just have to be here."

Katya was thinking that very same thing, hoping it might afford her a chance to mess with Amy's applecart. Flirt with the nerd, maybe take his eye off whatever prize Amy needed his help to win. People might think Katya was a bitch, but she could turn on the charm when she wanted to. And nobody was likely to contend she didn't have the physical tools to back that shit up. She'd had some manner of ski-lodge seduction in mind when she'd bought those new outfits, but one of them would be the perfect costume for this new occasion. Her calculating disposition was another thing that hadn't fallen very far from her mother's tree.

FIVE

Jeff figured he could have easily compressed those 3-D CAD work-ups into a Drop Box file and sent them to Amy online, but he was just as curious to see this PowerPoint presentation she planned to show to her father as he was to see where she lived, and so he'd elected to deliver that zip drive to her in person. The address she gave him was on the corner of Wooster and Charlton in SoHo, a dozen blocks south on Broadway from his own building on West 12th. It was a crisp and clear late-November day and so, being an inveterate people watcher, he'd elected to walk down past the east end of Washington Square and observe the always lively show there. Chess players at those permanent granite tables, bums and buskers, young mothers with dogs and strollers, joggers in a colorful array of bun-hugging spandex in perpetual pursuit of only God knew what. Perfection? Hipsters young and old of every stripe and persuasion.

Her building was one of those venerable 19th Century light-manufacturing structures with an ornate cast iron façade and two elaborate fire escapes climbing past floor-after-floor of immense, high-arched windows. Jeff took a moment to stand surveying the antiquated beauty of the place with something that approached reverence, always in awe of what the imaginations of his forebears had managed to conceive and execute.

Amy's loft was on the eleventh floor and when she opened her door to him he was amazed by how much natural sunlight flooded the space behind her. Considering how it had been transformed—a huge expanse of gleaming hardwood flooring, sleek white walls hung with an impressive collection of poster art and an eclectic array of mid-20th Century furnishings—it was hard to imagine those windows streaked with grime and machines churning out belt buckles or giant looms weaving textiles in an atmosphere filled with cutting-oil smoke.

"Nice," he commented as he entered. "Wanna trade? Mine comes with a resident slob porn junkie." He handed her the thumb drive as he spoke. "I suck at CAD and was up all night getting you that."

She stood barefoot, dressed in green leggings and an over-size denim work shirt, her hair confined to a bandana again. "You look like it," she said as she surveyed him. "How much Adderall did it take?"

He shook his head. "I hate that shit. It makes me crash too hard after. Just coffee. Around six this morning I managed to get a two-hour nap."

"Why don't I make you another cup and I'll show you what I've got. I was up most of the night, too."

He followed her as she led the way toward the kitchen. "How much Adderall did it take you?" he asked.

She smiled at him while approaching a huge ornate brass espresso machine that looked like salvage from an Italian train station. "We're both on the same page there, Prodigy-boy. I hate that shit, too. That's why I've got this baby." She patted the machine, grabbed two cups and poured coffee beans into a grinder.

Jeff was still looking around in wonder at the twelve-foot ceilings and views of the Financial District to the south and the Hudson River and Jersey City waterfront to the west. "You live in this whole giant space by yourself?"

"I don't generally play that well with others," she said. "Ask any of the half-dozen men I've tried to live with since high school."

He crossed to a stool at a bar separating her kitchen from the living room and climbed up to sit. "What's that say about the chances of our partnership surviving?" he asked.

He watched her work with practiced efficiency, tamping coffee grounds, clamping a pair of Portafilters in place and setting the cups beneath them. Once she switched the machine on, she turned to face him. There were those incredible green eyes again, flashing with their customary frank intensity. "I'm not proposing to live with you, Prodigy-boy. I'm just going to try to work with you. And just so we get one thing clear at the outset, I don't shit where I eat and neither should you. Any hooking-up I do will be outside the confines. Yours should be, too. You run a prosperous business and start blurring those lines, a hundred times out of a hundred you'll end up in deep doo-doo. You don't believe me, ask my dad."

Jeff was curious about that. She'd told him that her father had married this Bulgarian woman and gotten her pregnant before the ink was dry on his divorce papers. "You're saying it isn't all rose petals and bliss out there in East Hampton?"

"My step-mom is a cold, calculating bitch. I know my dad knows it and I think he's stayed with her these past twenty-two years out of self-hate. Kind of like an aesthetic wearing a hair shirt as penance for his sins. In this case, how he kicked my mom to the curb when she was down, just after I was born."

Wow. That was harsh. She'd told Jeff that her father travelled a lot on business. Now he thought he could understand why. At least for the duration of those trips he could leave the hair shirt at home in his closet. Listening to her, he wondered at the complexity of her own relationship with the man. There was no question in his mind that unlike himself, his own parents were small-minded bigots although both would vehemently deny it. So were a majority of his aunts, uncles, and cousins and the parents of the kids he'd gone to school with. That's just how things were when you got much north of the Dutchess County line, where the more rural upstate population was as redneck as anyone in the Deep South. He wondered how much empathy any of them would feel for a wife or sister suffering in the depths of post-partum depression. It was a thing that very few of them were equipped to understand.

Amy's PowerPoint presentation was impressive, making it clear to Jeff that she had, indeed, been thinking about and working on the details of this proposed venture for a long time before she'd ever found him. She'd managed to find P&L statements from three different European ventures that sought to succeed along similar lines, one Danish and two Italian. Using them, she'd tracked the history of their financial progress from launch to present day. There were no American ventures currently attempting to realize her same goals in the slightly upscale yet still mass market, and the fact that those three ventures in the EU were all still solvent, with two of them actually thriving, was a definite positive. Her proposed business plan depended heavily on creating a premier presence in the American marketplace and not at all on export, an area where protectionist tariffs could cripple initial growth. Instead, she was proposing to build her brand on the strength of the Amy Brock reputation alone, then let her brand create its own demand across the globe, sort of like how

Whack Job

Coca-Cola and Levi's jeans had become world-wide rages decades ago and still retained a large share of their foreign markets.

"I don't know your dad or how much of a tough-nut he is, but this looks pretty impressive," Jeff said. "And you seem confident that he'll bite."

She'd inserted his thumb drive and opened the first of those 3-D CAD files. They could be manipulated for views in all directions, the first depicting a gleaming white plastic chair on a sleek walnut base created using the digitally manipulated torso of Michelangelo's David with his spine straightened and him in a sitting position. It looked like the beautifully muscled marble giant had sat there and then gotten up, leaving behind a perfectly rendered imprint of himself in relief.

"I am now," Amy murmured. An obvious excitement tinged it. "This is so cool."

"As much as I'd like a party where I stick my naked ass into a vat full of wet plaster while a hundred drunks stare at me, I think I have a better solution now that I've worked on these a while," Jeff said. "Once I've had a chance to fine-tune them, I can turn these renderings into a digital map exactly the size we want them and then get a commercial pattern maker to 3-D print those molds for us. Check out the Venus de Milo."

After ten minutes spent playing around, spinning those images and looking at them from all aspects, Amy put them up side-by-side on her monitor and sat back in her chair.

"Nice work, Prodigy-boy," she said.

Jeff wondered how long she anticipated continuing to call him that, guessing it was kind of a defense mechanism meant to keep him at arm's length. No matter how much it rankled, it wasn't a bad strategy. The more time he spent around that green-eyed gaze, the deeper it was managing to worm its way in past his own meager defenses. Sure, she was too forward and brash and she was four years older than him and on most levels was probably a whole lot smarter, too. But still, prancing around barefoot in yet another t-shirt knotted at her waist and those spandex leggings, it was hard to deny the stirrings those things prompted in him.

So, tell me about this helicopter thing on Saturday," he said. "How does that work?"

"We go to Pier Six on the East River. That's the Downtown Heliport. They pick us up there."

"And where do we land at the other end?"

"There's another pad on the property."

"Jesus, how big is this place? Don't the neighbors mind the noise?"

"Fifty acres. The closest house is a quarter mile away. Unless the wind is bad, they make the approach from out over the water."

She said it as matter-of-factly as someone else might describe grabbing a six pack from the corner deli.

"And you've been doing this your whole life?"

"Daddy bought the place out there when I was ten. Before that they lived here in the city half the time and the rest in Pound Ridge. I used to either take a limo or ride the train when I visited in those days."

Jeff knew Pound Ridge. It was an exclusive enclave in Westchester just adjacent to Greenwich, Connecticut and thirty miles south of where he'd grown up. "Where in the city?" he asked.

"Dad has a penthouse in the Trump Tower."

"Fuck me. Really?"

"That's right, Prodigy-boy. He's one of them. And you're best advised to never forget that fact."

SIX

Milenka Brock watched the way her daughter had suddenly gone on point the moment she heard the helicopter's approach. It was 4:20 Saturday afternoon and dusk was gathering fast. The house staff had recently finished setting the table in the dining room and the odor of roast leg of lamb, her sainted step-daughter's favorite, wafted from the kitchen as the chef prepared dinner. Milenka had just finished mixing herself a gin Gibson in the cozy little entertainment parlor that opened onto the solarium. She was standing drink in hand and facing the beach when Katya appeared dressed to kill, her sights set on some hapless design nerd. The little wool knit dress she'd chosen wasn't much longer than most shirts, the fabric stretching to cover her like a second skin while still leaving plenty exposed. Perpetually concerned that her five-foot-four-inches in height weren't imposing enough, she'd chosen a pair of five-inch heels to make herself more formidable. How to dress for the hunt was only one of the many useful things that Milenka had taught her Baby Girl.

At that point Melinka's husband, Bert, emerged from his little man-cave in the west wing of the house to cross the pool terrace toward the solarium. With Thanksgiving just five days away and the weather finally turned chilly, he was dressed like a British country squire in brown corduroys, a Hebrides fisherman's sweater and an English tweed shooting jacket. He might be from Minnesota and of Swedish/Irish descent but his manner of dress for any specific leisure activity was one of his many pretensions, whether it be Big Game hunting in Africa or deep-sea marlin fishing off Mazatlán. Milenka had long-ago refused to accompany him on any of those excursions. They were mostly sponsored, she was certain, by panderers eager to curry favor by kissing her husband's ass and not hers.

On reaching the glass doors opening off the solarium, Bert poked his head in to shout, "Incoming!" like he was a platoon sergeant in some war movie. As if Milenka and Katya couldn't hear the chopper themselves.

"You look nice, Baby Girl," she told Katya. "Did you remember to file your teeth?"

Her daughter flashed her her best impatient smirk and sniffed the air. "Jesus, mom. Lamb? I hate fucking lamb."

Milenka might have offered a few words of consolation if Katya wasn't the fussiest eater she knew and pretty much hated everything. "You will be fine," she said. "It is not like either of us must stay all night. If you want, we can go get you something else afterwards." It wouldn't be the first time the two of them had done an Irish fade after dinner, leaving Bert and his guests to their devices. Her husband was usually so involved being his own center of attention that he rarely seemed to notice just as long as she was home in time to tuck his drunk ass into bed and maybe toss in a hand-job. He was rarely home more than six days out of the month and that ten minutes of conjugal contact with the evil she knew was a small enough price to pay for all the economic freedom this life otherwise afforded her.

Katya crossed to the bar to make herself a Manhattan, then raised her glass wearing one of her usual bored expressions. "Cheers then. If I'm not having any fun messing with the head of this guy Amy's brought, maybe I'll fake a stomach ache and meet you somewhere later," she said.

Milenka toasted back. "I will look forward to that. We do always manage to find ways to have our fun."

That past week while Bert was away in Hong Kong, it was two major league baseball players they'd met in the bar at Bobby Van's in Bridgehampton. A month ago, it was an actor with a new tequila company and his CEO. Milenka prided herself in how she'd managed to keep herself in tune over the past two decades and how many men often mistook her and Katya for sisters. She knew that one day it would no longer be so, but for the moment she was happy to push that time as far into the distant future as she could. Her daughter still had so much to learn about men and the art of twisting them around her little finger. And Milenka? She was more than happy to play the guide.

The turbine whine of the helicopter's engine died and moments later Bert appeared in the entry hall off the front door escorting Amy and a tall, unusually handsome younger man with a week's growth of beard and an unruly shock of dirty-blonde hair. Katya's sharpened attention was almost palpable as she nudged Milenka with an elbow while muttering under her breath.

"So, that's how they're building design prodigies these days? I think I know what I want for dessert."

"Down girl," Milenka murmured back. "I do not think he can afford you."

Amy made introductions as those three moved into the room. "Jeff Land, this is my step-mom, Milenka…and my half-sister, Katya."

This was supposed to be a dinner with Amy and some dipshit design student, not fucking Kurt Cobain. When he turned to Milenka and extended his hand, the directness of his blue-eyed gaze caused her to kick herself for not putting more effort into her own costuming. Try as he might to be cool, the guy hadn't missed anything about how Katya had managed to trick herself out.

"Nice to meet you, Milenka. Thanks for having us on such short notice. I hope we haven't ruined any other plans you had."

"Do not be silly," she said. "Bert says to me that you have just won some big design award. Congratulations." Bert hadn't actually told her any such thing but Amy had been on speaker with him Wednesday and she'd overheard her mention it.

"What's that I'm smelling?" he asked. "I haven't had roast lamb since I was home last Easter. It's one of my favorites."

Milenka continued to beam while feeling a little space open up between her and Katya regardless of how much less seductively she was dressed. There were other less obvious roads to a man's heart than surgically enhanced boobs in a skin-tight dresses.

"Oh? Where is your home?" she asked. He didn't sound like he was from Jersey or any of the five boroughs, but then people from all over the country attended Parsons.

"I'm from Pawling. That's upstate. In Dutchess County."

She'd actually heard of it from the time when she and Bert had lived in Pound Ridge. "Where Quaker Hill and Trinity-Pawling Prep are, yes?" Several power couples they knew had houses up there, in an area that was once a disputed territory between New York and Connecticut. Because of that dispute and a resultant lack of jurisdiction, robber barons seeking tax sanctuary had stashed large fortunes behind the gates of sprawling estates in the area.

"It is," he replied. "But I'm a townie and grew up in the cheap seats. Went to public school."

As long as he had those broad shoulders, soulful blue eyes, and that killer cleft chin, Milenka wasn't going to hold an unfortunate upbringing against him. Katya, on the other hand, was a bit more of a snob. She wondered how that information might be settling with her.

◎◎◎

Jeff had never been in a helicopter before, much less a thirty-room house manned by a small army of domestics, nestled on a fifty-acre estate insulated from the rest of the world by open meadows running to deep woods on three sides and the Atlantic Ocean on the fourth. And he had never met a mother-daughter duo quite like Milenka and Katya Brock.

The half-sister was more obvious about the kind of swath she thought she cut, but to him, the step-mother was the more intriguing of the pair. More polished, with more layers of innuendo. Less 'out there' in how she presented herself but still extremely attractive for a woman in her late forties. Jeff had never been into the cougar thing but guessed that if someone who looked like her came onto him in a bar, he might be seriously tempted.

He knew that Amy was hopeful of having their meeting with her dad before dinner, fearing that alcohol might cloud his perceptions afterwards, but that wasn't how things went. Milenka and Katya already had drinks and Amy's dad immediately jumped into playing bartender. With no choice but to go with the flow, Amy had a Negroni while Jeff, after requesting bourbon, got his first and hopefully not last taste of Pappy Van Winkle 23. Only recently of legal age he was just getting his feet wet in the world of whiskies, but it took no more than one sip for him to understand why this particular bourbon enjoyed such a reverential following. He'd had that Green Spot with Amy at the Black Sheep after she'd proclaimed her fondness for it. To him at least, this stuff was even better.

Whack Job

After their hostess invited them to have a seat in the parlor while they waited for the dinner bell, Amy led Jeff to a sofa set directly across from another chosen by Milenka and Katya. Bert Brock took a big leather chair with a view of the Solarium and the Atlantic beyond.

"I could get used to this," Jeff murmured as he sat.

"Easy," Amy murmured back. "It's mostly an illusion."

He smiled and clicked his glass to hers.

"So, tell us about yourself, Jeff," Bert urged him. "You mentioned a minute ago that you're from Pawling. Born and raised?"

Jeff felt all eyes on him as he nodded. "Yes, sir. Seventh generation. One side of my father's family were Dutch dairy farmers. They settled there in the Eighteenth Century."

"Amy tells me your father is a cabinet maker. That you grew up working in his shop."

"I did. He and my uncles mostly do work for custom kitchen contractors now. The retail shopfitting end of the business fell off after IBM pulled out of Poughkeepsie, before I was born."

Bert considered that information for a moment. "Good money in kitchens if you're in the right market I suppose. Up in that area, I expect he does okay."

Jeff hadn't realized this would involve Amy's dad vetting his father's Dunn & Bradstreet and found it a little irritating. If the man was trying to establish some sort of economic pecking order, the Sikorsky and a quarter mile of private beachfront had already managed that.

"My pop works hard and my parents are comfortable," he said, hoping to end it there. "I hear you're from Minnesota, sir. Did you ever do any ice-fishing?" From movies, he'd been led to believe it was all the rage up there.

"Never once. Didn't have the time. I was always a lot more interested in making money than freezing my ass off. I went to Carnegie Mellon in Pittsburg right out of high school, got my mechanical engineering degree, and then went to work for Rogers Crane."

Jeff didn't know who they were but assumed they were some big Pennsylvania outfit.

"I'd been there ten years when I met Amy's mother," Bert

continued. "Right around that same time a merchant banking group approached me, wanting to back me in a play they were planning. They were interested in buying up a half-dozen smaller, mom-and-pop crane leasing outfits around the country to consolidate them under one banner and needed someone like me to run that show. It meant quitting Rogers and going into direct competition with them, but they were privately held and top-heavy with heirs who didn't want to work very hard. I'd already realized I was never going to get promoted up past them, so I decided to take the risk. Those bankers kept up their end and consolidated seven different regional crane and heavy-hauling companies into the second largest crane-leasing company in the country. Eight years later, old man Rogers died. By that time, I'd added earth-moving equipment to our lease line, using the same trucks we used to haul cranes to move that other stuff around the country, and had grown us to be bigger than them in the process. Instead of rolling up their sleeves and getting to work trying to win back some of their old market share, the Rogers heirs approached me to broker a buy-out. For a piece of the whole pie, I came up with not only a consolidation plan but one to take the entire enterprise international. Once that deal was done, we were the largest crane, heavy hauling, and earthmoving equipment leasing company in the world."

Once he concluded that thumb-nail sketch of his impressive business career, Bert Brock sat back to sip a little of his Pappy's, beaming the most self-satisfied look Jeff had ever seen on another man's face. He knew the tweed hunting jacket was all part of a costume meant to impress and intimidate but he still wondered how long his host could suffer wearing it and that heavy wool sweater. It was hot as fuck in that house.

SEVEN

Katya saw her mother's cougar instincts kick in the moment this antithesis of a design nerd had first walked into view. And just as suddenly, she'd known that a different kind of game was afoot. Generally, when she and Milenka hit the town to play together there were plenty enough targets of opportunity to go around and so there was very little mother-daughter competition. Different men had different tastes, no two ever quite the same, and they most often were able to quickly recognize those preferences and divide up the prospective spoils like the white and dark meat on a turkey. Sometimes it was an older actor who preferred the young stuff and other times it was the young pro athlete who just couldn't get the prospect of hooking up with somebody's scorching hot mother out of his limbic brain. Katya had often wondered whether her mother actually enjoyed sex or whether if, like for her, it was more about the thrill of the hunt and the moment of conquest. It was something they'd never really talked about. Not like the things Katya talked about with her posse of girlfriends she'd known since high school; stuff like how to fake enjoying giving blowjobs or having some porn-addicted creep try to choke you out. She knew how much her mom liked them young and had a sneaking suspicion she might even enjoy those other things, too, but they'd never actually sat down to compare notes.

Once the dinner bell rang and they all rose to move toward the dining room, Milenka leaned close to whisper in Katya's ear, the scent of Tom Ford's Fucking Fabulous a little too strong on her.

"Scissors, paper, rock?"

"In your dreams," Katya murmured. "This one is mine."

"You give it your best shot, Baby Girl. Somehow, I do not think you have the staying power a project like him might take."

⊙⊙⊙

Jeff's hostess directed him to a seat alongside Amy on one side of her lavishly provisioned dinner table with Katya seated opposite. She and her husband took their places at either end, Amy adjacent to her dad, and Jeff next to her. It would have taken a much stronger twenty-one-year-old man than he was not to notice how Katya had purposely tugged at the neckline of that outrageously tight dress as she sat, pulling it a little wider to expose an even greater expanse of honey-colored flesh. Amy had already warned that this was one predatory beast and the last thing he wanted to do was endanger the prospects of their success with her dad by flirting with either of his daughters. And so, whenever the conversation required, he purposely gave more of his attention to Amy's step-mother, who also seemed treacherous but still like much safer territory.

It wasn't until a dessert course of tiramisu arrived along with a twenty-year-old vintage port and coffee that Jeff felt the toes of two separate feet brush against his shins almost simultaneously, one from straight ahead and one from his left. He barely managed to cover the start of surprise the contact gave him while he quickly tucked both his feet beneath his chair. The last woman who'd attempted to play footsie with him was a bridesmaid at a wedding that past summer and on that occasion he'd more-or-less invited the move with a lot of covert eye play. This dual contact had come out of nowhere, most surprisingly from the end of the table where his hostess was seated. Meanwhile, directly across from him, Katya Brock fed him a look full of question. When he shot a glance at her mother, he found that same look in her eyes, too.

Jesus, he thought. What kind of asylum were they running there? Thrown totally off his game, he turned to Amy, nudging her with an elbow.

"Are we gonna get a chance to show your dad that PowerPoint tonight?" he asked. "If he wants to talk about it again in the morning, it might not be a bad move to give him something to chew on." Then, without waiting for her to answer, he turned to Bert Brock. "I don't know what it'll take to get someone with a background and bona fides like yours excited, sir, but I think you'll be impressed by the work she's put into this project. My contribution is minimal by comparison."

"He's being modest," Amy said.

Jeff waved that away. "I'm no captain of industry, sir, but the numbers she's shown me feel super solid. Enough to persuade me to drop out of school and join her if you decide to back this venture."

Amy reached to place a hand on his arm, squeezed it, and also looked to her father. "You told me when we talked on the phone that you only have until noon tomorrow before you have to leave again. This pitch is a lot to digest."

Brock shrugged and looked to Jeff. "You smoke cigars, son? They're Cubans."

Jeff's experience with cigars fell far short of memorable. He'd attempted to smoke several in high school and they'd done nothing but turn him green. "You'd be wasting one on me," he replied. "I am enjoying this port though, sir. It's killer."

Bert reached for his own glass while looking down the table, first to Katya and then to his wife. "If you ladies will excuse us then, it sounds like our guests want to talk business."

It would have been hard for Jeff to miss the look of irritation that passed between Katya and her mother.

Two hours later, after bidding everyone a good night and heading for the guest cottage, Amy asked Jeff if he fancied a walk on the beach to clear his head.

"I'll show you your room and we can grab heavier jackets," she said. "We've got lots to talk about."

The so-called guest cottage turned out to be twice the size of Jeff's boyhood home in Pawling, with five bedrooms, each with a separate ensuite bath, a huge living room with spectacular views of the moonlit Atlantic, and even a game room with billiards and two card tables. Images of The Great Gatsby and The Wolf of Wall Street played in his mind as he explored the place while Amy changed into warmer clothes.

They were on the sand, trudging toward the tide line, when Jeff asked a question that had been on his mind all evening.

"When you said that your step-mother is Bulgarian, I never figured she'd still have such a heavy accent. How long has she been here?"

Hands shoved deep into the pockets of her coat and her chin buried in her muffler, Amy stared out across the gleaming water. "She moved here when she was sixteen, so thirty years. You'd think she would have lost it by now, wouldn't you?"

"Sort of like Arnold Schwarzenegger, right?"

"I told you she was a smoke show, huh?"

"Both of them are. It was Milenka's accent that threw me off. I wasn't expecting that."

A helicopter crossed above them beneath a waxing three-quarter moon that was as high in the night sky as it was going to get. Between it and the lights of Long Island, most of the Milky Way was washed out and only the brightest stars shone through. "I suppose I should have mentioned it, but I guess I don't really hear it anymore," she said. "To me she's just Milenka, a serious pain in my ass."

"They both tried to play footsies with me under the table. That's when I decided it was time we go show your dad your PowerPoint."

She looked at him in surprise. "You're bullshitting me. Both of them?"

"At practically the same time. When I felt that first toe prod from your step-mother, I almost pissed myself."

Amy tried to wrap her mind around the idea of Milenka making that kind of play.

"Katya I can see," she murmured. "The little bitch thinks any hot guy she meets should want to do her. Milenka's the surprise. I'm pretty sure my dad suspects she screws around on him when he's out of town, probably just as much as he does on her. But at least she isn't blatant about it. She wasn't the one with her boobs hanging half-out on the table."

Jeff chuckled. "You noticed too, huh?"

"How couldn't I? I also noticed how studied you were in your efforts to avoid staring at them. For which, I might add, you won points. I think I looked at them more than you did."

"Does she always dress like that? Or was that some kind of power play aimed at you?"

Amy took a moment to consider her answer before she spoke.

"Before you told me just now about Milenka's move, I might have thought so," she said. "But now I'm wondering if there isn't some other competition at work there. Between the two of them. I've heard of that kind of thing with mothers and daughters before."

"You're talking about Milenka trying to prove to Katya that she's still got the goods?"

She nodded. "I knew a girl at the University of Chicago whose mother had her when she was fifteen. She told me that when she was in high school, her mom tried to snake every boyfriend she brought home. She said she acted more like a hyper-competitive big sister than a parent."

"That's some sick shit."

"My guess? It's probably fairly common. I got lucky there. Since she had two more kids with my step-father, my mom has hardly paid attention to me."

Jeff turned his head to glance at her. "Meanwhile, even though your dad said he needs more time to look over your numbers, I could tell he was mega-impressed with what you showed him tonight."

"I think what influenced him most were those 3-D renderings of yours, Prodigy-boy. No matter how good the overall business concept is, it would still be dead in the water if the product we make has no commercial appeal. But with those Venus and David designs, Brocking Chair is gonna be a hit. I'm pretty sure he could see that, too."

When Amy had first mentioned her proposed brand name two days ago, it hadn't landed with any grace in Jeff's imagination. Now, he was still trying to decide if he could ever like it. He might appreciate the intention behind it, but the name itself felt too cute. Nothing had been carved in stone yet and he still had that veto power, but no nifty alternatives had yet sprung to mind.

"So, assuming he says yes. I guess we should start talking time-line," he said.

Initially, her plan called for the lease of a moderate-size industrial building somewhere in the 50,000 square foot range, within an easy commute of a large workforce skilled in all aspects of high-quality furniture production. Metalworkers, woodworkers, upholsterers, powder-coaters, chroming and lacquer finishing technicians. Brooklyn, Queens, and Nassau County on Long Island were chock full of custom fabrication operations that employed scores of craftspeople like them, many recent European immigrants. Once their design line was set and a small-scale production facility was built out, they needed to carefully recruit from those legions and then begin producing prototypes for entry into international design shows and competitions. They had to do all that and get some good notice in the design press before they even considered going into large-scale production.

"If he says yes, I want to start looking for real estate to lease right after the first of the year," she said. "With the liabilities that are involved in the type of work his company does, he's got a huge legal department. I can't imagine it taking them more than a couple of weeks to generate the contracts and for us to have our own counsel go over them."

"Whoa. Our own counsel?"

"I have an old boyfriend in Chicago who's willing to help out on a contingency basis."

"And what contingency is that?"

"That he and his firm become our corporate counsel if my dad's terms are acceptable and we decide to go ahead with this. He's good, Jeff. Graduated top of his class at Northwestern Law. And he's just as ambitious as I am. If this works, him bringing it to the big table at his law firm will pretty much guarantee him making partner."

"But old boyfriend? I thought we don't shit where we eat."

"Relax. I haven't eaten there in years. He's nothing more to me now than someone I think I can trust."

"Think?"

"Okay, know. As much as I know anything."

EIGHT

As she lay in her bed listening to the K-pop band Itzy's *Not Shy* album cranked loud through headphones, Katya studied herself in the mirror mounted overhead while trying to puzzle out just what her half-sister might have going with that smoking-hot Jeff dude. All through dinner she'd studied them hard, noticing that Amy had looked at her cleavage longer and more often than he had. So, what gave there? On TV and in the movies, most designers were queer, but this dude didn't give off that vibe, even if he and Amy never so much as touched hands or exchanged a look that might suggest intimacy. And it wasn't like her half-sister was a dog. As much as Katya hated to admit it, Amy was pretty hot, too, if you like Amazons. It pained her to have to acknowledge that about her but when sizing up the competition Katya had learned years ago that it paid to give an adversary her due, and then try to engineer an effective work-around. Clearly her partner wasn't a boob dude, so what else did she have to sell? All through dinner he'd paid a lot more attention to her mother, which would suggest he had no problem with that accent of hers or her age. Her mom, with all her regular Botox injections, didn't have a wrinkle in her face and was still sexy as hell at forty-six. Katya knew from the multiple forays they'd made together into the city that lots of younger guys seemed to dig that older shit, like they expected more experience might be some added plus. And she supposed there might even be some truth to that. Once, after the two of them had snagged a couple of Charlotte Hornets players in their hotel bar after a Knicks game, they'd headed upstairs with them to their suite where, after her Point Guard ran a sprint instead of a marathon and fell asleep, she'd spied on her mother in the other room. Somewhere along the line, somebody had taught her mom how to do things with her anatomy that Katya hadn't known were possible. She'd ridden that Power Forward like an Olympic Equestrienne and had his eyeballs rolling back in his head.

So, what was this Jeff's deal she wondered? Did he like his women with a little less baby fat in their faces and more sack-time on their odometers? Or was he really more attracted to her and just trying to be cautious in the house of a man who could either make or break his immediate future? She was hoping it was the latter and not the former because once she'd gotten a look at him and seen how much of her half-sister's ambition was hitched to his apparent talent, she was all about finding a way to drive a wedge in there to fuck all that up. It was the sort of challenge she'd lived for ever since first discovering her scheming inner-bitch and the kind of power that could be wielded by a woman with no qualms about turning that shit up full blast.

◎◎◎

"You do know that my sister isn't going to give up just because you did such a good job ignoring her," Amy said. "I've seen that look on her face before, whenever I brought a hot guy to the house with me."

Prior to calling it a night they were in the kitchen of the guest cottage where she was setting up the coffeemaker for the morning. Jeff handed her the joint they'd been smoking and grinned.

"Did you just say I was hot?"

She scowled, took a hit, and then spoke with smoke streaming from her nose.

"Fuck you, Prodigy-boy. You know you're hot. I'm pretty sure I'm not the first woman to mention that to you."

As a matter of fact, Jeff wasn't quite so sure of that as she seemed to be. Skinny and gawky all through his childhood and well into his freshman year in high school, he'd only filled out, his features finally catching up in proportion to his face, in the past few years. Even as he'd gotten ostensibly better looking, the girls he grew up with in Pawling hadn't treated him that much differently. He wasn't a gridiron star and while a decent basketball player, hadn't played for the high school team because the coach was an asshole. He had played in a variety of mediocre garage bands ever since junior high but the girls who hung around that scene were so Emo droll and cool that how they'd reacted to him wasn't much of a gauge. It wasn't until he'd joined his current band in Manhattan that for the first time in his life women had started to give him the time of day. But did those reactions mean he'd suddenly gotten hot? At least for the moment, he still thought not.

"Someday I'll show you a picture of me in the seventh grade," he said. "I used to stand in the middle of our vegetable garden to scare birds away."

She butted the roach in an ashtray and reached for the light switch. "Go sell your bullshit to somebody who's buying," she said. "Time to hit the hay."

"What's our schedule tomorrow?" he asked. "Your dad said he has to leave by noon."

"We'll probably do breakfast with him, somewhere in town. Depending on the availability of the chopper we might have to limo back to the city. You said you have a gig tomorrow night?"

"We're opening for Flymo at Arlene's. The show doesn't start 'til ten. You should come."

"I was thinking I might. At least for your first set."

"We're only doing one. Home in bed by eleven-thirty on a school night. The girls all think our drummer is hot."

"I thought you were the drummer."

He formed a gun with his hand and shot a finger at her as he rose from his stool. "I am. My new business partner has been building up my self-esteem."

Jeff left the window of his room open a crack in spite of the late-fall cold so he could hear the surf pound, then stripped down to his briefs, climbed in beneath a luxurious goose down comforter and lay staring at the ceiling while projecting images of the day onto it in his mind's eye. He'd learned that regardless of how opulent the interior appointments, a helicopter ride was loud. He'd seen what kind of isolation from the rest of society a few billion bucks could buy in the eastern reaches of Long Island. He'd been amused by the pretense attached to just about everything about international business tycoon Bertrand Brock, from how he dressed, ate, and lived, clear down to the Cuban cigars and the 23-year-old whiskey. He'd been interested to discover just how boldly secure Amy's step-mom seemed to be in that rarified world; safe enough in her station to flirt fairly outrageously with a much younger dinner guest she'd never met before.

He guessed that because he was the prospective business partner of a daughter who wasn't hers, any points she might score there would be seen as a win for the opposing team. And then there was the half-sister, who had probably made the biggest impression of all. As cool as he'd tried to play it, he was grateful for the napkin deployed in his lap at dinner to hide the throbbing erection sprung the moment she'd so obviously adjusted the neckline of her dress like that. Somehow, and he wasn't at all sure quite how, for the entire two hours it had taken them to consume a dinner served in three courses, and then coffee and dessert, he'd managed to keep his gaze averted from that quarter-acre of flesh on display directly across the table from him. Just like he'd never thought six-foot Amazons might be his thing until he first met Amy Brock, he hadn't considered high-maintenance blondes to be his brand, either. But Katya and Milenka were embodying a whole new epiphany there.

He wondered how much disloyalty he should feel, laying there in a bed across the hall from a partner forever off limits, thinking about how much he'd like to screw her half-sister. By all accounts those two were practically mortal enemies. He thought about shitting and nests and wondered where Katya fell in that particular equation. On the wrong side of the equal sign, for sure. Way on the wrong side.

He was still trying to push any fantasies being entertained in that arena aside and to instead concentrate on what had transpired business-wise that evening when across the room the door opened briefly to admit a shadowy figure not tall enough to be Amy. There was still enough light from a moon now lower in the night sky to partially illuminate her as she moved to the foot of his bed where he could make out gleaming blonde hair hanging to a pair of shoulders and then, as she unfastened the sash of her robe to shrug it off, he was hit by a first whiff of Tom Ford's Fucking Fabulous.

"You are awake?" Milenka Brock whispered.

⊚⊚⊚

Shortly after giving Bert just enough rudimentary carnal pleasure to get him out of her hair for the night, Milenka had retired to her own room and from her second-floor window spotted Amy and that tall, gorgeous boy walking together down on the sand. She'd studied them for the next half hour with the aid of binoculars, trying to discover what if any bond might exist there. Both of them had too many interests in common and were too pretty not to be in some way attracted to each other. And even if she thought Amy to be something of a cold fish, Milenka believed that all men and women had a deep-seated need to be desired. She couldn't imagine Amy not wishing to be desired by this particular man. He was young, apparently brilliant, and vibrant in his knowledge of the power those attributes gave him. He was also yummy enough to eat, with a rustic exterior, deliciously firm flesh, and a nice core of refreshing naïveté.

By the time those two had trudged up from the tideline and across the dune to the guest cottage, Milenka was convinced that nothing romantic was going on there, just as Amy had contended to her father earlier. Through those binocular lenses she'd watched the lights of the kitchen eventually extinguished and then those in two separate bedrooms come on. One was the room that Amy always used when she visited. The other was opposite it, at the end of the same hallway. Fifteen minutes after that, the guest cottage fell into darkness with only security lights illuminating the exterior terrace and walkways.

Replacing the field glasses in the cabinet across from her bed, Milenka stood in the gloom thinking about how much she enjoyed abandoning herself to actual unbridled passion and how good it felt to have a young, strapping man fuck her with the kind of frenzied urgency that only youth can employ. It wasn't about sensitivity or passion or finesse. It was about the pure animal act, like a stallion going at a mare in a breeding shed. She'd discovered over the past few years just how much she enjoyed and actually preferred such couplings and at least once a year had taken a vacation on her own in the interest of pursuing such singular satisfactions. There was that beach boy in the bungalow on Barbados. And the strapping young Greek fisherman on the tiny Aegean Island of Skyros. The young charter skipper in the forward berth of a sailboat floating over the Great Barrier Reef. The Charlotte Hornets Power Forward with that sneaky bitch Katya spying outside the door she'd purposely left cracked ajar a half-inch. And at no time had any of those trysts involved lovemaking, something Milenka didn't think she even knew how to do. They were couplings following conquests. Period. And goddamn how she loved and even craved them. She also found that the more jaded she became, the more she enjoyed taking risks. There was a night that past summer when she'd seduced a ruggedly-built friend of her neighbor's son, right there on the darkened beach in full view of her own house. The kid was a privileged brat and it wasn't about him being all that attractive, but because Katya had expressed a passing interest in him. One of Milenka's many mottoes was first come, first served. Another; finders keepers, losers weepers.

NINE

Over breakfast in a downtown East Hampton café Amy found herself wondering what might have transpired overnight to throw her new business partner so far off his game. While drinking coffee with him earlier in the guest cottage, he'd complained of not having gotten enough sleep, wondering if maybe it was the incessant pounding of surf that had produced a rare insomnia. Amy had always experienced the exact opposite phenomena whenever she slept there and so wondered if it might have been something else. Perhaps visions of her half-sister overflowing that dress had danced like sugar plums in his head all night. Or maybe he was having second-thoughts regarding their whole enterprise after meeting her dad. She really had no idea, but the way he was behaving, seated across the breakfast table from her and her father, was disconcerting. Since their meeting last night in his study her father had studied their Venus and David chairs and the rest of Jeff's designs in closer detail. Over breakfast, he'd heaped enthusiastic praise on him for the work. Rather than graciously acknowledge it, Jeff had not responded the way a prospective investment partner might. Instead, while struggling to at least appear affable, he'd seemed totally out of it.

It wasn't until they took their leave of her father—her stepmother and half-sister were nowhere to be seen—and were seated in the back of a limousine headed for Manhattan, that Amy finally had an opportunity to call Jeff on his curious behavior. She had the privacy screen run up between them and the driver, hoping that would make her partner more forthcoming.

"What the hell was going on back there, Prodigy-boy?" she asked. "When a man practically offers to suck your dick, I'd think you might want to be a little more enthusiastic. He all but agreed to give us the keys to the castle."

Jeff turned from staring out the window at the winter-barren landscape to look at her with tired eyes.

"I wish you'd stop calling me that," he said. "My name is Jeff."

Amy had figured he'd weary of the teasing moniker sooner-or-later and supposed she'd had as much fun with it as she was likely to get. "Okay. So, Jeff. What the fuck was that about? Are you having second thoughts?"

He forced a wan smile and shrugged. "I guess maybe I am. But not for any of the reasons you might think."

"What other reasons could there be? You don't trust my dad? You don't trust me? You don't like the split? You don't like the risk involved in going into business for yourself, especially on this scale?"

When he broke eye contact to turn away toward that window again, Amy watched his reflection in the glass. He wasn't staring out like he had before. He'd closed his eyes.

"I don't think I trust myself," he murmured.

Something was clearly bothering him. With her dad having just agreed to back their project pending the ironing out of some specific contractual details, she needed it out on the table, right then and there. "Trust yourself with what?" she insisted. "Out with it, Prodi…Jeff."

He turned back to stare at her with an intensity that approached anger. At who or what, she couldn't imagine.

"It's hard to sit there and talk to some dude about going into business with him when you just fucked his wife," he said.

Boom. Right between the eyes. The instant she realized he was serious, Amy felt her breath catch.

"What? How could you have? You were in the guest…"

"Right after we went to bed she showed up in my room. I didn't invite her there or even act like I might want her to come. I was lying there sorting through a bunch of shit in my head when she opened the door and just walked in."

Amy now had a vivid image working of her stepmother and the scores of times she'd seen her brazenly flirt with other men when she knew her husband wasn't looking. Last night on the beach, when Jeff had told her about how Milenka and Katya had both attempted to play footsies with him under the table, why hadn't she at least seen the possibility of something like this happening? All she could do now was close her eyes, shake her head and murmur, "Jesus."

Jeff's tone was subdued and contrite when he spoke next. "I know I should have found some way to tell her to leave but I didn't want to cause a scene. And there she was, crawling into my bed."

Amy couldn't exactly put herself in his shoes, but she did have enough experience with men and their libidos to know that at that particular juncture all cerebral function would abandon ship. As cold and calculating as she knew Milenka to be, she couldn't deny that even at forty-six she was still a lot hotter than most twenty-year-olds. And when she got it in her mind to really turn on the seductive charm, men of all ages practically drooled over her.

"Aw, fuck," she muttered.

"I know. This is probably a deal breaker, right? But I swear to God, Amy. I don't think I'm capable of ever saying no to something like that. Not when a woman who looks like her crawls naked into my bed out of the blue. It was crazy."

It was Amy's turn to stare past him out a window, her mind racing as she weighed the implications of what she'd just heard. "I'm sure it was," she said, her tone neutral and distant. And then she turned back to him.

"I'm not ready to call it a dealbreaker. At least not just yet. And I appreciate your candor. From the way you're reacting, I'm guessing you've never done anything like that before?"

He looked puzzled. "What? Fuck someone else's wife? No. It wasn't even on my bucket list."

"A friend's girlfriend? Mother?"

"No!"

She reached to pat his thigh with a calming hand. "Okay. I'm just trying to clear the air here. So, you're not a schemer like Milenka or Katya. You're just a basic twenty-one-year-old dude who found himself in a fantasy sitch and couldn't say no."

"It wasn't even a fantasy. You want me to be totally honest? I was a lot more attracted to your sister than I was to her."

"Of course, you were. She practically had her boobs out on your dinner plate." She paused to think about where she thought she wanted this to go from there. So far as she was concerned, there was no reason that Jeff would ever have to see her stepmother again. The rest of their negotiation with her dad could be done over the phone and through their lawyers. "Somebody told me once that guilt is a useless emotion," she said. "That it only affects the person suffering it. If I saw any advantage, I might try to make you feel guilty, but I'm looking at it more like you were the victim of a drive-by shooting. You didn't see it coming. And I doubt I've ever met a man who could have dodged something like that. Not unless he was gay."

His return look was frown-heavy with uncertainty. "So, what are you saying?"

"I'm saying that no, I don't see this as a deal breaker. We're gonna try to make sure my dad never finds out and then forget this ever happened."

"Don't you think that's easier said than done? I'm pretty sure shit like this tends to linger."

"We'll try. We need to get on with our show and we have a ton of work to do."

"Is there any point in me registering for the spring term or are we gonna be too busy for that?"

While he'd been occupied with fucking himself to exhaustion last night, she'd spent at least part of that same interval thinking about their timeline and just what their next several moves needed to be."

"We should talk about that," she said. "It's going to take the lawyers at least a month to hammer out the details and I can't imagine Parson's letting you stay in that apartment once you drop out. We might have to double-up so you won't have to worry about rent and can concentrate on doing the fabrication specs for those chairs while we start looking for a space and recruit the rest of our team."

"Double-up like me move in with you?" All that guilt had been replaced by surprise.

"Just temporarily, until we sign on the dotted line and get some cash-flow going. I have a painting studio in the back of my place that I never use. There's another bathroom back there with a shower. We can get you a bed and you can do your design work there."

"I thought you said you don't play nicely with others."

"I don't. You leave dirty dishes in the kitchen sink you'd better start wearing a helmet because I'll throw them at you. And this will be a good way for me to keep an eye on you, at least until you can afford to get your own place. If Katya gets even a hint that her mother went there, I wouldn't put it past her to come looking, just to even the score. I don't know it for a fact, but I get the sense they're keeping some sort of tally in that regard."

◎◎◎

Jeff had started to see Amy in a whole new light while watching his new partner try to process what had happened that past night. She had been dealing with her step-mother and half-sister and their scheming natures all of her life while he'd only just met them yesterday. And now, rather than hate him for having gone where he had, she'd surprised him by suggesting they create a sanctuary, if for no reason other than to protect her own interest in the investment she was about to make. He had no idea how having her act like Cerberus at his gate was likely to cramp his social style but after last night he figured some kind of cooling-off period might be required, regardless. He was still as inclined as most other twenty-one-year-olds toward the occasional hook-up, which happened most often after he finished playing a gig at one club or another either downtown or in Brooklyn or Hoboken. He doubted that Amy would be pleased to wake up and find one of those women trying to figure out her espresso machine or raiding her refrigerator. Fortunately, he wasn't in the habit of taking women home with him. It was all about having an escape hatch and the better chance of sleeping on clean sheets.

They were on the L.I.E approaching the Midtown Tunnel when he tore himself from thoughts of a long nap and turned to her. "Are you still thinking about coming out to see us play tonight?"

She looked at him and sighed. "I don't know. Do you think you'll have the strength to stay awake?"

"I hope so. The second you drop me off I'm headed straight to bed. Our lead guitarist has this new booking agent coming to see us. He says she listened to our demo and was impressed. Supposedly, she can get us choice gigs if she likes us live."

Yesterday, when he'd mentioned the thing at Arlene's Grocery, he figured Amy had only expressed an interest in coming out of courtesy, like he might if she'd told him she had a dance recital or poetry slam. But now she was focusing more closely.

"How serious are you about this band?" she asked.

"I've played drums and sung in them since I was thirteen, but none were even close to as good as these guys are. Foster, our lead guitarist, goes to Julliard, plays jazz in quintet there, and can totally shred it. Our bass and keys players are super-solid, too. I really love making music with these guys."

"Are you doing covers or original material?"

"All original tunes," he replied. "Written by Foster."

"And who else but you sings?"

"All of us, but I do the leads. We aren't exactly Queen, but our harmonies are pretty tight. I definitely think you should see for yourself. Scream. Throw your panties at me. Help us impress this booking agent."

"You're disgusting."

He got a sudden mental image of her stepmother riding him reverse-cowgirl and demanding that he slap her ass like she'd just made the clubhouse turn at Saratoga. He sighed, suddenly overwhelmed with exhaustion. "Yeah, I probably am," he admitted. "The show starts at ten. Don't be late. Most Sunday nights we actually start on time."

TEN

Katya was steaming. When she'd gotten up to pee just before dawn that morning some sixth sense had told her to look out her bedroom window. Her mother had chosen that same moment to skulk out of the guest cottage through the side terrace door and hurry in her robe to the storm cellar entrance one story below. It was the same basement access door that Katya had used as a means of clandestine ingress and egress all through her high school years and she knew its convenience all too well. It was a knowledge that forced her to realize with infuriating certainty that her mother had just snaked her again and that all her own efforts at titillating Amy's new partner at dinner had done nothing but prime his pump.

Her mother managed to avoid her for the first half of the day by locking herself in her room, most likely to catch up on some much-needed sleep. By the time she emerged, Katya had already vented at least a portion of her ire by doing some power shopping on Milenka's Amex Black Card at the Reformation Beach House on East Hampton's Main Street. Between that and a light but expensive lunch of oysters, beluga caviar, and a whole bottle of Louis Latour Chevalier Montrachet, she didn't arrive back at the house until almost four o'clock, drunk and ornery. When she found her mother in the parlor pouring herself a glass of Champagne, she shot hate darts at her while standing defiantly in the doorway.

"I can't believe you went and fucking did that!"

Unperturbed, her mother smiled with unnerving serenity. "Did what, dear? Or should I just assume that you have been spying on me again?"

Katya wasn't sure what that 'again' meant, but seeing as she had certainly done it more than once, decided to let it pass. "I'll bet you money he was thinking about me while he was fucking you," she snapped.

The smile on her mother's face turned smirk. "That is possible, maybe. Before I get there, he has definitely been inspired by something. You would think that a man his age, so primed as he was, would not have his kind of staying power. That has not been my usual experience."

"Oh, Jesus, mother. He was supposed to be mine."

Her mother took a sip of Champagne, eyebrows arched. "Who says he cannot still be, Baby Girl? I do not make a down payment, I just rent him for one night. You must know by now I am not possessive."

Still pouting, Katya crossed to grab her mother's bottle and another glass. She might already be drunk, but suddenly she wasn't drunk enough. "Was he really that good or are you just trying to piss me off?"

"On the one-to-ten scale? I will give him a solid nine."

"Jesus. I fucking hate you. A nine compared to that guy from the Hornets, or the soccer player from Argentina?"

"Both of those were tens, dear, but I must say. This one does have that upside potential."

"Do you know he's in a band? I overheard him tell Amy he's got a gig at Arlene's Grocery tonight. That's like one of the hippest downtown clubs right now."

Katya saw a funny look cross her mother's face. The cougar had just crawled back out of her den. "Oh, for fuck's sake, mother! You can't. It's my turn."

"So, go," her mother insisted. "Your father is in Pittsburgh. No one will be at the city apartment."

Katya thought about the logistics of that. She didn't have class again until Tuesday. On a Sunday night, traffic on the L.I.E. headed back into the city was always brutal, but she could take the…ugh…train. She'd seen how Jeff Land's eyes had lingered on her when he thought she wasn't looking. And the idea of seducing her half-sister's new business partner right in front of her sounded like as much good sport as she could imagine. "Did you make him wear a condom?" she asked.

"I have my tubes tied after you were born."

"Great. But I still don't want to catch any of your skanky shit. I wonder how daddy will react when you finally give him a dose of something."

Her mother reached to pat her on the shoulder, smiling. "Not much chance of that, Baby Girl. I always make him wear one. The man will fuck anything that walks on two legs."

Katya smirked back at her. "I guess that makes you both about even then, huh? Though I sometimes wonder if you've managed to limit yourself to just two legs."

With a quickness that shocked as much as the sting of it, her mother slapped her across the face. "You must understand there are limits to how far you can push me, Baby Girl," she snapped. "Have fun with your sloppy seconds. And perhaps do not let him to kiss you. That would be eating my *barnha* by proxy."

⊙⊙⊙

A five-hour nap went a long way toward restoring Jeff. He rose from bed at seven that evening to scour the refrigerator for something to eat and found DeShawn and a woman he recognized from the Fashion Design program at Parsons watching porn and eating Chinese take-out in the living room.

His roomie lifted his chopsticks and waved. "Plenty more of this, you hungry, Homes. How'd it go with the Brock chick's daddio?"

A hulking porn actor onscreen was gripping a fistful of a fake red-head's hair to force her down hard on his erect penis, trying to get himself all the way to the back of her throat. Jeff couldn't imagine watching something like that with any woman he might invite home. But then, for the three years that DeShawn had shared an apartment with him, the man had continually surprised him. So had his wide circle of friends and acquaintances. DeShawn's current visitor wasn't squirming uncomfortably or casting sidelong looks of horror at him. Instead, she seemed to be every bit as into it as he was. It reminded Jeff yet again that he didn't live in some upstate hick town anymore. New York City was a brave new world.

He wandered toward the kitchen to help himself to whatever it was that DeShawn and his friend had ordered in, calling out to ask if either of them wanted another beer. They both nodded while riveted to the action onscreen, Deshawn's guest with her fingernails dug into his thigh. Apparently, watching some muscle-bound cretin choke another woman with his dick was a turn-on for some people.

Jeff spent a couple of hours in his room tinkering with a new chair idea and by nine o'clock was ready to head out for his gig at Arlene's. That night, doing a single set at a venue with its own excellent set of house drums, amps and microphones would be a simple matter of showing up with a few extra pairs of sticks and a fair-size helping of attitude. As the band member seated on a stool behind a screen of drums, cymbals and hi-hats, he generally let the other three do most of the showboating, save for the two minutes when he took his obligatory drum solo. And all of that was just fine with him. Over the three years that Whack Job had been playing together, his voice had improved dramatically. He was hardly any Freddie Mercury but as a drummer who could sing he was certainly capable of holding his own. That particular night, mostly because they were hoping to impress some hot booking agent, he was determined to bring his A-game, which meant he needed to make the audience forget about the headliner, Flymo, an older Downtown band with a more established following.

When he stepped out of a cab onto Stanton Street, he found Amy waiting anxiously on the sidewalk outside the former Puerto Rican bodega. To judge from her expression, something was wrong.

"What's up? You look upset."

Her green eyes flashed anger. "You told her you're playing here tonight?"

Thinking Milenka, Jeff felt a knot suddenly form in the pit of his stomach. But that was impossible. Hardly twenty words had passed between them all night, most of them demands made by her. "Her who?" he asked.

"Fucking Katya. She's sitting at a table in there with three guys I'm pretty sure are the rest of your band. Dressed even skankier than she was last night. I can't believe you'd do that and then invite me, too."

"I didn't do anything," he protested. "She must have overheard you and me talking. I didn't tell her shit."

Some of the venom leaked out of her expression as she scrutinized his face for the truth of it. All the same, she was nowhere near mollified. "Jesus, Jeff. First my step-mother and now her? They're like a pair of fucking tag-team wrestlers."

Whack Job

"I just told you I didn't invite her. I swear to God."

She waved a dismissive hand. "I mean I'll admit you're kinda cute," she continued, "but not that fucking cute."

It was just the second time she'd said anything about the way he looked. Beyond their first intersection when she'd ordered him to take off his shirt, grabbed his ass, and growled in his ear, she'd since made a studied point of comporting herself with total neutrality whenever they were around each other. There'd been that 'shitting where you eat speech' and ever since, she'd pretty much treated him like a eunuch.

"So, just what is it you're worried about here?" he asked. "That I might be just slutty enough to fuck your step-mother one night and then turn around and do your step-sister the next?"

Even as he said it he wondered how much lying he was doing to both her and himself. Katya was the one responsible for the erection he'd been sporting when her mother climbed into his bed last night.

"C'mon. Try to get real here," she countered. "I happen to know for a fact that I could walk up to any twenty-one-year-old male on the planet, tell him I want to fuck, and he'd be incapable of saying no. Maybe not if his girlfriend, mother, or wife was standing right there next to him, but otherwise? He'd fold like a beach chair. Deny you wouldn't and you're just another liar."

Jeff was starting to sweat beneath the hot intensity of her gaze. No way he'd ever admit it but he'd already entertained any number of fantasies involving her, ever since she'd grabbed that handful of his ass and filled his nose with the hot scent of patchouli, frankincense and cloves. While she might not have Katya's ridiculous way of comporting herself, she was still more attractive than her half-sister in the ways that tended to endure for years. She was quick-witted and insightful, with a much stronger self-image. And she also had those eyes. By making him her business partner and forbidding him to even think of her in any other terms, she had also made her beauty inaccessible in ways that he knew might ultimately make him crazy.

"I know we've both got big days tomorrow so maybe you should stick around until the end of our set and then drop me home," he said. "That way you can be sure I don't wake up inside

Trump Tower."

She took a deep breath and shook her head, still glaring at him. "Jesus. Are you really that pathetic?"

"I think you already know the answer to that, which is why you're gonna take me up on my suggestion." He nodded toward the door to the club. "We'd better get in there. This place gets mobbed. That table where you saw Katya sitting is probably the band's. Can you sit and try to enjoy the show without clawing her eyes out?"

"You're very funny."

"If you want, I'm sure I can get our bass player to make a move on her. Chicks like her seem to really dig him."

ELEVEN

The next morning Jeff woke up alone in his own bed. Whack Job had managed to put on what he believed to be their most dynamic performance to date, his own singing as much inspired by the presence of his new business partner as it was by a desire to impress that booking agent. In his experience, those agent-types when coming out to give a band a listen generally tended to play their cards close to the vest but this one had actually been openly enthusiastic about their prospects. If there was an off-note it was played by Amy's half-sister, who was clearly displeased by how close he and she had remained huddled-up when he wasn't on stage, effectively preventing her from getting anywhere near him. She'd come loaded for bear, in black thigh-boots with five-inch heels, a skirt short enough where even a casual observer could see clear to East Jesus, and a gauzy white blouse with a near see-through black bra worn beneath. His two unattached bandmates, Tanner Upton on bass and Rick Carlisle on keys, practically tripped over each other vying for her attention. He was pretty sure it was Tanner who would either end up with her in Trump Tower or on the dirty sheets of his shitty studio apartment in Bed Sty. His money was on the Tower. While many of Tanner's conquests seemed to think it exotic to screw a bad-boy bass player in his Bohemian Brooklyn shit-pit, Jeff didn't have Katya Brock pegged as one of those.

⊚⊚⊚

Come early December, the Parsons School's five-week winter break found Jeff and Amy spending almost all of their time together plotting the immediate future of their manufacturing enterprise. This involved traipsing all over the boroughs of Queens and Brooklyn and even venturing into the nearer reaches of Nassau County and across the Hudson River into Hoboken and Jersey City looking for just the right building to house their operation. Because Jeff also had his Whack Job gigs and preferred to not commute great distances to get to them, he'd lobbied for a location like East Williamsburg in Brooklyn or Long Island City in Queens because of their proximity to Manhattan. With the pressures of gentrification, both of those areas were rapidly becoming more expensive and the pickings within them were slim. Still, there were opportunities to be found, a task made easier by Amy's willingness to exploit her father's New York commercial real estate connections.

Christmas came and went with Jeff venturing home to Pawling for the holiday and Amy spending it at her mother's house in Scarsdale in Westchester County. Then, during the week between Christmas and New Year's, they lucked into the perfect building on 9th Street near 37th Avenue in Long Island City. Zoned multi-use light industrial, it was a two-story, 60,000 square foot red-brick former tool-and-die works, built in the middle of the 19th Century. It had been through a number of incarnations since, the most recent a custom cabinet fabrication plant owned by three bullheaded German immigrant brothers, two of whom had outgrown their use for the third, split their business into two separate entities, and relocated. Jeff appreciated the fact that much of the infrastructure from that latest enterprise was still in place, eliminating the need to start from scratch with new dust abatement systems and upgraded power panels.

After arranging with the broker representing the property to have the lease details sent to their attorney in Chicago, Amy and Jeff cabbed it back to Manhattan via the Queensborough Bridge. It was mid-afternoon, the last Friday in December. In the middle of the holiday dead-week, traffic was light.

"I just realized we've been so pre-occupied, I haven't asked what you're doing for New Year's Eve," Amy said. It fell on a Sunday that year, just two days away.

"Our new agent's gotten us a co-headliner gig at Brooklyn Steel," Jeff replied. "We alternate with another band, playing sets from nine o'clock 'til two. You should come."

"Is your bass player still hooking up with my sister?" A heavy helping of disdain was served with the question.

Jeff shrugged. "I dunno. I expect only if she's willing to take a number and put up with him fucking a shit-load of other chicks, too. The word exclusive's not even in his vocabulary."

"It's not in hers, either," she said. "The only reason she banged him in the first place was to get her foot in your door."

Jeff knew she was likely right. Tanner might be hot in a sleazy bad-boy rocker kind of way, but Katya Brock had cut her eye-teeth in a completely other realm; one populated by men dripping with cash. Most months Tanner had trouble paying his rent.

"Still, I get the impression her attention span isn't much longer than his," he said. "He challenges the common fruit fly in that department."

"New Year's Eve I'm supposed to get together with an old boyfriend I haven't seen since high school," she said. "He probably won't be up for spending the whole evening in Brooklyn."

Was that a little pang of jealousy Jeff felt? In one of their many conversations he'd learned that Amy had attended Brearley, the exclusive all-girls school on Manhattan's Upper East Side. He guessed that this old flame had gone to some other school with that same kind of pedigree.

"Does he live here in town or just home for the holidays?" he asked.

"Visiting," she replied. "He hasn't lived here in years. Midway through high school his dad moved them to LA to start a new record label. He was the love of my life at that point. When he left, I thought I would die."

Jeff realized how little he actually knew about her personal life, other than the segment that existed in the far reaches of eastern Long Island.

"How weird will it be to see him again after all this time?" he asked.

He watched her let her mind drift back over what he assumed were old memories. It probably wasn't the first time she'd done that since learning of this guy's impending visit. "How would I know?" she said. "He could be anybody now. It's been ten years."

"So why not meet him early? See how it goes. If it's going okay, drag him along with you. If not, escape and come by yourself. There's nothing worse than being caught with somebody you don't want to be with, come midnight New Year's Eve."

"I don't know about coming alone that late. I don't want to cramp your style."

He looked at her sharply. "What's that supposed to mean?"

She shrugged. "I don't know. It's not like I've been keeping tabs but with all the time you've spent with me lately it's probably been a while since you got laid."

They were halfway across the Queensborough Bridge, the Empire State Building's red and green holiday season lighting just becoming visible as the shadows of dusk gathered. Jeff didn't think there could ever come a time when he wouldn't be awed by the sheer drama of the Manhattan skyline, no matter how many times he saw it. Just staring out the cab windshield at it helped distract him from how that last comment of hers was making him feel. It had prompted a memory of the last time he'd been with anyone, in this case a random one-off after a gig at the Bowery Ballroom two weeks ago. Right in the middle of that hook-up, in an Avenue C apartment with the woman's roommate smoking weed in the living room on the other side of a flimsy bedroom door, he'd suddenly been visited by the strangest feeling of guilt, like he was cheating on Amy even though no relationship of that kind existed between them. And now, first that earlier pang of jealousy and then, with her comment about the last time he'd gotten laid, it felt like she'd just stuck a knife in his gut and twisted the blade. What the hell was that about?

"I don't think it's really your business when or if I get laid," he muttered. "That's an area both you and I should probably stay out of."

She turned in her seat to look at him more sharply. "Where did that come from?"

He shook his head and continued to stare straight ahead. He knew he probably looked like an ass but right then he had no control over it.

"Jeffrey?"

"It's Jefferson, and don't fucking go there. You sound like my mother."

"I don't understand what's eating at you. We just found the building of our dreams."

He suddenly realized that if he didn't get control of himself right then and there he ran the risk of throwing a grenade into their works and blowing everything up. Okay, so he cared a lot more about her esteem than he ever realized and that fact had just hit him like a truck-load of wet cement, but that was on him to deal with, not her.

He took a quick breath and turned to meet those remarkable green eyes again, every ounce of will producing what he hoped was an acceptable smile.

"You're right. We did. And I think we need to celebrate with a drink. I'm buying."

"You don't have any money. Let me."

He was trying as hard as he could to loosen up and forget the fact that within forty-eight hours she'd likely be spending the night with some old preppie flame. To that end, he fed her his best sly smile. "Actually, I do. The last gig we played at the Ballroom? I made a five hundred bucks. Heck, I can even pop for Champagne."

With things threatening to go south between them just a moment earlier, he saw a look of confusion mixed with relief on her face.

"Keep your wallet in your pants, Mr. Big Spender. Save the Champagne for our first feature in Architectural Digest."

"Okay, but you need to promise me something," he said. "I read somewhere recently that ninety-five percent of all partnerships fail. I'm sure there's a whole list of reasons, but you and me are in a kinda unique situation here."

Those eyes were boring in on him now. "And just what would situation that be?" she asked. "That we're both attracted to each other, that we know that if this is going to work we can't go there, and that at this point in our lives we're both still horny as hell?"

He stared at her in astonishment. Damn, had she really just read his mind? There was no doubt in his own that he found her desirable but in spite of that naked butt-grab and her hot breath in his ear early on in their program, he'd managed to convince himself that she had no actual physical interest of her own. He swallowed hard.

"So, what do we do about that?" he asked.

She averted her gaze to look down at her folded hands. "I'm hoping we can find some means of building on that tension. Maybe even use it to stay friends. How we do that, I'm not really sure. At least not right now."

He had problems imagining how they could do that, too. At an age when spontaneous erections occurred as often as commercials during ballgames and when almost any woman walking down the street appealed to some primitive impulse generated by his lizard brain, he already had more sexual tension in his life than he knew what to do with.

"We might have better luck if we agree to take all mention of our respective sex lives totally off the table," he said. "You don't worry about the last time I got laid and I don't worry about that same thing with you. Or at least if we do, we don't talk about it to each other."

"So, if Katya makes another run at you, which we both know she will, you're not going to say anything about it to me?"

"And if you end up fucking your old high school boyfriend New Year's Eve? You're not gonna mention that either."

"Who said I have any interest in fucking him?"

He'd already seen the spark of curious interest there in her eyes but knew, if this was going to work, he couldn't challenge her. Instead, he lifted his hands in surrender. "According to the new rules we can't even go there," he said. "From now on that subject is off-limits. Verboten."

She caught one of his hands in both of hers and pulled it down to the seat between them, that green-eyed gaze boring in again. "I've never said it outright to you, Jeff, but I think you're a genius. And I know that the chance to take those designs of yours and turn them into things the whole world can use and enjoy is something that comes along once in a lifetime, if ever at all. I have the means and I have the ambition, but it's the luck part I really don't want to fuck up."

Without also mentioning her intention to take credit for those designs as their female entrepreneur front person, she'd just made as clear and concise a declaration of their mission as he was ever likely to hear from her. He inverted his hand to intertwine fingers and squeeze back.

"I don't want to fuck it up, either," he said.

She nodded while disengaging, then folded her hands in her lap again. "I guess this means that the offer I made earlier, about the two of us doubling up at my place, should be taken off the table, huh?"

"I'm thinking that once we sign that building lease I can turn one of those office spaces there into a bedroom, plumb in a shower, and move in," he said. "We're gonna need a break-room with a kitchen. I can use that as mine, too."

"Really? You'd live all alone in a factory?"

The building they'd just found had an office mezzanine that ran the full length of the first-floor production area, front-to-back with a pair of restrooms in the middle. Always quick to conceptualize, Jeff could already see himself installed there. He could set up a bedroom with direct access to his design studio; make it a sort of suite. Amy and any other management personnel could use the offices closer to the head of the stairs, with a conference room and that kitchen/break-room between them. He usually got his most serious creative work done at night, so a factory sitting idle in the wee hours, with no social distractions, might actually be beneficial to his process.

TWELVE

As events actually transpired, Jeff's Whack Job gig at Brooklyn Steel that New Year's Eve turned out to be almost disappointingly drama free. According to bass player Tanner Upton, Katya had lost interest almost as quickly as Amy had predicted she might. She was nowhere to be found among the crowd of fifteen hundred revelers high on Molly, coke, mushrooms, and excessive amounts of alcohol. Amy and her former high school beau never showed and at three AM Jeff let two women visiting from Charlotte, North Carolina take him back to the city in a rented limo. The next morning he awoke, ironically, in the master bedroom of a Trump Tower condo owned by his bedmate's hedge fund manager father. Hungover, he'd managed to slip out from under the ochre satin sheets without waking her and avoided the embarrassment of not remembering her name. He left the building thinking that Amy no longer had to worry about the last time he'd gotten laid and suspecting that he likely didn't need to worry about the last time she had, either.

He didn't see her again until the morning of January 2nd when she invited him to her place to discuss their next moves over coffee. When she didn't mention her failure to show at his gig, he left the subject of that old boyfriend alone.

"Yesterday, I spent some time sketching out a proposed layout for that mezzanine area on the first floor," he told her. And with that he pulled a drawing more elaborate than any simple sketch from a tubular blueprint case and unrolled it onto her coffee table, pinning one edge with his coffee mug.

"Check it out. Because you're the head honcho, I've got your office here, at the top of the stairs." He pointed. "Right next to the production manager, with our marketing department in the offices next along. Then two more offices for whomever, a conference room, kitchen-slash-break area, and the two executive restrooms, with my design studio, bedroom and separate bath at the far end." He tossed the pencil he'd been using as a pointer onto the drawing and sat back on her sofa. "Home sweet home."

She seemed impressed. "You came up with all this just yesterday?"

He nodded. "For at least the first couple years, I'm guessing those thirty thousand square feet on the first floor will be all we need. So maybe we can rent out that upstairs to some other business on a short-term lease. You know. To help defray some of our start-up costs."

He'd stolen glances around the loft while loitering in her kitchen earlier, looking for signs that someone else might have spent the New Year's weekend there. Now seated in her living room he realized he was doing the same thing again while also trying to gauge her demeanor. She was dressed for what looked to him like a comfortable day at home; barefoot, baggy flannel pants, and an oversize University of Chicago sweatshirt. Her hair was semi-contained in another one of her ubiquitous bandanas. There was no sign of anything being out of place in either her house or her world.

"I think this is killer," she said. "So, you're really serious about wanting to live there?"

"Hell yeah. Living in an industrial building like that has always been one of my secret fantasies, ever since I joined the band and had my first loft practice in Gowanus." That building had been even grungier than the one they were leasing; divided up into spaces rented to musicians and studio artists in search of the cheap square footage they needed to pursue their crafts. The design he'd come up with would be considerably less basic, but he imagined the feel would be roughly the same. Lots of space for him and no one around to bother him after hours. He figured that Amy, living in an old loft building like she did, had to be sympathetic to at least some of what he was talking about.

"I kind of like the idea of always knowing where to find you," she said. "Maybe more than you will once I start showing up at your door at all hours with crazy new ideas."

He winced. "We'll probably need to enforce an after-hours call-ahead policy."

She wasn't done sticking the needle in there. "It might be your house but it's still just down the hall from my office." She tapped that drawing with an index finger.

"Not that this isn't great work, but are you sure about this? I've got money set aside. I can help you get an apartment somewhere if you want."

At least in his head, once he'd started doing those renderings he was already living there. "After we get some basic plumbing roughed in so I can set a toilet and rig a shower, I'm moving in. I can do the rest of the carpentry myself."

"You don't mind living in the middle of a construction site?"

"I grew up breathing sawdust."

He surveyed her sitting there in the equivalent of her PJs and considered how relieved he felt, seeing no evidence that another male had occupied that space over the weekend. Maybe she was just a neat-freak who always cleaned up really well after herself, but just the fact that he cared at all was still something he needed to find ways to deal with.

"Meanwhile, depending on when the school wants me out of my apartment, Foster's got a futon in his music room. He says I can crash there."

Whack Job's lead guitarist also had an intrusive girlfriend who drove Jeff crazy, but right then he was talking ports in storms. She might end up functioning as motivation for him to work even harder to get his new living quarters together quickly.

Amy was looking at that floor plan again. "I hope you know that once we sign that lease, you can't spend all of your time just working on this," she said. "We'll need you to focus hard on our product line; to get prototypes of those first two chairs built and into production as fast as possible. I know you just said you can do a lot of the carpentry yourself, but let's hire a contractor to do all that stuff. We'll need you in the game."

He didn't know why it shocked him so much when the efficient pragmatist in her came out so strongly like that. Was it just because she was from such a different background and he'd always assumed that people like her wouldn't be quite so practical? In the upstate, male-dominated construction world from whence he came, women like her were usually clients, seen by people like his father and uncles as needing a lot of guidance from strong, knowledgeable men. Listening to her now, he realized he'd better get his head out of his provincial ass. Pronto.

"You're right," he agreed. "Your dad rents equipment to

Whack Job

people who build dams and skyscrapers. That's way bigger than I've ever learned to think."

She removed his coffee mug from the edge of his drawing and proceeded to roll it up. "I'm planning to rely a lot on advice from people he's connected to here in the city; on how to get us built out and up-and-running quickly. They'll all be commercial contractors, many of whom can also point us to the kind of fabrication expertise we need." She slid the drawing back into its tube. "I'll give this to one of them. Once they've had a look, we'll set up a meeting with an architect and you can fill in any missing details."

Jeff was getting the message. He was thinking baby-steps and she was already on the fast track. "I get it. I need to focus on those chairs and nothing else."

"Pretty much. You need to spec every detail of them, which I imagine will involve research. What materials you'll want to use, stuff like that. I know those might change once we talk to a production expert, but you need to have a good idea about how you want them to go together."

"I think I have a pretty good notion of that already," he said. "It's part of my own fabrication background."

"Well, spell it all out. In as much detail as possible. That will help me with production cost analysis. And keep in mind what our target market is. These won't be six-thousand-dollar chairs, but they won't be cheap pieces of shit, either."

They'd never really talked about a price point before, only agreeing that they wanted to make their designs accessible enough so that somebody who wasn't rich could afford them. "The prototypes will still be expensive, no matter," he said. "The main way we bring down the cost will be through mass production."

"Definitely. But while we do that we'll still need to do competitive bidding for all of our materials. We aren't the Pentagon."

Jeff chuckled at that.

"Speaking of my dad," she said. "He invited us out to East Hampton again this weekend to talk the finer points." This was punctuated with a knowing look. "I told him I could make it but you already have other plans."

◉◉◉

Milenka Brock knew that no reasonable mother would gloat on hearing her daughter admit defeat, but after making a half-dozen trips into Manhattan trying to even-up their sexual conquest score, Katya's failures saw her doing just that. But then again, Milenka wasn't an ordinary mother or at all reasonable. If forced by some arcane means of torture to admit a truth, she might allow that Katya currently embodied more physical allure than she any longer did, but she would still contend that with her wiles she continued to have a slight seductive advantage; one born out of simple boldness. Katya, in her youthful pride, preferred to dangle her physicality out there like a flashy lure tied to 80-pound test and trust that any fish she was after would sooner-or-later bite. Milenka preferred the snorkel and speargun approach. Swim right up, take aim, and shoot. Drag him to shore impaled and squirming on the end of her pike.

If pressed to give an answer, she probably couldn't say precisely why she was so obsessed with her stepdaughter Amy's new partner, other than the fact that, in spite of being repeatedly thwarted in her pursuits, Katya was continuing to express a keen interest. Sure, Jeff Land had been a decent-enough lay, but that certainly wasn't factor enough to sustain Milenka's current preoccupation. As she'd learned over the years Eastern Long Island was littered with attractive men who were decent lays. Instead, it had to be the competition with her daughter, plain and simple; the thrilling ripeness of Katya's youth versus her own nearly three decades of honing her craft. That, and proving yet again that regardless of her age, she still had what it took to win any fishing tournament she chose to enter.

Clandestine information-gathering was crucial to Milenka's current quest and so, as Katya's frustration with her own strategy continued to grow in direct proportion to the indifference being shown to her by the bass player in Jeff Land's band, Milenka worked to remain encouraging. Bert was away in Dubai until Friday and the two of them had just been served breakfast together in the solarium.

"I know this Tanner boy was just a means of getting close but I think you are sort of into him now, too. No?" she asked.

"He's a total skeev," Katya replied. "Which might be fine if he were my primary target, but not as a stepping stone. I need a guy like him to be totally into me. That way it's me who gets to fuck with his head while I'm playing him and not the other way around."

"You think he is playing you?"

"He gets too much random pussy to bother. Once he's tasted the fruit, he just doesn't really care all that that much anymore."

"What about the others in the band?"

Milenka was watching Katya nibble at the edge of her croissant like she was still debating whether or not to commit. She knew that her daughter watched the scale like a cat watches a mouse hole. But Katya also didn't work-out as zealously as she did and over the holidays her face had filled out a tiny bit, which likely meant her ass had as well.

"Don't think I haven't thought about them," Katya replied. "Foster, the lead guitarist, is out. He's got a girlfriend. A real bitch. If she's at one of their gigs, he's not even allowed to talk to anyone else. And the keys player, Rick? He's a no, too. Too big a step down."

"Not hot enough you mean?"

"Not even lukewarm."

"So, why do you not go straight for the jugular?" Milenka asked. "I assume you have Jeff's address by now."

"What? Just walk up and ring his bell? That's more your game than mine."

"If you wear the dress you wear the first night we meet him, I am sure he will ask you in."

"I'm just different than you are," Katya said. "For me, it never feels like a conquest unless it's the dude who takes the bait; makes the play."

"And this has worked for you so far how? You see him how many times now? Five? Six? I do not understand why you even care anymore. Just because I am fucking him first?"

Katya finally took an actual bite of her pastry, chewing slowly as she thought about what Milenka had just asked. "That's part of it, sure. But even more is because I knew I had him that night and it was only a matter of reeling him in. Then you went and messed with my rhythm. Once I set the hook, I'm never really satisfied until I have that fish flopping around in the bottom of my boat."

"Your father called to say that Amy she is coming out Saturday to meet again. I ask if her partner comes too and he says no, that he has other plans. I assume this means he and his band will play another show."

Katya nodded. "At Terminal 5 in Hell's Kitchen. They're headlining."

"So, why do we not both go? Leave your father and sister here to have their little pow-wow. You wear your dress and bring your fishing pole. I will bring my speargun. May the best woman win."

THIRTEEN

Amy called Jeff that Friday evening to tell him their lawyer had just contacted her from Chicago, saying that he and Bert Brock's attorneys had finished drawing up those contracts and they'd been overnighted to East Hampton. They should be there by the time she arrived out there for dinner Saturday. Jeff asked if that meant he needed to be there to sign something and she said no. She would bring a copy back into the city where the two of them could go over it together, Sunday. Toward that end, she offered to cook them brunch. They made a date for noon at her place.

After Whack Job did a sound check at Terminal 5 Saturday evening, Jeff took a pass when the other guys asked if he wanted to join them for dinner at Victor's. As much as he loved Cuban food, for the past week he'd been working hard on those materials specs for the Venus and David prototypes that he and Amy would feature as their venture's first offerings. She needed that data to get an initial cost analysis done as quickly as possible and he was confident he could have them wrapped up and ready for her before tomorrow's brunch if he worked the several hours before the band was scheduled to step onstage at 11:00 PM.

Amy had worked just as diligently as he had over that past week on her own end of organizing the business, meeting with several of her father's contractor associates and compiling lists of fabrication and production consultants they would want to put on retainer as well as hands-on people they hoped to hire. The organization he'd seen her bring to her home life appeared to reflect how she approached every task she tackled.

He'd just finished putting his finalized notes together when she called from East Hampton. It was pushing ten o'clock and was time for him to think about grabbing a cab.

"Hey. How did dinner go?" he asked.

"Good. Either my friend in Chicago really did us a solid or someone with some serious muscle at his firm did. Dad's guys tried to shave us a little bit here and there but our team stuck to their guns. We've gotten pretty much everything we wanted."

"The whole ten million up-front?" That was their ask for a phase-one build-out and for prototype fabrication, a number that still boggled his mind.

"Yep. And if we hit our goals with the kind of reviews in the trades that we'll need and then pull off the gallery show we'll want to mount to launch this enterprise, there's that other twenty million to take us into full production and marketing. It means that as soon as the ink is dry he cuts us our first check and we can start paying ourselves enough for you live on."

Another thing they'd had a serious discussion about was how big their initial salaries should be. Not having earned a dime yet and with no prospect of doing so in the immediate future, they both knew they couldn't pay themselves more than a subsistence minimum. Anything in excess of that would raise all sorts of red flags and lead her father to question his daughter's business acumen. Apparently, the eighty thousand-per-person they'd proposed to sustain themselves through their first year of operation had landed safely inside his ballpark.

"That's not the reason I'm calling though," she continued. "I need to give you a heads-up. Milenka and Katya weren't at dinner tonight. They told my father there's a hot new band playing in the city that they really want to hear. After that show they're planning on staying at the condo in town. I'll bet you my first year's salary I know just which hot new band that is."

Jeff felt a little quiver of dread run down his spine.

"Fuck me," he muttered.

"I hope not. But those two are nothing if not determined."

He'd collected his jacket and the half-dozen pairs of drumsticks he might need while flashing on Milenka Brock climbing into his bed and the wild ride that then ensued. Conniving bitch or not, she'd brought a kind of fervent energy to the act that he'd never encountered before and that recollection had the sex-maniac area of his twenty-one-year-old limbic brain firing on all cylinders while another more reasoning part of his consciousness was telling him that if he ever went there again it might be the worst mistake he ever made. The woman's husband had just committed to feeding his dream of a lifetime ten million dollars. How badly did he want

Whack Job

to risk fucking that up just to get his dick wet?

"Do me a favor and find yourself some cute little groupie and latch onto her like she's a goddamn life preserver," Amy said. "And don't dare let go no matter what kind of tsunami hits your beach."

He laughed outright at that. "You're suggesting I fight fire with fire? How very kind of you, partner."

"Just stay focused on what we've got at stake here, asshole."

Before he could respond she cut the connection, those last words still echoing in his ear.

☉☉☉

Perpetually late, Whack Job's bass player Tanner Upton showed up backstage at Terminal 5 in the company of Katya and Milenka Brock while Jeff was in a corner of the green room doing neck rolls and light vocal work to loosen up his chords. If there had been any doubt about what "hot band" the mother-daughter pair had traveled into the city from East Hampton to see, the way Milenka caught Jeff's eye told him exactly what sort of game was afoot there. This play had been carefully engineered. Neither of them could have possibly left Long Island dressed like a pair of high-end Las Vegas hookers so he guessed they must have stopped at the city apartment to change. Milenka had her hair up with little stray wisps let hang free to frame her exotic Slavic face and was turned out in a pair of black leather capri pants that looked like they'd been sprayed on paired with an off-the-shoulder crop top that left half-an-acre of toned ab, arms, shoulders and back bared. Katya wore a black lace bustier from which she all but overflowed and a little pair of Lycra shorts so brief that left several inches of butt cheek were left exposed. When Milenka's first eye contact changed ever-so-slightly to let a sly smirk leak out, the memory of her naked body glistening with sweat in the moonlight was suddenly front-and-center in his mind's eye.

Aw fuck, he thought. No way this was happening.

As Jeff settled in front of his drum kit and adjusted his mic boom a few minutes later, Tanner drifted over, the body of his bass guitar slung low against his right hip and a fox-in-the-henhouse grin plastered across his face.

"I can't believe Katya's mom, dude. Holy shit. They want you to come hang with us at their place after the show."

Jeff had seen this coming with that sly smirk of Milenka's and had since walked onstage scanning faces in the crowd for any possible port in this brewing storm.

"I told this chick who's here I would hook up with her later," he lied.

"Ghost her, dude. We play this right, I bet we can double-dip. Each of us fuck both of them, bro."

Jeff adjusted his sticks in his hands and nodded toward the Terminal 5 emcee then crossing the stage to join Foster at his microphone and scream, "Are you ready for this?!!"

He leaned toward Tanner, barely able to hear himself over the frenzied roar of the crowd. "Not happening, bro. But you have a ball. And if I were you I'd save most of my energy for the mom."

◉◉◉

Jeff managed to sneak offstage at their first break and talk to two women from Hunter College at the bar. One seemed particularly keen on getting better acquainted but he couldn't shake the feeling that the air had been let out of his balloon that night. He still hadn't quite comprehended what Amy meant when she'd described the competition that she'd sensed between her half-sister and stepmother but when they'd appeared backstage together dressed like that, it had all come clear as spring water. The two of them were on some sort of strange, manipulative crusade and by all appearances he was their Holy Grail. Tanner was just the ship they'd boarded to make their voyage to the Promised Land.

He'd repeated the number ten-million to himself like a mantra throughout both of their sets and ten minutes after the end of their second encore, his shirt soaked with sweat inside a leather bomber jacket and a bar towel wrapped around his neck like a gasket to keep out the frigid February air, he hiked two blocks east to the corner of 57th Street and Ninth Avenue looking for a cab. He pulled his phone out of his pocket when it buzzed to find a text from a

Whack Job

number he failed to recognize.

Where the fuck are you?

631 Area Code. He punched Amy's number on speed dial rather than respond. She answered from her father's guest cottage.

"Kinda late, isn't it?" she growled. "I'm in bed."

"Any idea where the 631 Area Code is?" he asked.

"Yeah. Here. Why?"

"I just got a text from a number I don't recognize."

"Is your show over?"

"Yep. I'm headed for Ninth Avenue looking for a cab."

"And Katya and Milenka both showed, right? What does the text say?"

"Where the fuck are you? They tried to get Tanner to recruit me to their place for some after-hours fun."

"Left alone with those two he's liable to get hurt. You might want to start looking for a new bass player. Jesus. How did you manage to escape?"

"I used your advice and kept thinking about that ten mil."

"I'm thinking you might be smarter than you look, Prodigy-boy."

It was late and it sounded like he'd just awakened her from a dead sleep so he let the Prodigy-boy slide. "What does a smart guy look like?" he asked.

"In my experience? They're usually not quite as cute as you or play drums in a rock band. Where's Foster? I thought you were crashing at his place."

"He wanted to hang. I needed to get out of there, fast."

His phone dinged as another text came through.

"Well?"

"You might want to block that number," Amy said. "Katya's next move will be to send you a picture of her boobs."

"She probably doesn't realize they aren't worth ten million dollars," Jeff said. "Am I mistaken, or did you just call me cute?"

"Fuck you and go get some sleep. Dad gave me a whole bunch of great new leads tonight. We've got a big week ahead of us. I'll see you at noon for brunch."

As soon as Jeff hung up his phone rang. It was Tanner,

face-timing him. When he answered, he saw Katya holding the phone out at arm's length to show the two of them in the back seat of a limo, Tanner with one of her breasts in his mouth like a hungry baby. Milenka was nowhere to be seen. She then turned the camera to look directly into it, a craziness in her eyes as she smiled and hit the disconnect. Jeff stood there in the bitter cold staring at his blank screen. His phone rang again.

This time it was DeShawn.

"Yo," he answered. "What's up?"

"I just thought you should know some dope-ass older bitch was just here knocking on my door. She was looking for your ass. I told her you don't live here no more and she was pissed. Fuck was that about?"

"That was Amy Brock's step-mother. Long story, bro. I'm sorry she rousted you. I owe you a beer."

"No big, Homie. I almost invited her in. Bitch is smoking." Seconds later, Jeff reached Ninth Avenue and raised his hand to flag a lit cab, feeling like he'd just missed being hit by a bus.

Whack Job

FOURTEEN

Jeff was amazed to see what could be accomplished in a short period of time when you had the right connections and enough money to see a concept realized. He had tired of sleeping on Foster Bragg's sofa and dealing with lead guitarist's perpetually ornery girlfriend in less than two weeks and had found himself a sublet upstairs from a Korean BBQ restaurant on 11th Street in Long Island City just two blocks from their new site. From there he'd been able to keep closer tabs on the building project and to also meet with the fabricators who would engage in helping him produce prototypes of the Venus and David designs in three different formats; desk, dining, and rocking chair. After three months of that, he'd moved into his new digs and design studio at the plant, Amy then moving into her new offices in mid-April with construction on their production floor well underway. Meanwhile, in a smaller fabrication shop, his prototypes were being realized by a team of pattern and mold makers, welders, and specialty carpenters. Their first chairs, in the dining format, with body reliefs formed in white plastic with faint gray veins and blemishes in them to resemble sheets of antique white marble, were all but finished.

In the interim, Amy had hired Tamara Wilson, a young, twenty-seven-year-old black woman with an MBA from Columbia as their director of marketing and had installed her in an office just down the mezzanine. Tamara was already deep into ramping up a campaign to garner some serious notice as a new woman-owned business with big ambitions. Jeff, meanwhile, had turned a majority of his attention to designing a batch of new 'Lifestyle' offerings; a dining table and chairs, a sofa, loveseat and reading-chair ensemble with a coffee table and two different side table options, a credenza, and three distinct free-standing lighting fixtures. These would be reproduced as three-dimensional digital files and projected onto the walls of the high-profile SoHo art gallery where Amy would introduce those first Venus and David prototypes to the design world at a mid-September show. For him, it was a heady and exciting time spent working late most nights in his studio. Most days he could be found in the fabrication shop with his sleeves rolled up and hands dirty, working alongside everyone else involved in making those first designs a physical reality.

Late one May afternoon at quitting time he was washing up at one of the downstairs industrial sinks when Amy appeared, walking toward him across the production floor.

"I see you down here so much, I'm wondering how those 3-D projections for our opening are coming along."

That was one of the problems with having an office mezzanine that overlooked the nuts-and-bolts end of the business. Like nosey neighbors, Amy and everyone else working up there could watch his every move.

"When you're in the building you might see me down here a lot," he replied, "but you've gotta realize that aside from band practice and playing the occasional gig, I have no other life. The creative end of things comes a lot easier when no one is around to distract me."

"Don't give me that no social life crap," she countered. "I've seen the write-ups Whack Job has been getting."

Since the band had started to make a bigger name for themselves, they'd been getting a lot more notice in social media and on all the hippest New York music scene blogs and websites. With it had come more women wanting to party after their shows, a number that had increased in direct proportion to Jeff's current dwindling interest in one-night stands. Finished washing his hands and drying them, he gestured toward the fabrication shop. "Tanner and Rick might be having the times of their lives right now, but as pathetic as it might sound? Those people working on our chairs are most of my social life these days."

"When's the last time you saw Katya or my step-mother?"

"Not since that gig at Terminal 5. They've quit showing up, thank God.'

"Is Tanner still doing Katya?"

He frowned at that. "Hell if I know. Not that I've heard, but it's not like I keep tabs."

"From that little Facetime clip you said she sent you, I can't imagine why he'd want to quit."

He was starting to regret ever telling her about that. "Tanner? Shit. I doubt he could care less. Dude gets more pussy in a month than most guys get in their entire lives. But you didn't walk downstairs and all the way across the floor just to get my commentary on Tanner's sex life. What's really on your mind?"

"I was wondering if maybe we could have dinner tonight? Something other than Korean Barbeque or whatever it is you're living on these days."

Ever since that Sunday on her living room sofa when she'd slipped and admitted an attraction, they'd both purposely stayed at arms-length whenever they weren't working together. He hadn't been to Manhattan for anything but band gigs for what felt like an eternity. "Got somewhere in mind?" he asked.

"There's a hot new Caribbean-Low Country fusion place just opened in my neighborhood," she said. "I thought maybe we could try that."

"Sure. What time?"

"I'll call and see if I can get us an early reservation. That way we can ride in together; save you the cab or train ride." She still had that Porsche Carrera convertible her daddy had given her for her sixteenth birthday and drove it to the office most days now rather than take cabs. Jeff couldn't blame her. It was a sweet car and had to be a lot of fun to drive, even on New York City's crowded streets.

"Sure. Meanwhile, if you've got a minute I can show you those new renderings," he said. "I wasn't really liking them much until just recently, but now I think they're starting to finally come together."

It had been a while since she'd last paid a visit to his studio, which had him wondering if it felt too much like his house to her. He'd gotten in the bad habit of leaving his bedroom door hanging open, his slovenly bachelor's lifestyle on clear display. While he'd made any number of pledges to get better about making his bed every morning and picking up after himself, they'd thus far proven to be about as effective as most New Year's resolutions or gym memberships generally were.

Upstairs, they passed Tamara's Art Department where she and an advertising whiz-girl recently graduated from Syracuse University were busy creating an in-house ad campaign. In the break room, three fabricators just off work were talking loudly and laughing over beers. In his studio, he invited Amy to pull up one of the rolling stools while he fired up a digital projector aimed at a screen on an opposite wall. At his desk, he clicked onto the first design file he wanted to show her. It depicted a bulky sofa supported by a graceful, inconspicuous chrome frame that made it look almost like a cloud floating on air.

"I think I've finally managed to get the proportions right," he said. "What do you think?"

She stared at the 3-D rendering as it slowly began to spin clockwise, revealing the piece's sleek but sumptuously inviting lines. "I think I want one in my living room," she murmured. "That thing looks like you could spend your life on it."

"That's the basic idea," he said. "So, you like, huh?"

Amy spun on her stool to face him again and he got a faint whiff of that scent he'd caught during their first meeting in the Parson's fabrication shop so long ago. Frankincense, Patchouli and Clove. It instantly conjured his initial memory of those remarkable green eyes, her hot breath in his ear, and her fingers with a firm grasp on his naked butt. Any attraction to her had been buried beneath layers of complication in recent months but as he absorbed her frank, totally forthright gaze now, he couldn't deny how strong it still was.

Almost as if she could read his mind, she said, "Do you realize just how lucky we were to have found each other, partner? I get to be the one who introduces this stuff to the world and you don't have to sell your soul to La-Z-Boy."

One part of his brain was basking in the warmth of her open admiration while another was still wondering how it was going to feel to have her take full public credit for his designs. Sure, he knew it was a genius marketing ploy, but personal pride had always been a powerful motivator for him. More than money. With each day that they got another step closer to Brocking Chair becoming an actual, up-and-running commercial enterprise, his feelings about that idea had gotten more complex and confusing.

Amy stared at that projection of the sofa design again. "Between a Brock and a Soft Place," she murmured.

"Say what?"

She looked back at him. "I think I just came up with our ad campaign slogan for this stuff. You like?"

She did have a knack for catchy product concepts involving her last name. For the Venus and David desk chairs they were introducing, she'd come up with Brock and Roll. And for the three casual rocking chairs, Brock Around the Clock.

"I do," he admitted.

"Super work, Jeff. I love this stuff." She checked the time on her phone. "I'd better go and see if I can get us that reservation."

"Please do. Caribbean and Low Country fusion, huh? That sounds interesting."

⊚⊚⊚

Amy parked her car in the commercial garage up the block from the building where she lived and she and Jeff started to walk the three blocks to Carolibbean. All through her drive into Manhattan she'd found herself plagued by some serious and confusing misgivings because even after that don't-shit-where-you-eat speech she'd served up to Jeff when he first agreed to their partnership, she'd secretly suspected that sooner-or-later they might end up going there anyway. If he'd been nothing more than just a design genius, the temptation probably wouldn't have been quite so powerful as it was, but the fact that the bastard was so damned humble and pretty had made the eventuality seem all but a fait accompli. But then, a lot of that initial attraction she'd felt through their first few interactions had been annihilated on that limo ride back to Manhattan from East Hampton, the morning after Milenka had ambushed him. Now, six months later, time had slowly eroded the edges of her revulsion. Earlier that afternoon she'd stood at the mezzanine railing watching him working on those prototypes in the fabrication shop downstairs. She'd felt a surge of that same attraction flood through her once more as he moved,. The confidence and strength in his hands, sparks flying as he ran a body-grinder over a weld. The way he thought nothing of lifting and throwing a 4 X 8 sheet of three-quarter ply onto a table saw and pushing it through like he was cutting cardboard. The man was a stud. Just an hour ago, as she'd glanced past the open door from his design studio into his bedroom and seen the rumpled sheets of his unmade bed, she'd started to second-guess everything she was about to do. And it wasn't the first time. Thankfully, his head was in some totally other place at that moment, which she knew was a good thing because it had to be.

"Did I ever tell you my mother was born on St. Simon's Island in Georgia?" he asked. "And that I practically grew up on shrimp and grits?"

She glanced over at him. "How did she end up in upstate New York?"

"Her father was the Academy Superintendent at West Point and she was going to college at Vassar in Poughkeepsie when she met my dad," he said. "He and my uncles had this job building cabinets for a new infirmary at the college," he said. "She was getting drunk with friends in a local bar on her twenty-first birthday when they met. A month later, she was pregnant with me and eloping to Niagara Falls." He paused to grin. "As I'm sure you can imagine, that triggered a serious shit-storm."

Amy didn't know how any guy from a tiny rural town upstate could continue to surprise her the way that Jeff Land always seemed able to, but every month or so it felt like she was uncovering another layer. No guy as good-looking as him could be that smart. Or as insanely creative. And no one that smart could also be the drummer in a rock band of ever-increasing popularity and be able to sing like he could while also being so good with his hands, and also be so fucking guileless.

"Who do you favor," she asked. "Your mother or your father? Looks-wise, I mean."

"Pictures of my dad at my age look just like me," he said. "But my mom's the creative one. She was an art major and I'm pretty sure it's her who I got my design sense from. Dad wanted me to go into the business straight out of high school but she's the one who encouraged me to apply to Parsons instead."

"How often do you see your grandparents on your mother's side?" she asked

"Almost never. My grandma left the General when I was in third grade. He's an asshole. She moved back to St. Simon's and last I heard, he'd remarried for like the third time and was living in Hope Mills, North Carolina. That's close to Fort Bragg. He pretty much disowned my mom when she ran off and married my dad."

"That's a wild story."

He smiled. "Not as wild as having a billionaire father who practically abandoned you after you were born. That one takes the cake."

She bumped shoulders, laughing. "Touche'. Meanwhile, what were you starting to say about Low Country cooking?"

"My mom cooked dozens of her mother's recipes while I was growing up. Lotta stews. Frogmore, Brunswick, Catfish, but things like Charleston Red Rice, Shrimp Kedgeree, and Crab Cakes, too."

By then, they'd reached the front door to Carolibbean. When Jeff opened and held it for her, Amy guessed the gesture was little bit of his mother's Southern influence, probably beat into him as a kid.

Seated and having ordered cocktails after listening to the specials, Amy saw Jeff peering at her over the top of his menu. "Enough about my parents," he said. "Back at the shop you said there was something on your mind. So, spill. What's up?"

Amy felt her abdominal muscles tighten and realized she was white-knuckling the napkin in her lap. A moment of unavoidable truth was upon her and while every fiber of her being was screaming, Don't go there!, she knew that she had to. She swallowed hard.

"You remember that boyfriend from high school I told you about? The one who visited over New Year's?"

He frowned. "Jason something-or-other. Dude from LA."

"Jason Wuthrich. Last weekend he asked me to marry him."

Jeff looked at her with in confusion. "Say again?"

"He's been spending a lot of time in New York these past few months on business. We've been seeing each other a lot. Next month he's moving back here to take over a recording studio that his father just bought in the Brill Building."

She watched Jeff set his menu on the placemat before him, any of the tempting fare described therein apparently forgotten. "You serious? About marrying him, I mean?"

It was the slightly stricken look he wore that Amy was now trying to puzzle out.

"I think we're a really good fit, yeah," she replied. "His parents are sort of freaking out about him marrying a shiksa, but I've told him I'll convert."

That had him blinking in disbelief. "You don't even believe in God. What the fuck, Aim? Not that kind of God at any rate."

"It would be more like a formality. I'm not planning to drink the Kool-Aid."

He was taking a moment to digest all he'd just heard while she listened to the echo of it in her head. She knew the anger that she saw on his face was probably justified. There was more than just surface hypocrisy there. It ran deep and counter to everything he knew about her.

"Just so you realize how fucked up that is," he said. "I know you do. I can see it in your eyes."

Rather than confront him she pulled another one of those patented Amy switcheroos she was so good at. The wearing of a cool veneer and engaging in lots of emotional avoidance was buried deep in her DNA. "He's somebody you and the guys in your band will want to know," she said. "He won't just be running that recording studio. He's also taking control of DogPound Records. That's one of his father's hottest labels."

From previous conversations with him, Amy knew how well-versed Jeff was in the lore of the music business. He surely knew that the Brill Building, located at the corner of 49th and Broadway in Manhattan, was to the music business what the Vatican was to the Catholic church, with labels headquartered there cranking out one number-one hit after another for the past eighty years. He probably also knew that Abe Wuthrich's DogPound label was currently producing several Grammy winning hip-hop artists and other acts. According to Jason, one or another of those talents currently on his roster was mentioned in the music trades nearly every week.

"And what exactly is it about this dude that makes him such a good fit for you?" Jeff asked.

She scrambled to think of an answer that wouldn't sound

shallow and trite to him while feeling a little twinge of chagrin. "He went to Dalton, I went to Brearley. We lived in buildings a block away from each other and grew up knowing all the same people." Yep. Both shallow and trite.

"And his living in LA for the past ten years hasn't changed any of that?" he asked. "For sure I'm not the same dude I was when I was twelve."

She was losing patience. "Can't you just be happy for me? He's a good guy, Jeff. We click. He's solid. And he doesn't have a problem with me having my own company."

"So, then what? You'll make the perfect New York power couple? Because you're a pair of kids with rich daddies, your skids greased with dollars and all the right doors opened to you at the drop of a name?"

She felt heat rise in her face. "That's not fair," she retorted. "Neither of us had any control over who our parents are."

"Okay, so answer me this then. Are you actually in love with this guy or does he just tick all the right boxes on your Brearley Girl checklist?"

She realized then that she should have seen this coming. She knew how much she hated being challenged on anything that she'd made up her mind to do. In both college and grad school she'd cloaked that stubbornness in a Kevlar blanket of aloofness that was often mistaken for confidence. She'd watched how Jeff drew his creations with such assured directness, much in the same manner as he handled power tools. That kind of true confidence was something she could only dream about.

Feeling more vulnerable than she would want to admit, she set her own menu down to look at him without that barrier between them. "I'm not sure I even know what romantic love is," she said. "Do you?"

If she'd hoped to pin him with a question like that, even before he opened his mouth to answer it she saw in his eyes that she'd failed.

"No, I don't. And I sure as shit wouldn't marry anyone until I was pretty sure that I did. Why not skip all that for-better-or-worse, in-sickness-and-in-health bullshit and just form a corporation? To me, that sounds exactly like what you're proposing. If access to hot sex is part of your motivation, work some conjugal rights into your charter."

There was an undeniable vehemence in how he'd spoken and she wondered how much jealousy was responsible for generating it. As part of her learned-defense mechanism, she decided to confront his anger point-blank.

"I think you're upset because it isn't you."

Rather than call bullshit, he surprised her again. "That's probably part of it. You're as close to being my best friend as anyone in my life right now. How about I bring your sister Katya to your wedding as my plus-one?"

Wow. Harsh. But then again, when it came to this kind of combat, she was a seasoned pro. Years of fighting for her rightful place in her own fucked-up family had made her an expert in the field. "It's going to be a small, family affair, but if you ask nicely, maybe she'll bring you as hers," she said. "I'm pretty sure that Milenka already has a date."

FIFTEEN

By the time mid-September and Brocking Chair's big SoHo gallery launch event rolled around, an uneasy truce had existed between Jeff and Amy for the better part of four months. All six Venus and David prototypes were finished and unbeknownst to him, Amy had directed Tamara Wilson to send photographs of them to four of the most prestigious international design award competitions in the world, one in New York, one in Italy, and two in Germany. No winners in any of those would be announced until after the New Year, but his designs had already been announced as finalists in one of them, creating just the right kind of pre-opening buzz that Amy had hoped for. Two days before the show, Jeff also learned from her that Parsons had nominated her for the German Design Awards Newcomer Prize, one of the most coveted awards for newbies in the industry. Then, literally on the eve of their gallery opening, Jason Wuthrich contacted Whack Job's booking agent to say he wanted to discuss offering them a record deal.

It was Foster who called Jeff with that news, catching him going nuts with last-minute details at the gallery.

"This guy told our agent he's Amy's fiancé. I Googled him. His dad is fucking Abe Wuthrich, dude. Owns like six labels and is one of the most powerful record producers in America."

Jeff felt his stomach tighten. Now that Amy's name had been put forward by Parsons for that Newcomer Prize in Germany, her fiancé's interest felt like a weird kind of peace offering; something that she had engineered to salve her conscience. The first time that Jason Wuthrich had shown up in Long Island City for the obligatory tour of Brocking Chair's manufacturing facility, Jeff had forced himself to make nice while witnessing a dynamic that was far worse than anything he'd been able to imagine. Considering what Amy embodied physically, he'd expected her fiancé to cut an impressive figure, too, and in that regard he'd been seriously disappointed. The man was three inches shorter than her and pudgy, with a fleshy face and hair buzzed close to his scalp. Beneath that surface he oozed a strong sense of entitlement that made his Hollywood huckster's line of slick bullshit that much more offensive. Instead of embodying any sort of authenticity, it felt like he was playing a role he'd written for himself, in a movie where he was the star and everyone else, including Amy, was little more than a character playing a supporting role.

"Do me a favor, at least here at the jump," he told Foster. "Let's play hard-to-get for a while. Once word gets around that Dog-Pound is after us, other labels will be interested, too. They're all a bunch of sheep, everybody waiting for someone else bold enough to make the first move. We should see what other offers come in. Maybe get a bidding war going."

There was a pause at the other end of the line as Foster digested this. "The dude is Abe Wuthrich's son, bro. They don't come any bigger than that."

"He's also my business partner's fiancé and to me this feels like some kind of conflict of interest. I've met him and you haven't. He shakes your hand and you feel like you need to wash it after."

"So, I tell our agent what? Not to take any more of his calls? I'm not sure I can convince her to do that, Bro-mine. She's in this to make money, too."

"Just ask her to stall him off is all I'm asking. Say we're real busy with other shit and can't sit down with him right now. Maybe in a couple of weeks. Then tell her to spread the word that he called to everybody she knows in the business. My bet? It'll spread like wildfire."

Down the line, he heard Foster chuckle. "Listen to you, Mr. Businessman. That actually sounds like a decent strategy."

"Right now, I'm learning at the knees of several different masters," Jeff said. "Just tell her to hold her fire."

⊚⊚⊚

It wasn't just due to the efforts of Tamara Wilson and her ad team that the turn-out at their SoHo gallery opening a week after Labor Day was impressive by any design industry measure. The Parsons School's public relations department had also done its part, eager to enhance the institution's stature through the accomplishments of an alumnus. Movers and shakers from all corners of the New York design world had caught the buzz. Figuring that the daughter of business tycoon Bert Brock would at least put out a spread of decent food and booze, they'd come flocking. By six that evening, that crowd of curiosity seekers was overflowing the place and spilling out onto the sidewalk. In one corner, Foster's jazz quintet from Julliard played a steady stream of up-beat Bebop. Champagne flowed and designer-of-the-moment Amy Brock circulated, answering questions and making small talk. Jason Wuthrich, apparently having the wherewithal to know his place at an event like that, had managed to restrain himself from hitching his wagon to his fiance's star and instead loitered on the sidelines with Bert and Milenka Brock, shaking hands and exchanging Manhattan-style pleasantries with magazine editors, design critics, and various acquaintances.

Jeff, meanwhile, hung back with his production team to watch the show. It was the first time he'd seen Milenka since the night of his last Terminal 5 gig. When she and Bert Brock came face-to-face with him, she'd acted like she only vaguely recalled ever having met him.

Sooner or later, Amy drifted over to stand at his side and murmur in his ear. "They're loving these chairs, Prodigy Boy. How good does that make you feel?" It was at least six months since she'd last hung that moniker on him.

"Either that, or they're loving the fact that a woman designed them," he replied. "Though I'll admit that just seeing how they're looking at them does make me feel pretty good. I mean, I like to think I know what people want, but it's always touch-and-go until someone sits their butt in one of your chairs, smiles, and says, ah."

She chuckled at that. "It would appear that whole lot of people are saying ah tonight," she said. "That was a great idea to let everyone actually sit in them. Kudos there."

Six of their dining chairs, three Venus and three David, had been arranged boy/girl around a simple plate-glass table. One each of the office chairs faced each other over a pair of butted desks, and the two rocking chairs stood side-by-side on a simple square of plush jade-green carpeting.

"It's what furniture is made for. Not just to look pretty," he said. "I've been keeping a mental tally of which of them both genders prefer. So far, the gays and lesbians are mostly staying with their own sexes. It's with the heteros that I can't seem to see a clear pattern. The liberal feminist types are sticking with the Venus, but a lot of other women are definitely digging Dave."

"What about the straight guys?" she asked.

"Oh, Venus all the way. I didn't think you'd have to ask."

She grabbed his sleeve to tug at it. "I bet Tamara can get one of her interns to take over that survey. You need to relax and come enjoy the party."

"That's how I'm enjoying the party," he said. "By watching people sit in our chairs and smile and laugh."

Katya Brock entered the gallery at that point and Jeff watched her make a beeline for the bar without even looking around. After grabbing a glass of Champagne, she moved to join her mother, Bert Brock and her half-sister's fiancé. From the familiar way that Jason reacted when she kissed his cheek it was clear this wasn't the first time they'd met. She'd worn another one of those ubiquitous rigs of hers for the occasion, the late summer weather too warm for thigh boots but everything else pretty much the same. Five-inch heels, a skirt so short it could barely be called one, and a backless halter crop top that left very little to the imagination. It was going on six months now and she looked a bit more tuned-up than the last time he'd seen her, like she and her mother might be sharing the same personal trainer as well as their other mutual interests. Jason Wuthrich hadn't failed to notice, too.

"It looks like the B-team just arrived," Amy muttered. "I try to picture her in the hotel bar at, say, the Four Seasons, and how long it would be before they asked her to leave."

Jeff laughed. "Which one? In Vegas they'd probably pay her to sit there."

He'd made his first trip to Sin City a month earlier to attend a design materials convention with several of Brocking Chair's fabrication team. The scene had been something of an eye-opener for him.

"My fiancé seems to be enjoying the view," she growled. "But then, so is every other male in the room. When it comes to getting attention, that bitch is shameless."

He smiled and clicked glasses with her. "Maybe you should go lay claim to your future husband," he said. "Before your demi-sibling decides to eat him."

Pete O'Brien

BOOK TWO

Too Many Cooks

SIXTEEN

Amy's wedding was a small early October ceremony at her family's East Hampton estate that Jeff opted not to attend. Things had started to really jump in their world when, in the wake of that gallery show, the fledgling Brocking Chair Furniture Company was written up in a controversial article in the Sunday New York Times Style section. In it, an ardently woke feminist reviewer had attacked Amy for her gender-specific creations, calling them anti-progressive and an insult to contemporary feminism's pioneering position in helping make manifest a truly non-gender-specific, they/their world. The Monday after that article appeared, the Brocking Chair sales team was inundated with a flood of higher-end furniture retailer enquiries, all of them eager to know how soon the pieces featured in that article would be available to the general public.

Meanwhile, Whack Job's booking agent had taken Jeff's advice and stonewalled DogPound Records while word of their interest circulated throughout the industry. Approaches were made by three other reputable labels, all of them with a significant streaming music presence; the new industry-wide name-of-the-game. In mid-November the band signed with Nashville-based Ardent, a newer, forward-thinking label with a stable of clients getting at least as much on-line notice as any other in the business. Whack Job might not be a household name yet, but their visibility had started to climb with Foster's songwriting and guitar work along with Jeff's vocals, getting them some very positive notice in the Indy press.

Based on an impressive first batch of orders, Brocking Chair received their next twenty-million-dollar capital infusion, enabling the partners to prioritize completion of construction with the aim to quickly kick production into high gear. By the time the holidays rolled around, three separate areas of the plant were fabricating chair components. The assembly line would to be ready to roll by the end of January and their Production Manager was busy interviewing a small army of new-hires.

Now that her marrying Jason was a done deal, Amy and Jeff had reached a sort of truce. He still thought Jason was a douche, not that Jason, his nose out of joint over Whack Job's snubbing him to sign with Ardent, had made any attempts to court his favor. Whenever they found themselves together in the same room they mostly engaged in avoidance. Amy was less than happy to see it, but was also so busy with the distractions of trying to launch a successful business to pay it much mind. Her interactions with Jeff were primarily at the plant and generally cordial.

In mid-February, two weeks after their chairs started coming off the production line in real numbers, things started to get really crazy. Word came that Amy had won the prestigious German Design Awards Newcomer prize in Frankfort; news that was followed almost immediately by her winning an iF Design Award for furniture, also in Frankfort. Then, in April, she won a Red Dot award in Como, Italy, after which orders for their chairs suddenly skyrocketed all over the globe, pushing them to seek extra financing from her father to expand upstairs into their building's additional 30,000 square feet. They were already thinking about needing a much larger space and had their commercial real estate agent putting feelers out. Then Vanity Fair did a splashy cover article on Amy and Tamara in a Young Female Entrepreneurs issue that once again stirred up the controversy over the gender specificity of Amy's designs. Various social and political scientists had weighed in on both sides of it, in the process creating even more interest in their products.

After a Whack Job gig at Brooklyn Steel in early March, Jeff found himself escaped to a dive bar on Metropolitan Avenue in East Williamsburg with the other guys in the band to talk about where they were and what they were expecting to happen next.

"I don't know about you dudes, but I've barely got time to eat, shit, and sleep," he told them. "I know the rest of you probably don't think I'm holding up my end, but just showing up for practice and gigs is about all I can manage these days."

"So long as you ain't thinking about quitting, I don't give a shit," keyboardist Rick Carlisle said. "We could find another drummer, but not another voice like yours. It's such a big part of our fucking sound now."

It wasn't like Jeff hadn't thought a lot about that and so many other factors involved in trying to live his strange dual life. Playing

Whack Job

drums had always been his way of getting away into a world where he could totally let his hair down and do some serious de-stressing. Lately, it had become an outlet he felt he needed desperately, just to keep himself sane. Not that he had to be a rock star to accomplish that end. He could go find himself some shitty garage band and probably achieve the same goal, but a four-year bond existed between him and these guys and what they'd managed to accomplish together. And as it was with all of his work, he took serious pride in it, especially whenever he managed to achieve something significant.

"Don't worry. As long as you dudes will still have me, I'm not going anywhere," he said. "I mean, just like David Byrne was with the Talking Heads or Mark Knopfler with Dire Straits, I think we all know that Foster is the real heart and soul of this band. I expect that down life's road, other opportunities will start to make the rest of us feel a little limiting for him." He was looking at their front man and tunesmith as he said it. "But for now, I think all of us should just enjoy the ride and try to avoid overthinking where we are or how we got here."

He realized as he said it and watched their faces that the possibility of his deciding to leave the band was something they were all worried about and had previously discussed among themselves.

Tanner, while tracing patterns in the dew on his glass looked across the table to meet Jeff's eyes. "You don't know how fucking relieved we are to hear you say that," he said. "With you guys winning all them design awards, we were afraid you might decide you don't got time for this anymore."

Jeff appreciated the relief he heard in the bass player's tone. "Fuck, dude," he said. "I need to find the time. There are days when this band is about the only thing that keeps me sane. Vanity Fair made it look like what Amy and I are doing is all glitz and glitter, but the pressures of building something like what we have, especially with the amount of money involved, would probably have turned me into an alcoholic by now if I didn't have these gigs to play."

Tanner lifted his glass in toast. The rest of them met his in mid-air above the center of the table.

"We're gonna need to get together on our calendars for the

next few months," Jeff continued. "When does Ardent want us in the studio?"

He'd already warned Amy that he would need to be out of town in Nashville for two weeks, sometime that summer.

"If all of us can swing it, they want us there by mid-June," Foster said. He paused for a moment and then looked directly at Jeff again. "I think everything you're doing is the bomb, bro. I mean shit. We all knew you with hay seed still in your hair, fresh from Bumfuck. Every art student who comes to this town thinks he's gonna be a star and ninety-nine percent of them get back on the plane and go home. But you? You didn't just get hit once with the lucky stick. That fickle bitch done tapped you twice."

A woman from a table across the way rose to approach them; early twenties, dressed for a Brooklyn hipster's Saturday night out, a copper Moscow Mule mug in one hand.

"You're the guys in Whack Job, right? My friends and me? We think you're awesome. Right now, you're our favorite band."

Jeff liked that 'right now', like she and her pals were musical hummingbirds moving from bright flower to bright flower. He noticed that his bandmates were all close to empty and excused himself to head for the bar to buy another round.

The bartender, a slender redhead with a slightly bored, I've-seen-everything attitude, nodded to acknowledge his presence as he pulled up a stool. Once she finished mixing drinks for another patron, she wandered languidly down the duckboards.

"What'll it be?"

He ordered another round of drinks for his bandmates and a Green Spot Irish whiskey on ice for himself.

As she started setting them up, she glanced over again. "That person talking to your buddies over there just told me you guys are in a band that just signed a major record deal."

"Fraid so," Jeff replied.

"Why are you afraid?"

"Because I think I liked it better when nobody knew who we were."

"What do you play?"

"Drums. And I sing."

"Like Phil Collins or Levon Helm." It wasn't a question.

He smiled at that. "I've got a better voice, but yeah."
He examined her a bit more closely. Thirty, maybe? From what she purposely seemed determined to hide, he guessed she was a lot smarter than her bored demeanor might initially suggest.

She carried his drinks over to set them before him. "Okay, so I've got to ask. How does it feel to find yourself on the brink of possible serious fame? Kind of trippy, no?"

"It's definitely that," he replied. "Are you dating anyone?"

It provoked a snorted laugh. "What? Your girlfriend was too busy to come see you play tonight?"

"I'm currently one short in that department. Not that I'm much good at sustaining long-term relationships."

"So, is this your game instead? Hit on random bartenders, thinking your good-looks might get you into their beds, if only for a night?"

He lifted his whiskey and took a little sip, leaving the liquid in his mouth for a long moment to savor that tiny tongue-burn before swallowing it. All the while, he maintained steady eye contact. Hers were brown and soulful in spite of her slight sneer.

"Matter of fact, you're the first bartender I've had more than a five-word exchange with in over a year. If I want to get laid, I generally hang around backstage after a show and wait for some chick to hit me up, but it's been at least eight months since I took anyone up on one of those offers, too."

He watched the sneer disappear, replaced by puzzled curiosity.

"Serious? What are you? A monk?"

A slow nod. "Something happened last year that made me re-evaluate my priorities there. I'm still working on it."

"And what was that?"

"I accidentally fucked my business partner's step-mother."

If any of her attention had been elsewhere, it was all front-and-center now. "Accidentally."

"She crawled naked into my bed."

"You're not bullshitting me."

"I wish I was."

"How old?"

"Forty-six. I didn't have that particular fact in hand at the time, but I knew she had to be close."

"Your business partner? You do something besides play in the band?"

"I design furniture. My partner was on the cover of Vanity Fair last month."

"Which issue?"

"Young Women Entrepreneurs."

"I saw that. Is your partner the taller Eurasian one or the black woman?"

"The taller one."

"She's hot."

He took another sip of his whiskey. "That, she is."

"And she's the actual designer, right? You just said that's what you do."

"She's more like the face of the business. Straight white men aren't selling so well at the moment, us all currently mired in a super-woke, post-post-modernist market."

She chuckled at that. "Do I detect a little bitterness there?"

"A little, but her daddy's rich and mine isn't, so it's always been her ball anyway. I'm just happy to get to play."

"In that article, it mentioned her having just gotten married. How'd you manage to miss out on that? The two of you being so pretty an all."

He was in the middle of taking another sip of his whiskey and almost blew it out his nose. "Damn! Don't do that!"

"What? Call you pretty? C'mon. I'm sure you own a mirror."

"Just the same, it's not how I prefer to think of myself."

She lifted the bottle of Green Spot and poured a little more into his glass to top him off. "Well, indulge me anyway," she said. "And you still haven't answered my question. What? Tall gorgeous Eurasian women aren't your thing?"

"We have an agreement about not shitting where we eat."

Maybe just to keep her hands busy, she shot some club soda

into a glass and took a swig. "It sounds like you've at least talked about it. That's unusual in this day and age."

"You saw her picture. We had to talk about it. And she's smart, too."

"From the look I just saw in your eyes, I'm guessing you did more than just talk about it. What's going on there?"

For the last minute or so Jeff had been marveling at this conversation he was having. With a bartender, no less.

"I'm not sure I even know," he said.

"Does she know about you and the step-mother?"

"Oh, yeah. I told her the morning after."

"And how did she react?"

With his head tilted slightly to one side he thought about her question for a moment before answering. It was a good one. "Not well. She'd been more concerned about her half-sister, who'd flirted with me at dinner all evening. She was afraid I might take her up on it."

"But you didn't."

The ice was melting in his buddies' drinks. He needed to wrap this up and get them over to them. "Nope. I went to bed in their guest cottage expecting to get a good night's sleep."

"Because you're really more attracted to your business partner."

"I never said that."

That earned him an impatient eye-roll. "Trust me," she said. "I'm your bartender. I know things about you that even you don't know about yourself. You're probably even in love with her. I'm just as convinced of that as I am that once my shift is over, I'm going to take you home with me."

SEVENTEEN

Her name was Patty Conlon, thirty-one years old and the frustrated owner of a PhD in Cultural Anthropology from the Ohio State University. She'd moved to New York a year earlier to take a job at the New York Museum of Natural History only to see the job evaporate before her plane touched down at LaGuardia Airport. She lived with a cat and $150,000 in student debt in a second floor sub-let in an old East Williamsburg redbrick industrial building on Morgan Avenue. It was one of those that a slumlord had chopped up into a rabbit warren of mini-lofts. The actual tenant who'd been there for years had followed a soul-mate-actress-girlfriend to Los Angeles and didn't plan to return for a long time, but you never knew about those things. Just a three-block walk from the bar where she worked, it was both relatively cheap and handy.

With the exception perhaps of her cat, Jeff took an immediate shine to Patty, based mostly on how she thought and lived, but also on how uncomplicated and non-neurotic their first sexual encounter had been. In other words, after discounting the facts that neither of them was interested in anything long-term or had any interest in even a short-lived mutually exclusive relationship, they'd found each other agreeably convenient. They both liked to drink in moderation and spark a little reefer when the mood hit. Neither was into harder drugs. They found they never ran out of lively topics of conversation and that they liked the same music, the same food, and lots of exhausting sex. And so, after several weeks of returning repeatedly to feed from that same interactive trough, eating the occasional meal out together, and sitting around her place having fun conversations about art and ideas, they eventually had the talk.

"You're starting to seem like more than just a booty call, Jeff. Is it just me, or are you feeling that, too?"

They were slouched on her couch with yet another Netflix series episode on the flat-screen, her with one leg extended and a bare foot in his lap where he idly massaged it. It was mid-March and still cold outside. The radiator clanked like all of those old steam-fed units do. Jeff liked the fifty-or-so houseplants she'd inherited with the place and how they gave it a sort of jungle feel. The cat was lying stretched across the back of the couch like he owned the place, which to judge from the carpeted cat-tower and the myriad toys strewn across the floor, he probably did.

With Patty's last utterance Jeff saw the caution flag come out. In reaction, he slowed. "That sounds like you're on the verge of proposing some sort of agreement. Am I reading that right?"

She wriggled to get even more comfortable, pushing her foot deeper into his lap so her bare calf now occupied it, too. She seemed to love his massaging her calves almost as much as him pulling gently on her individual toes.

"I was just thinking it's been a while since I've had a friend-with-benefits rather than just a fuck-buddy and how nice it feels. We have great sex, your career is suddenly all over the map, and nobody could ever hope to pin you down right now. And me? For all I know, if I can't find a real job in my field, I'll be moving back home to Indiana in another six months. So, how are you feeling about this right now?"

He liked how her bare calf felt in his hand and how, in a strong, smart, self-assured way, she embodied a whole lot of other things he found beautiful in a woman. And from that first exchange they'd had at her bar, and over the score of times they'd seen each other since, he'd never gotten any sense that there crazy might be lurking under all that practical intelligence.

"I've never had a friend-with-benefits," he said. "I assume there are rules? Kind of like with polyamory?"

"Less bullshit involved," she said. "You've just got to agree to always say how you really feel. If it's working, you enjoy it, no strings attached. If it isn't, you say it and then don't hang around long enough to make it any worse. No harm, no foul."

"What about other people?" he asked.

"I don't expect we can ask each other to be exclusive, but frankly? I'd prefer it if you kept those other things to a minimum. You finish a gig, walk offstage and some hot-to-trot gal just insists on sucking your cock, how can I expect you to say no? That's a similar situation to your partner's stepmother crawling naked into your bed.

The Nucleus Accumbens area of the male brain isn't wired with an off-stitch once stimulation there reaches fever pitch. But there is a lot of disease going around. I'd like to minimize my risk there."

Jeff had never met a cultural anthropologist before, let alone hooked-up with one, and he found her observations on the human animal, both male and female, to always be both enlightening and refreshing. Seven years of doctoral studies in that realm appeared to have beaten any notion of romanticism clean out of her.

She continued. "The most important thing is to remain clear on exactly what this thing between us is. We're friends who fuck because we're attracted to each other. Not because we feel obliged to or because we're trying to build something bigger out of that."

At twenty-two years and several months, Jeff didn't have the same wealth of experience in those realms as she seemed to have. With the exception of a girlfriend who'd lasted six months in high school, all he'd ever done was meet women at parties or after playing gigs and hook up. He wasn't old enough to have spent very much time in the bar scene, but figured from what little he had that there wouldn't be that much difference there, either. It was how he'd met Patty, after all. But none of those other experiences had the same edge of friendship that this one had developed. He actually knew her name, knew that she had two sisters and a brother, that her father was a middle-level functionary in a commercial real estate management company in Batesville, Indiana, and that her mother taught second grade at a Catholic school. That might not be much, but when examined alongside the things he'd learned about his other random bed mates, it read like an entire biography.

"If we're gonna do this, do you want to sleep at my place every once in a while, too?" he asked.

She shrugged. "If you want me to, sure. I've never fucked in a factory."

"It's a nice factory. And I could show you the shit I'm working on if that has any appeal."

She withdrew her one leg from his lap to exchange it with the other. "I make you listen to my bullshit cultural theories all the time, I figure turnabout is fair play. Your hands on my calves and feet have given you quite the stiffy, by the way."

He eased her foot down to nestle it deeper into his crotch. "I didn't think you'd noticed."

"I wanted to make sure you were good and primed before I demanded to have my way with you."

"Mission accomplished. Is that the next item on our agenda?"

"Are we done with our conversation here? Do we have a deal?"

"I think maybe so."

"No maybes. Either you're in or you're out. It's not like I don't have other offers."

He swung his legs around to plant his feet on the floor. "I'm in," he said. "Tell those other dudes to take a number."

EIGHTEEN

The first time that Amy met Jeff's new friend Patty Conlon, the woman was walking barefoot down the factory mezzanine walkway from the kitchen toward his bedroom dressed in nothing but a long-sleeve t-shirt, her flaming red hair pulled up in a topknot. Other than the fact that a half-naked stranger was parading around her place of business in the middle of the morning, the other thing that stood out was how shockingly white the woman was—perhaps the whitest woman Amy had ever seen. She'd just reached the top of the mezzanine stairs, headed for her office, and in her surprise had dropped a box of promotional materials she was carrying. The noise caused the stranger to turn with a start, slopping coffee from the two mugs she carried.

"Oh," the woman exclaimed, her eyes gone wide. "You're Amy. I don't think Jeff was expecting you."

There was the noise of scrambling from down the walkway and Jeff emerged from his studio clad only in a pair of sweat pants.

"Amy. Hell are you doing here? It's a Sunday. I thought you were out on the Island."

Right after the New Year, her new husband had made a big deal about how much he missed living near the beach and they had bought a house in Amagansett, the next hamlet east of her family's place in East Hampton. For the past several months they'd been going out there most weekends.

"I had too much to do and stayed in," she said. "I was just dropping off these galleys for a promotion we're doing. I probably should have called ahead."

Jeff waved it off. "This is my friend Patty. She had to work late last night so we're only just getting up."

He didn't say work at what. He hadn't had a gig that weekend so this woman wasn't someone he'd just picked after a show. The fact that he even knew her name was interesting. "Well, sorry I disturbed you," she said. "I'll just drop these and head out. Nice to meet you, Patty."

"Nice to meet you, too," Patty said. "You're even prettier than you were in those *Vanity Fair* pictures."

Amy had no idea what this redhead might look like in a picture, but from what she could see of her in the flesh, she imagined she'd probably look just peachy, too. It had been a while since she'd felt one of those pangs of jealousy she used to feel when she saw another woman taking Jeff's measure, but she was feeling one now.

"Thanks," she said. "You guys have a nice day."

"You got time for a cup of coffee?" Jeff asked. "We don't mean to run you off like this. Patty's already got the water hot."

Amy wondered if he realized how much double-entendre he'd just loaded onto that statement. "I feel like I'm intruding here," she said.

Patty started forward, one of those two cups of coffee she held extended toward her. "Here. Take this one. I'll make myself another right after I go find some pants."

Before Amy could further object, a steaming mug was in her hands and Jeff's friend was turning to hand him the other.

"You might want to put a shirt on, too, hot shot," she said as he took it. "Your business partner is blushing."

And with that, Amy was left standing alone outside the break room as her partner and his guest disappeared to find more clothes. She asked herself what was she doing there and then she took a first sip while staring past the railing onto the production floor, marveling at what they'd managed to create in so short a period of time. Brocking Chair was shipping Venus and David chairs in all three configurations as fast as they could produce them and was still nowhere near able to keep up with demand. That next week they would be firing up their second-floor phase-two, 30,000 square foot production annex. And the prototype shop was hard at work on Jeff's new dining and living room furniture designs.

This Patty emerged barefoot from his studio in a long, low-cut brown cashmere sweater, cinched at her slender waist with a wide belt, and a pair of black spandex leggings. She hurried into the kitchen to grab a bag of coffee beans while Amy followed to watch her pour them into the grinder, fire it up, grab a portafilter and knock spent grounds out into the trash like a pro. While not as elaborate as the ornate brass machine in her loft, she had budgeted enough money for a high quality Breville appliance for the business. Patty Conlon was handling it with the crisp efficiency of a trained barista.

The newcomer saw her watching and smiled. "I worked at a Starbucks while I was an undergrad. We used to get swamped and I got pretty fast."

When she was an undergrad? That seemed to imply that she'd gone beyond and Amy wondered in what field. You didn't wear a sweater like that working late for an accounting firm or law office. By way of making conversation, she asked where she'd gone to school.

"I did my undergrad at Purdue, then grad school at Ohio State."

"In what?" Amy asked.

"I have a Doctorate in Anthropology. Not that it's done me much good in the current job market. I really like what you've done with your hair."

Just that past week, Amy had finally relented and let her Madison Avenue stylist put in two blonde streaks that framed her face. She'd hoped that her father might be mortified, but he'd blown the same smoke up her ass that he always did, telling her he thought she looked more beautiful than ever.

"Thanks," she said. "Jeff mentioned you had to work late. What do you do?"

"I tend bar in Williamsburg. That's where we met."

That would explain the sweater. With all of that creamy white skin working in contrast to the ginger-bread brown fabric, she imagined the male patrons there might get competitive, vying to see who could out-tip the other.

Jeff appeared in the long-sleeve t-shirt Patty had just been wearing along with jeans and a pair of wool shearling slippers.

"You two act like you've known each other a while," Amy observed.

Her partner pulled up one of the break-room chairs to join her at the table, setting his coffee before him. "The better part of three months now."

Amy had trouble gauging ages but guessed that Patty was a few years older than she was. There were tiny little crows' feet at the corners of her gray-blue Irish eyes, visible only when she smiled. She was slender like a runner or maybe a dancer and looked like she was in fairly decent shape. It wasn't hard to see why Jeff might be attracted to her.

"Not that it's any of my business, but what is someone with a doctorate in Anthropology doing tending bar?" she asked.

Patty moved the little stainless-steel pitcher in a slow, circular motion to steam milk for her latte as she replied. "Paying the rent and the interest on my student loans, mostly. Once in a while I grab a bag of groceries. A job offer I got from the Museum of Natural History evaporated somewhere in the air between Columbus and Queens. I didn't know that until I'd spent my last dollar on a plane ticket and landed here."

Just from the way she talked it was obvious she was whip smart and had that special gift of bitch-wit. Those were also things that would appeal to Jeff, who was so much smarter than he knew. "That's awful," she said. "Who would do that?"

"They told me they were feeling a budget crunch, had a board meeting, and decided to defund my part of their educational outreach program. It would have been nice if they'd said something earlier. I'd just turned down a research fellowship at the University of Missouri."

She finished pouring the frothed milk into her coffee, producing one of those little lotus flower-shaped barista things on the surface like it was second-nature. As she pulled up a chair to join them, she smiled at Amy again. "It's fun to meet the partner Jeff has told me so much about. Cheers."

Amy clicked mugs with her.

"And before you get any wrong ideas here, this isn't some hot romance you just walked in on," Patty continued. "We're just friends who fuck."

Said just like that. Bold as spit-shined brass. As much as Amy hated to acknowledge it, she felt herself blink. She'd always been the one who controlled the tempo of these exchanges; the cool, ballsy, aloof one. But this gal had just trumped her before she could even get traction. What was she supposed to say to something like that?

As if she could read her thoughts, Patty moved to relieve her of the need to say anything. "I like to think I don't look it, but I'm nine years older than him," she said. "And right now, he's on a trajectory that will take him places he can't even imagine. Not like the rest of us ever can, but his situation is fairly unique. I just finished spending ten years studying cultural anthropology and I might look like a bimbo red-head but I'm not stupid. Even so, I'll never go to the kinds places he's going to go, for more reasons than I can list. Heck, I don't even want to try." She paused to look at Jeff and smiled. "But he is awfully cute. And for the moment, seeing as we seem to enjoy each other's company as much as we do, why not?"

Any shock Amy was feeling had since been replaced by surprise. Who was this person? Too many women in New York would see the trajectory Jeff was on as one of the hottest tickets in town. They'd be working every wile in their arsenal to secure a seat on board that gravy train for the entire ride. This Patty could also be entertaining those same notions and just have a really good line of shit, but Amy didn't think so. There weren't any baby-cow eyes accompanying that little speech. She hadn't reached earnestly across the table to grab Jeff's hand. And him? He was sitting back as nonchalantly as he might while on a break with a couple of their mechanical engineers or fabrication techs. Smiling, but not in any kind of infatuated way. It was almost maddening.

Amy struggled to keep it light, speaking while flashing a grin that had to look slightly forced. "So, what you're saying is, I don't need to worry about you moving in here."

"Ha! Not any more than I need to worry about him moving into my place. I have no idea how long this might work and neither does he, but we both know it wouldn't if we didn't give each other lots of space."

Seeing as everyone was being blunt, Amy figured she might as well join the fun. She looked directly at Jeff. "What happened to Mr. One-night-stand? He in retirement?"

There was nothing abashed about the grin he flashed Patty before answering that question. "When we met, Patty was my first in like eight months. But the morning after, once we got to talking and realized that neither of us was really much interested in that shit, this started to evolve." He waved a hand back and forth in the air between him and her. "Sure, we both liked the idea of getting laid, but the random stranger thing just wasn't working out for either of us anymore."

Patty took up their narrative from there. "So, we decided to hook up again a couple of nights later," she said. "And then again after that, and again, until we both realized it was becoming a habit. We always find fun stuff to talk about and enjoy not eating alone every night. All of those things considered, we decided to form a sort of alliance. I can't speak for him, but for me it's been fun."

Just her saying all that got Amy to thinking about how much fun she wasn't having in her marriage, and never really had. Jason was by no means an inspired lover or a particularly scintillating conversationalist when he wasn't talking about some hot new musical act and how much money they could make him. The first time they'd slept together he'd seemed awestruck enough by the fact that he'd finally gotten into her pants that she'd mistaken his response as being hopeful and thought she might be able to teach him a move or two to improve his skillset. Instead, it turned out that he was just as self-involved as most every other male she'd ever slept with. He didn't think about anything but himself, both in and out of bed, and his group of friends were all just as vapid and boring as he was. If it weren't for the amazing success her company was having, she might even be miserable, but because Brocking Chair was such a great distraction she was more-or-less just pissed off at herself for having fallen into a trap of her own making. She was also too stubborn to ever admit that to anyone but herself. And so she downed the rest of her coffee and smiled serenely at Jeff's new friend. "Whatever works I guess, right?" she said.

"Another cup?" Patty asked. "I can make you one in a jiff."

"I appreciate it, but no," Amy replied. "I've got like a million non-work-related things to do today. I really should be going." She pushed back her chair, stood, crossed to the sink and rinsed her mug before placing it in the dishwasher.

NINETEEN

With all of the sophisticated security technology that her new brother-in-law and half-sister had installed at their Amagansett house, Katya was surprised that Jason would risk inviting her there in the wee hours of that Sunday morning. Maybe it was because they'd been up all night drinking and snorting coke with a hip-hop artist he was trying to sign and he wasn't thinking as clearly as he might have been if he hadn't been so wasted. That was probably it, she guessed, and the fact that ever since they'd first met, he hadn't been able to stop drooling over her.

Katya had run into him by design midway through Saturday night at his favorite local club during a party he was throwing for Easy-F in the club's VIP room. She'd learned that Amy wasn't coming out that weekend and had slipped the muscled-up bouncer at the foot of the stairs a half-gram of coke, telling him that the host was her brother-in-law while knowing that, with the way she was dressed and carried herself, it didn't even need to be the truth. Jason was already pretty lit by the time she found him on a sofa wedged between two women with considerably less firepower than she was bringing to the fight, and a bottle of Cristal on ice on the table before them. Rather than wait for a server to bring her a clean glass, she picked up Jason's, drained it, and then reached for a re-fill while the bimbos on either side of him went wide-eyed. He'd just grinned.

The party went late into the night and the more wasted he got, the closer Katya had let him get to her. His father might not have quite as much money as hers but they were both in the same ballpark and Abe Wuthrich's world was a whole lot sexier than Bert Brock's. She doubted that her dad had ever even tried cocaine while she was pretty sure that over his lifetime, Abe had snorted a truckload of it. At Amy's wedding she'd watched him and his fourth wife constantly fiddling with their noses after frequent disappearances into their guest cottage bedroom. The wife had at one point emerged with white powder dusting her considerable decolletage.

They'd eventually reached Amagansett at four-thirty, high on coke and Champagne. Even after taking an insurance Viagra, Jason's performance in those wee hours of Sunday morning was nothing he'd ever want to brag on. After a year of drooling he'd finally been able to access her naked but still wasn't able to get more than semi-hard. When she'd mounted him in hopes of getting at least some moderate satisfaction for herself, he'd artlessly thrust his hips only twice before spending all of his currency. He was dead asleep and doing a fair imitation of a freight train before she could even dismount and grab a Summer's Eve from her purse. It wasn't until one o'clock that next afternoon when she climbed naked from his bed and wandered into the kitchen looking for some sort of analgesic and coffee that she saw that first camera aimed right at her.

☻☻☻

In retrospect, Amy couldn't pinpoint exactly why she'd done it. Was it because she'd been having a shitty day after a string of so many good ones that she'd started to foolishly believe she might never have another one of those? Silly her. Sunday morning after finding Jeff and his new gal pal acting so well-adjusted and content in their little domestic moment, she'd descended into a deeper funk than any she'd suffered in recent memory.

Mid-morning she'd left Brocking Chair's Long Island City plant feeling suddenly depressed over her own romantic choices made and returned to Manhattan in a mood that made no logical sense. Her entrepreneurial dream had come true. How many people in the world could say that? So, was it really all that important that she wasn't in love with her husband, or that their so-called marriage had turned out to be such a disappointment? She had a whole other life which kept her so busy most days that she could barely catch her breath. She had dozens of people who depended on her for guidance, looked up to her, and told her on a daily basis how fabulous they thought she was. And not just them. Newspaper and magazine writers and business pundits, too. Amy Brock wasn't just Bertrand Brock's daughter anymore. She was a design and marketing dynamo; in her own right an economic force to be reckoned with. So why was she so down? Because the design genius part of the public's perception of her was a lie? Heck, lots of things perceived as truths in life were lies, especially in recent times. Was it because her business partner had found a way to at least temporarily accept that fact, while she really hadn't? That kind of thinking was crazy, right? From the very outset she'd called the shots and made those rules they were now playing by. All he'd managed was to do was swallow his pride, do brilliant work, and find ways to live with the obvious compromises he'd agreed to make.

And so it was, after twice calling Jason to ask him to bring a book back to the city that she'd forgotten and not hearing back from him that she'd opened her laptop and clicked onto the security system at the house in Amagansett while catching up on e-mails, just to see what might be going on out there. As soon as a dozen little camera thumbnails popped up on her screen, framed there like the images on Hollywood Squares, she saw Katya standing naked in her kitchen in one of them, reaching into an over-counter cupboard for a coffee mug. And just as she clicked onto that image to enlarge it, her half-sister turned to look up at the camera, almost like she'd just realized she was being watched.

Amy gaped, feeling like she'd just been punched in the gut. "Holy shit," she murmured. "You fucking cunt."

ⓔⓔⓔ

Jeff had just walked Patty outside to see her into an Uber and was returning upstairs to his design studio when his phone rang. On seeing it was Amy calling he smiled as he swiped to answer, an image of her first encounter with Patty that morning bright in his mind's eye. He still had very complex feelings regarding her and knew, as much as she might try to hide them, that she had similar feelings of her own. It had given him a kick when the three of them sat down to coffee together, especially seeing he look on her face when she learned that Patty had a doctorate in Anthropology.

"Hey, Aim. What's up?"

"Jason is fucking Katya."

He didn't know what he'd been expecting, but that sure wasn't it. "How do you know that?" he asked.

"I just now clicked onto the security feed from my house at the beach. She was standing naked in my kitchen."

He'd seen her half-sister in too many of those get-ups she wore and didn't need to strain his imagination to generate a pretty good picture of what that might look like. Jesus. "Where was Jason?"

"Still in bed. We have cameras all over the house."

"Did you see anyone else?" He didn't know why he was trying to imagine some scenario other than the one with which he'd just been presented. He'd pegged Jason for a smarmy, smoke-blowing douche the first moment they'd ever met.

"Just the two of them," she said. "Why? You think there might be some other explanation? You saw how she flirted with him at our opening. She did the same thing at my wedding. I was just fool enough to think she does that with everyone and that he was at least smart enough to see through her manipulative bullshit."

"He's a dude with a lot of insecurities," Jeff said. He was thinking about the expensive clothes, the multiple neck chains, the Lamborghini SUV he drove, and the power that he believed his job gave him. "The fact that you never seemed to see any of that has always baffled me. Remember that I did try to play Devil's Advocate once upon a time."

"Oh, fuck you. What the hell am I going to do about this? Drive out there and confront them?"

"She'll probably be gone by the time you get there. I assume your system has some kind of memory back-up?"

"It's programmed to hold images for a week and then refresh. You're telling me I need to download it onto a separate drive, right?"

"And then call your pal Greg Logan in Chicago. Ask him to recommend a good divorce attorney."

"I don't need to," she said. "I'll probably use the same woman who represented my mom when she divorced dad. It's been twenty-six years but I'm pretty sure she's still practicing."

"Or knows someone good who is. Yeah, do that. And meanwhile, I know what I wouldn't do," he said.

"What's that?"

"Look at any of the earlier footage from your bedroom. From the shape it sounds like you're in, I'm pretty sure whatever's there might make you blow a gasket."

TWENTY

That next week got crazy. Amy descended down a my-life-is-ruined rabbit hole while Brocking Chair's new expanded, second-floor assembly capacity went online. The responsibility for overseeing that transition fell mostly to Jeff and the company's Production Manager, along with their recently promoted Manufacturing Foreman. Work on the prototypes of his new 'Brockstyle' dining set and living room ensemble were nearing completion and where Amy would usually be working tirelessly to plan a show to promote the roll-out of those items and make sure the global design community was full-aware of them, most of that task now landed on Tamara Wilson's back. Jeff tried to wear two hats as much as he could, watching out for any quality control issues for half his day and then huddling up with Tamara and her marketing staff for the rest of it. It made for a long week and by the end of it, as he headed into Manhattan Friday evening to meet with Amy at her place to make sure she hadn't slit her wrists, he was bone-weary.

Once arrived outside her SoHo loft building, he tried to prepare himself for what he might find upstairs. She'd thrown Jason out of her loft and banished him to a hotel whenever he was in the city and then taken a week of personal time to wallow and try to deal with her marital train-wreck. Jeff knew that when the guy had first moved in with her just eight months ago, much of the décor in her loft had been changed to accommodate his tastes, too. Rather than store her old furniture, they'd donated most of it. He half-expected to find the burned-out husk of her marital bed mattress still smoldering on the sidewalk.

He found her eleventh-floor front door open a crack and rapped lightly on the panel. It produced a brusque, "It's open." He could hear one end of a subdued conversation as he entered and saw his business partner sitting on a stool at her kitchen bar, on the phone. Save for a single pair of Venus and David rocking chairs and a reading lamp, her living room was bare. No more poster art on the walls. Not even a side table. There were three empty coffee cups and a wine glass on the floor alongside the chair.

Wearing a slightly panicked expression, Amy held up a finger, then pointed to her espresso machine while continuing her conversation.

"What the hell was he doing in Riyadh? He told me he was going to Dubai again." There was a lapse. "And what exactly are their demands?" Another lapse. "What do you mean there aren't any? They must want money. Everybody wants money." Through another lapse, her already strained expression grew more exasperated. Then, "Okay. Please keep me posted. If they need me to be anywhere, please tell me." Yet another lapse, then, "I appreciate it. Goodbye."

She terminated the call and set her phone on the island's granite surface as Jeff finished grinding coffee beans.

"What's going on?" he asked. "You look like someone just stole your puppy. What's this about demands?"

"That was Agnes, my dad's executive assistant. She and Brock's Chief Operating Officer just talked to an Undersecretary of State in Washington. A Yemeni rebel faction has kidnapped my dad and Crown Prince Ahmad ibn Abdullah off some golf course in Riyadh. Apparently, they had help from a disgruntled faction of the Saudi royal family and were able to breach some really tight security."

This had nothing to do with those chairs looking like orphans in her living room. "Oh, shit. Fucking gnarly," he murmured. "And they haven't made any demands?"

He wondered why he was surprised she looked as distraught she did. It wasn't like she really liked her father all that much, but then again, the dude was her dad. He tried to imagine how he'd feel if his own difficult father had just been kidnapped. Not good about it. That much he knew.

She shook her head. "I'm reading between the lines here, but after what's been going on in Yemen ever since Prince ibn Abdullah took over the reins from his father in Saudi Arabia, I'm inclined to guess those rebels and their royal family accomplices can only want him dead. That's generally how they settle that kind of thing in their neck of the woods."

From pictures he'd seen of the generally treeless Saudi landscape, Jeff was pretty sure that wasn't the right analogy. Regardless, he'd gotten so he could read Amy's mind almost as well as she could, his, and right then he thought he knew what she was thinking. If those rebels had the anger, balls, and wherewithal to kidnap one of the richest and most politically powerful men in the world and maybe switch his lights off, things weren't looking good for an incidental American billionaire.

"They've got to know how much money your dad is worth and want to get their hands on some of it," he said. "They won't be able to do that if they kill him."

He watched Amy wince at his last words. "Oh, Christ. Please don't even say that."

"I'm sorry," was all he could think of to say.

"I mean, I've always thought he was an asshole, but the man is still my father."

Jeff was still trying to put himself in her shoes. His dad was at least as big an asshole as Bert Brock, albeit on a significantly different scale. But he was also a huge presence who'd always been there in his life. He couldn't imagine him not always being there. "It sounds like all you can do right now is sit tight and hope," he said.

She squeezed her eyes shut and pinched the bridge of her nose. "Oh, God, Prodigy Boy," she said. "I've been doing a little bit too much of it this past week but think I need a drink."

It had been nearly a year since she'd called him that, and it seemed like a sure sign of just how much stress she was under right then. Her subconscious was reaching desperately for the comfort of the familiar.

"I saw the empty wine glass. How many have you had today?" he asked.

"Fuck that. There's an open bottle in the fridge and another glass in the cabinet next to the broom closet." When she opened her eyes again, he saw tears in them. "God, what a nightmare."

He collected her empty from the living room, then headed for the refrigerator. "What's the State Department doing?" he asked. "Lining up a Delta Force extraction team, I hope."

"According to Agnes, they have no idea where he even is. They've been studying satellite pictures and haven't been able to pinpoint any unusual traffic overland into Yemen, or boat movement into the Persian Gulf. It's their guess that he's being held somewhere in-country, probably under the protection of some ingrate who thinks he should be sitting on the royal throne and not the other guy."

"Just keep remembering that there's no point in killing him," he said. "You need to hang onto that."

"He's a rich American businessman and during the last administration, people he's publicly supported sold like a gazillion dollars-worth of armaments to ibn Abdullah and the United Arab Emirates, specifically for the purpose of suppressing the Houthi rebels in Yemen."

Amy was a more ardent follower of the news while Jeff only knew from scattered CNN reports and articles in the Times that the Saudis and the Emirates had been shitting all over the impoverished people of Yemen for decades, working to keep them destabilized mostly because they sat right on their borders and were too poor and hungry not to want a piece of their pie.

Once he'd filled two glasses he handed hers to her and glanced around the empty living room. "I like what you've done with the place. Extreme minimalism has its place in the design canon now."

She took a deep breath and shook her head. "That sounded a little too much like an I-told-you-so."

"Naw. That would be kicking you while you were down. I may be shallow, but I'm not that kind of guy. Any chance you can get some of your old poster art back? That stuff was awesome."

For the first time since he'd walked in the door, she smiled, albeit wanly. "That I didn't sell. It's in storage."

"So, you were hedging your bets. Glad to hear it."

"I've been sleeping on an air mattress until I can get a new bed delivered," she said. "It's supposed to come tomorrow morning. I sure hope so. That other piece of shit is killing my back."

So, he'd been right. He couldn't imagine her wanting to sleep in the same bed she'd shared with a man who'd stooped low enough to screw her sister.

"I know it must feel like your sky is falling right now, but you might want to consider hiding somewhere else for a while," he said. "Once the media gets wind of what's happened to your dad, they're gonna be all over you."

She slid from her stool to cross the empty living room and stand at one of her big south-facing windows, staring out at lower Manhattan, the Statue of Liberty, Verrazano Bridge, and Staten Island beyond. But for the load of crap her world had just dumped on it, it would have been a beautiful day. "And where would you suggest I go? East Hampton?"

Not hardly, he thought. "A hotel, maybe? At least for the duration?"

"I have no idea how long that might be. I still have a fucking business to run."

"We seem to be doing okay for the moment without you."

"Tamara tells me you worked sixteen-hour days all week. I'm supposed to be okay with that?"

"Nobody just threw a grenade into my life. I'll survive. The guys are doing an awesome job on the new production line. There's hardly been a glitch. Tam's team has that launch event for the new line covered. The prototypes are all but finished. You've got other things to worry about right now."

"You mean like whether some jihadist who's been fucked over for like a hundred years by people like my dad decides to cut his head off? I've been wallowing for a week over my marriage, and now this. I need distraction right now, Jeff, not more hiding out and wallowing. Work seems like the best option I have there."

"So, pack a change of clothes and your toothbrush and come stay at the plant," he said. "That sofa in your office looks pretty comfy. You can use my shower. They might be able to find you there during the day, but nobody will expect you to be there at night."

She turned back from that view to look at him, no small measure of surprise in her eyes. "Did that idea just come out of your mouth or did you actually think about it first?"

"Probably more the former than the latter, but you know me. Mr. Spontaneity. It's actually not a bad idea. You're feeling guilty about being away from the business at a pivotal time. It's a better option than you sitting here, trapped by an army of paparazzi and licking your wounds."

She moved to sit in the David chair, leaving the Venus for him. Ever since that ultra-woke feminist attack in the Times, he'd noticed that she seemed to prefer him to her. Which was fine. He was definitely a Venus man himself.

"You know what's strange," she said. "I can so believe Jason did what he did. With him, that kind of predictability is almost a fucking cliché."

"Even when the other woman is his sister-in-law?" Jeff asked. "That strays into Biblical no-no territory."

She sighed and shook her head. "So, tell me something," she said. "Is that little twat really that much more attractive than me? I mean, enough to make him unable to resist going there?"

Jeff laughed outright. Ever since first looking into those remarkable green eyes of hers and getting a snootful of that brash confidence, he'd thought she was the most attractive woman he'd ever met. Everything he'd seen in the two years since hadn't served to dissuade him there; the quick wit and precise analytical brain combined with her imposing physical dynamic. Sure, at the moment she might look like someone who'd had the air let out of all her tires, but the only things required to fix that were a compressor and air hose.

"I wish I thought you were kidding," he said. "But I also know you're not and you don't know how sad that makes me feel. Your scumbag husband didn't fuck Katya because he thought she was hotter than you. He fucked her because he's pathetically insecure and believes that some is good and more is always better. What he doesn't realize is that Katya wasn't even a conquest. She scaled his walls and crawled into his bed, not the other way around."

She looked far from convinced. "I've seen the way men look at her."

"Hell, I've seen how you look at her. If you decided to hang your shit out there like she does, I'm pretty sure they'd look at you like that, too."

There was almost a shyness in the smile she flashed him next. "Pretty sure?" She drained her wine rather than sip at it and stared down into her empty glass. "I'm kind of in the mood to get drunk right now," she said. "Wanna join me? I've got no idea what might be coming next, but I think we need to drink to my dad."

TWENTY-ONE

Crown Prince Ahmad ibn Abdullah's head, secured in a plastic garbage bag and a cardboard box, was left on the hood of a car parked a block from the Saudi Royal residence in Riyadh just a day after his abduction. Meanwhile, American billionaire industrialist Bertrand Brock seemed to have vanished from the face of the earth. Neither Ahmad ibn Abdullah's body nor any parts of Bert Brock's were found anywhere else, although speculation in the international press was rampant. Like those persistent rumors that Jimmy Hoffa's murdered remains had been buried in the concrete poured beneath the endzone of the Meadowlands Stadium in suburban New Jersey, theories regarding the lower portion of the Saudi Crown Prince and the whole of Amy's dad abounded. They were at the bottom of the Persian Gulf off the massive Ras Tanura oil refinery just east of Riyadh. They were buried beneath a freshly poured new runway extension at the King Khalid International Airport.

For weeks after the discovery of the prince's severed head, Amy had clung to the hope that the Yemeni Houthi rebels laying claim to responsibility for removing it might surface to make some sort of ransom demand for the safe return of her dad. To her, it made no sense that they wouldn't. In the avalanche of media coverage that followed the kidnapping, plenty of mention had been made of just how wealthy and influential he was. Killing him would be analogous to killing the Golden Goose. She found herself in touch with a liaison assigned to monitoring the situation at the U.S. State Department sometimes multiple times a day, only to learn that every enquiry that the American intelligence gathering apparatus endeavored to make in the region had met with total radio silence. It was like Bert Brock had simply vanished from the face of the earth.

Then, six months after the launch of Brocking Chair's new line of "Brockstyle" dining and living room furniture, and three months after Amy's trip to Como, Italy to collect the last of her four international design prizes for her previous year's work, Milenka Brock started proceedings to have her missing husband declared legally dead. Those would likely take several years to complete but in the interim, she also petitioned the New York courts for the green light to begin overseeing any of his far-flung business affairs in which she also had a shared financial stake.

At the same time, the release of Whack Job's first extended-play recording and the critical acclaim it received, combined with Brocking Chair Ltd's super-fast take off, combined with all the turmoil surrounding Amy, was making Jeff Land feel like his life was spinning more and more out of control. Patty had worked an early shift at the bar the day he heard from Amy about Milenka's legal filing and as he walked her home, he knew she could feel his current anxiety.

"Talk to me," she said. "You seem more tightly wound than usual tonight."

"We got an interesting letter from Milenka Brock's lawyers today. Even though Amy's dad hasn't been declared legally dead, the bitch is suing to take a more active role in his business affairs. Specifically, a merchant banking fund he controlled with a billion dollars in assets."

"Ah. And how could that affect your business?"

His expression was glum. "Apparently, there's some clause in Milenka's pre-nup that says, in the event that Bert pre-deceases her, a big chunk of certain assets will be liquidated and go directly to her. Of the rest, half will go to Amy and half to Katya. Amy isn't quite sure how it happened, but her father's equity in Brocking Chair comes from the fund I just mentioned, and somehow it's ended up on Milenka's side of the tally sheet."

"I thought you had some contractual stipulation," she said. "That even though he's the majority stakeholder, he couldn't interfere with your actual operations."

"We do," he said. "But apparently, she's threatened to challenge that, saying he had no right to make that stipulation in the first place without her agreeing to it."

"Jesus. Can't she and Amy just trade?"

"In a civilized world, that would make the most sense. But Milenka's not civilized. She's always hated how Bert, at least in her estimation, seemed to favor Amy over Katya. Right now, that's motivation enough for her to want to fuck us."

"But with Amy's dad not officially declared dead, I don't see how she can do that," Patty said.

Jeff had spent the past two days in extended conversations with Amy and Greg Logan in Chicago on that very subject. "Our counsel is telling us there's a lot of gray area there," he replied. "If a person simply disappears, it usually takes seven years to declare them dead. But there are lots of potentially extenuating circumstances. Say a dude is in a plane crash in the Andes and they can't find his body. Or he goes missing playing golf with a foreign potentate whose head is delivered up in a cardboard box. Depending on the court and the judge, that could be construed as enough reasonable cause to shorten those seven years considerably."

"Like how much shorter?"

"That will probably depend on how good her lawyers are and how much money she's willing to pay them. Our guy says that under the right circumstances it might be a year, give-or-take. But either way, there's nobody at the helm of that investment fund right now and as the widow with the largest stake, he thinks Milenka can make a strong case for assuming stewardship."

Patty continued walking, now deep in thought. Summer had recently turned to fall and Jeff could feel it in the air. He'd donned a wool hat and light jacket and now zipped it up to his throat.

"But you guys plan to fight her, right?" Patty said.

"We need to see what she's planning, first. If she can succeed in dissolving that non-participation clause in our contract, and decides to start telling us how to run our business, things could get really nasty."

"Didn't you tell me Amy's dad was already getting half your revenue? Why would she want to mess with that? It would be like cutting her own throat out of spite."

Jeff felt another wave of weariness wash over him as he leaned to kiss her cheek. She might have a doctorate in Cultural Anthropology and know a lot about human tendencies from an academic standpoint, but she was still a babe in the woods when it came to business and how it was all-too-often run. "She'll mess with us for no reason other than that she hates Amy. The only reason she crawled into my bed and fucked me that night was to get one over on her. It was nothing more than a power play."

"Something you didn't understand at the time."

"How much understanding are you doing when you're thinking with nothing but your dick?"

"I don't have one of those, so a rhetorical question." She reached to hook an arm with his and pulled herself closer. "But to judge by all the opportunities being thrown your way these days, it seems like you're doing a lot less of that now. What do you want to eat tonight? We should go somewhere special. My treat."

He looked over at her, his interest suddenly piqued in a different direction. Patty was so broke from trying to service her student loan debt that most months she could barely pay her rent. "What's this about?" he asked.

"I've got news," she replied. "But let's save it until we're both sitting down."

◉◉◉

Katya Brock was still trying to get a handle on the idea that one day before not too long the fact that her father had been murdered in Saudi Arabia was going to make her filthy rich. On her own terms. She'd lived her entire indulged life in the shadow of great wealth and benefited from it in myriad ways but had never had control of the actual purse strings. In terms of new options being open to her, this would be a game changer.

For the moment, she was continuing to see her brother-in-law whenever he was out at the Amagansett house, not because he was much by way of company—the man couldn't fuck for shit and talked ceaselessly about himself—but because he was willing to spend lavishly on her and she relished in the idea of how that had to be frying her half-sister's circuits. It was just a matter of time before she got tired of him but by then she imagined Amy would have moved on and she would need to find some new way to torture her. Maybe she would make a run at Jeff Land again, although she'd heard from Tanner Upton that at least for the time being he had some bartender girlfriend covering his action. Because guys who looked like him and sang in rock bands weren't usually the long-haul types, she was sure that just a little patience was all that would be required there.

Katya had taken to rising late most mornings since her graduation from Stony Brook six months earlier and was in the kitchen of the East Hampton house waiting for the cook to make her coffee when her mother swept in from a work-out, dressed in one of her ubiquitous thong-leotard and leggings outfits, her hair tied up in a disheveled knot atop her head. Damn. The woman worked so hard trying to keep up with her and the strain was starting to show. Of late, she'd lost some of the muscle mass in her once fabulous ass and even with periodic maintenance nips and tucks, her face was finally beginning to look just ever-so-slightly gaunt. She knew that Milenka would still be considered hot by most middle-class standards, but compared to her, who was not quite twenty-three and still in her post-pubescent ascendency, she could no longer stake claim to a level playing field. Not that she would ever admit that. Hell, no. Before Katya had managed the coup with her brother-in-law, her mother had always insisted on treating her as an understudy. But now, with that feat since accomplished, Katya believed she could now lay claim to the family crown.

"What are your plans for the next month or so, Baby Girl?" Milenka asked.

Katya had just accepted a mug of coffee from the cook and taken a first sip in an effort to get some basic synapses kicked into gear. She and two high school friends had taken a limo to the Hulk-O-Mania male strip club in Freeport last night where she'd ended up partying in the parking lot drunk and snorting coke off the head of some muscled-up dancer's Viagra-hard dick.

"You mean, like, between now and Thanksgiving?"

Her mother nodded. "I need you to take a trip to Bulgaria for us."

"This time of year? It's cold as fuck there, mother. How about Tulum or Barbados?" She'd been to Sofia to visit Milenka's relatives any number of times throughout her childhood and hated the place. Everyone there was so fucking Bulgarian, while she was just half, didn't speak the language, and could barely relate to them.

"This will not be a vacation," her mother said. "It will be

business. I think it is time for you to start earning your keep here."

Katya knew that the part of her dad's will that cut her in for nearly half of his net worth wouldn't kick in until she reached thirty. The same for Amy, who was almost twenty-eight and for whom that big-casino pay-out wasn't so far off. For Katya, it seemed like an eternity. When she spoke next, her tone grew cautious.

"What kind of business?"

"I have looked at your sister's deal she signs with your father," her mother replied. "It is based on the notion that their designs should be manufactured here, in United States. Her wish is to revive some silly, long-lost tradition of American manufacturing excellence. Apple and Google and everyone else has recognized the stupidity of that. I think that we should do this, too."

Katya was confused. "We? I thought Daddy gave Amy and her partner control of how they operate."

Milenka waved a dismissive hand. "He did, but my lawyers believe they can break that clause, to help me take control from them."

Katya stared at her, feeling a strange mix of pride and admiration in what she saw there. "Damn, Mama. I think you might be an even meaner bitch than me."

Milenka smiled. "But you are learning, correct?"

"So why fucking Bulgaria? Other than the fact that you're from there?"

"I am not quite certain yet," her mother replied. "But I am working on it."

TWENTY-TWO

Jeff and Patty ended up at Testo, a Northern Italian place on Leonard Street that was a favorite of theirs, Jeff grateful for the distraction after the last conversation he'd had with Amy and their attorney that afternoon. Ever since the first of last year, things had been going so well for him that he'd started to wonder if maybe he shouldn't pinch himself. Then along had come Milenka Brock, raising her avaricious head to inject a note of reality and remind him of what the world was really like. Their waiter had just poured them wine and taken their orders. Jeff lifted his glass.

"So, what's this news?" he asked. "I hope it's better than mine." With the way his day had gone, he was half-expecting her to tell him she was pregnant.

"You know the job that I flew out to interview for last summer? The one I thought I didn't get?" she asked.

That past July she'd flown to San Diego to interview for a teaching position at the University of California there.
"They finally finished their vetting process and just offered me an Assistant Professorship," she said. "Tenure-track. They want me to start teaching winter quarter, which starts four days after New Year's."

For some crazy reason, the first thing that popped into Jeff's mind was an image of Patty, the whitest woman in the world, on a beach in Southern California. She'd once told him it was impossible for her to tan. "Oh, wow," he said. "That's only two months from now."

"I know. Crazy, right? They were down to four candidates and the Dean just called me today. Right when I had started to think I might be working as a bartender for the rest of my life."

Undeniably stunned by her news, Jeff forced himself to rally. This was her dream and what she'd spent over a decade studying for, accumulating a mountain of student debt in the process. For some reason, he'd never thought enough about it to consider the possibility that the job she might eventually land would take her so far away from him. San Diego. Damn. He'd never been there but she'd said it was nice. Seventy degrees in the dead middle of winter.

"That's fabulous news, babe. Tenure track. Shit. A month

Whack Job

ago, you were convinced they don't make those jobs anymore."

"They don't make many. I mean, I did great work at Ohio State and published some cutting-edge research, but I was starting to feel like nobody really cared about it. The Chair of my new department called me right after the Dean to say how excited she is about having me there. She told me she's been teaching my dissertation as part of one of her courses."

Jeff thought about first meeting her that past February and how much fun he'd had with her in the ten months since. He'd never imagined being quite so comfortable with a woman as he was with her. There was no artifice, no posing, no bullshit; just straight-up who they were. The fact that she was nine years older had never really seemed to matter. He loved it that she was tempered by life in a way that women his own age just weren't yet. He'd learned a lot from her, being around all that maturity and strong sensibility, and believed that she had helped ground him at a time when there was so much turmoil in his life. Amy's dad had been kidnapped and was presumed dead. Her mother was conspiring to steal their company. He was a fledgling rock star now, the lead singer of a band getting national attention, which all seemed just a little bit crazy.

"I'd be a liar to say I'm not gonna really miss you," he said.

She grinned back at him. "Miss what? The fact that I help keep you level-headed, or my fabulous butt?"

"Can't I miss both?"

"I'm gonna miss you, too, hot-shot," she said. "And be forever grateful for the fact that you kept believing in me, even in those times when I got so discouraged."

"That's because I saw something special in you the first time we ever talked, and I always knew that this would happen," he said. "Sooner or later, someone else was going to see what I saw, too. That shit's not so easy to hide."

She took a sip of her wine while meeting his gaze with a frank one of her own. At length she said, "I kind of figured it would be time for me to be going soon anyway. Before too much longer, you're going to need to figure out this stuff between you and Amy. I don't want to be in the way of that. She may have set out a bunch of rules before you two started down this road, maybe even before she really knew how she actually felt, but that woman is in love with you. Any fool can see that. And I'm pretty sure you're in love with her, too."

It was a harsher truth than he wanted to admit to, probably because he wasn't so sure that the door there actually swung both ways. Amy had a lot on her mind those days and in subtle ways those things had changed her. The disappearance of her father had really rocked her. Her hatred for Milenka had hardened her. When he started to open his mouth to protest, she held up a hand to stop him.

"Don't even try to bullshit me, dude. A woman can feel these things. And don't get me wrong. I'm thrilled to have gotten to know you and get to share the kind of stuff that we have. That shit is rare, for lovers and friends-with-benefits. The fact that we've gotten so close as we have is something I hope you'll always treasure as much as I know I will."

He was unable to find words, his throat thick with emotion. All he could do was nod.

"I also know that you guys are going to need to get on the same page pretty quickly now," she continued. "From what you just told me it sounds like you're under siege."

Jeff was thinking about the factory and the business that he and Amy had built together in such a remarkably short period of time. There was an undeniable magic in their partnership and the trust they seemed to share, a lot of it based on how their interests fit so perfectly together. He was also thinking about Milenka and the deep animosity she was so intent on focusing on the one daughter of her dead husband who wasn't hers. Because of what the woman had managed to engineer the first time they'd met, his own resentment of her was almost as strong as Amy's was.

"I'm not sure that anything between Amy and me can be quite as simple as you imagine," he said. "There's way more complexity there than meets the eye."

"Of course, there is," she said. "Just for starters, she's taking credit on the world stage for work that's mostly yours. To me, the fact that you're willing to go along with that is nothing short of amazing."

He smiled. "In the current woke atmosphere, I never really

had a choice. She's a smart and driven bi-racial woman while I'm a straight white dude named after Thomas Jefferson. My kind ran the show for centuries and we've finally been caught with our pants around our ankles. The idea that she and Tamara are coming up with all these innovative design and marketing ideas has generated a kind of excitement that a straight white dude just can't achieve anymore. I'd rather see my ideas in their hands and flourishing than filling a Dumpster somewhere."

"It's still remarkable that you've been able to harness any resentment you might feel over that," she said. "Your shitty moment in history and all that."

He chuckled. "I may be only twenty-three, but I'm smart enough to know you need to play the hand you're dealt. Either that, or fold. Right now, I'm having way too much fun with all this to not keep playing. I know in my heart that those awards that Amy keeps winning should really be mine. And thankfully, so does she."

"That's how it's been with all the world's great love affairs," Patty said. "Anthony and Cleopatra, Romeo and Juliet, Tristan and Isolde. The fact that those connections were all born in tension seemed to have somehow fueled them."

"I'd rather go the Jimmy and Rosalyn Carter route," Jeff countered. "They both got to live to a ripe old age."

⊙⊙⊙

Jeff's new 'Brockstyle' designs were introduced to the public at their second gala gallery opening held in early November. Meanwhile, actual production of them was already being implemented in Brocking Chair's Long Island City factory. After that opening, Jeff suggested to Amy that she use the prototype pieces to replace the furniture removed from her loft in the wake of her separation. Because of how enthusiastically they'd been received by several major international design critics, Amy was convinced they would be museum pieces one day, but meanwhile loved the idea of having them in her home for everyday use, just to look at and feel the sense of pride and accomplishment that they gave her. For the several years she'd spent as an MFA candidate before meeting Jeff Land, she'd dreamt big but never imagined getting quite this big. The smart-ass kid with balls big enough to tell her that her chair design sucked without being the least bit mean about it had proven himself an anomaly in so many other ways, too. He'd not just lived up to every accolade that members of the Parsons School faculty had heaped on him, he'd proven that even that high praise was significantly under-rated. He might be a hick kid from the sticks, but he was that rare individual who absorbed information like kitty litter, had a genius for extrapolating from a host of different design forms and creating inspired amalgams from them, and had the tireless work ethic of a 19th Century Iowa farmer. He also seemed to be impossibly humble and she wished she could say that he was unprepossessing, too, but that wasn't remotely true. He had a world-class rock and roll voice, was gorgeous, and was so irritatingly unassuming it only added to his overall charm.

It was mid-November, with the holiday sales season suddenly upon them, and nothing had been heard regarding her father in over a year. That flood of calls made regularly to her contact at the State Department had slowed to a trickle while Brocking Chair was now being slammed with orders they would never be able to fill as quickly as retail design galleries all over the country wanted them. Pressure was on from European retailers to begin direct sales to them as well, any tariffs be damned. Because they loved the team they had assembled and didn't want to lose any of them by forcing an inconveniently long commute, she and Jeff had been in discussions aimed at finding a bigger manufacturing space somewhere in the same immediate area. Square footage of that sort in any of New York's five boroughs or even in the closer cities of Long Island's Nassau County was expensive. Any move was sure to put serious pressure on their price point but in that area Jeff was proving himself more progressive in his philosophy than even she was, talking profit-sharing and employee ownership, handsome returns remaining a secondary objective for him. He liked to point out that because of his music he was going to get rich either way and that, at least on paper, she already was. They were fortunate to be where they were and they needed to keep the people who'd helped them get there happy. To do that, they would need to share the wealth. It was a mindset so dead-opposite everything that her father had stood for that she found herself resisting at first, purely out of habit. In order to force herself onto Jeff's more egalitarian wavelength she'd had to remind herself of what a selfish and ruthless prick her father could be, and to ask herself if she wanted that to be her legacy, too.

It was the Saturday morning before Thanksgiving when she was surprised to receive a call from Patty Conlon, asking if they could meet face-to-face to talk. When Patty offered to come into Manhattan for lunch and told her to pick the spot, Amy suggested she come to her place. She could make coffee and order something in.

It was two weeks since Jeff had mentioned Patty taking that teaching job in San Diego and that she would be moving to the West Coast the week before Christmas. They hadn't really talked about how he felt about that. When it came to personal matters, she'd found it safest to maintain an emotional distance. He was already too well aware of how the unceremonious end to her embarrassingly brief marriage and then the kidnapping of her father had trashed her and how she was still in recovery from them. Added to it was the stress of Milenka and the equally treacherous Katya both looming ever larger now in her overall picture. She knew that regardless of how Jeff chose to define his connection with Patty, a bond had been forged there that he wasn't excited to see move twenty-eight hundred miles away. And the fact of the matter was, she felt for him. She'd found herself in Patty's company on at least a dozen occasions since that first Sunday morning and over time the woman had grown on her. Patty had been really sympathetic over the loss of her father and was not only really smart, but also capable of some serious depth. Amy could see her in front of a classroom full of smart kids, engaging them with that rare kind of frankness she had, and being a wild success at it.

Later, on greeting Jeff's lover at her door, she wondered how surprised she should be when her visitor planted a light kiss on her cheek.

"Jeff's told me about the trouble your step-mother is trying to make," Patty said. "That sucks, hon. I feel for you. Any more word from the State Department?"

New York was in the middle of a nasty cold snap and her

guest took a moment to unburden herself of a heavy winter coat, wool hat, scarf, and gloves. Amy hung them in the coat closet before leading the way toward her kitchen.

"I think the guy I talk to there was getting really tired of hearing from me," she said. "And my bitch of a step-mother hasn't won anything just yet. Right now, with the pressure on us to expand, if a judge gives her control of my dad's money and allows her to participate in our business, she could really tie things up for us. Your boyfriend's dream of employee profit-sharing could be put on hold for years. Coffee?"

"I'd love some," Patty said. "And we need to talk about that 'my boyfriend' thing." She pulled up a stool to sit at the island while Amy got busy with the brass behemoth. "Jeff and I have become much better friends than either of us ever expected, but I've never been anything more than a placeholder for him."

Amy glanced over a shoulder at her, puzzled. "A placeholder for what?"

"Until you two could get your romantic shit together."

In the middle of loading a portafilter, Amy stiffened and turned to look at her in shock, a tiny knot suddenly formed in the pit of her stomach. "Say what?"

Patty smiled, a surprising warmth in her frank gray eyes. "You heard me the first time. And I know that you know exactly what I'm talking about. We both know that you married that two-timing cheesedick record producer as much in denial of the obvious as anything else. You and Jeff are meant for each other. You know it. I know it. And I know that he knows it, too."

That was a whole lot of painful truth to be dumped on a woman at any one time. Amy's heart was suddenly racing, making it difficult for her to catch her breath.

"He's told you that?"

"He didn't have to. I've got a doctorate in the human condition. I can stand behind a bar, watch two people at a table and within five minutes know exactly what's going on between them. Sometimes I even scare myself with that shit." Patty pointed to the portafilter in Amy's hand. "Are we going to have coffee or just hang here staring at each other?"

Amy managed to jerk herself out of whatever place she'd momentarily drifted off to and turned to fit those fresh grounds into place and switch on her machine. "Latte or straight up?" she asked. This was crazy. Out of the blue she was suddenly engaged in a woman-to-woman conversation about who should rightfully be tending to her business partner's romantic interests…with his current lover of all people.

"I'd love a latte. Thanks." Patty shifted on her stool to lean forward and plant both elbows on the granite while staring straight at Amy. "I didn't come here to make you uncomfortable, hon," she said. "I came here to tell you to quit denying things. That it's time to get real. You and Jeff share almost the exact same ambitions. You're both scary smart, each of you in your own way. That first time we ever sat down in the break room at your plant, I saw the way he looked at you and could see it in his eyes how beautiful he thinks you are. It was a whole other way than he's ever looked at me, and I know he thinks I'm plenty hot. He likes me a lot, but he's in love with you. That's not something he's capable of hiding, no matter how hard he tries."

Feeling a little bit like she was having an out-of-body experience Amy broke that eye contact to hurry to the refrigerator for milk. She suddenly needed to keep her hands busy, like the mere fact of action might buy her time to think. As seemed to always be the case in her life, whenever she felt herself being trapped in a corner, her defenses went up with an unsettling abruptness. "You do realize that it takes two to tango, right?" It sounded dumb but at that moment it was the only thing she could think of to say.

"I saw that same look in your eyes, too, hon. The first moment when you saw me standing there in nothing but his t-shirt. It hit you like a sledgehammer. It was that same, oh shit, the guy I've got a crush on is fucking someone else look that I've seen a hundred times in my work. You can stand there, lie to me all you want and try to tell me it wasn't. But believe me, I know it when I see it."

What was Amy supposed to say? What would be the point of fruitlessly trying to deny something that she also knew was true? She did have a crush on Jeff Land. It had hurt like hell to see him relaxing so comfortably in that intimate physical space with another woman.

For some reason the idea of his one-night-stands after band gigs had never bothered her all that much, mostly because she'd known he wouldn't likely ever see those women again, but with Patty it had been different. Patty was someone who'd seen him most every day for most of the past year and who was, in many ways, her equal.

Almost as if her guest could read her thoughts, Patty stood and crossed to remove the milk carton from her hands, taking over those frothing duties as she spoke. "You need to understand that there's no competition for him here," she said. "He's always been yours and I've always known that. I like to think I may have taught him a few things that you might benefit from someday, but a month from now I'm gone and it's going to be time for you two to get on with it." She paused to top their lattes off with frothed milk and do her little lotus flower thing. "Some smart person once told me that two people in the right kind of relationship can have the strength of twenty once they've bonded. I really think you two have that potential." The cup of coffee she handed to Amy felt like a peace offering.

TWENTY-THREE

The idea of screwing over her half-sister twice in the same year, first by stealing her husband and then stealing her business, had more than sustained Katya Brock for the two miserably cold weeks she'd spent in Sofia and then in the Black Sea port city of Varna. Still, once all of the various enquiries made at her mother's behest were concluded, she was more than ready to fly home. For starters, she'd always found Bulgarian men more condescending and difficult to manipulate than their American counterparts, them making it abundantly clear that they thought dealing with her, regardless of the fact that she was a future major stakeholder in Brock International, to be beneath them. All the same, her mother had sent her there with an interesting product to sell, and if all of the men she'd met there seemed mostly interested in getting into her pants, they were all of them still keen to make money.

Just to make her trip a little more bearable, she'd stopped for two days in Mallorca on the way home, managing to find warmer weather there and a ruggedly built local in a Santa Ponsa beach bar who'd helped her get the bad taste of Bulgaria out of her mouth. It was late on the Saturday night before Thanksgiving when her mother and their driver collected her from JFK, Milenka suggesting that they spend the night at Trump Tower rather than ride all the way back out to East Hampton. Once dropped off there they could send the car on its way and take the chopper back out to the beach the next morning.

"I know you are tired, Baby Girl, but our new business partner's band is playing at Terminal 5 again tonight. I thought we might see what kind of trouble we can get into." To sweeten her proposition, Milenka fished a little cocaine-containing silver bullet from her bra and handed it across.

So far as Katya knew, her mother had never snorted coke before her politically and socially conservative father had disappeared. Or if she had, she'd kept it a closely guarded secret. But over the past year it seemed as if her consumption of the stuff had become a more-or-less routine thing. She'd even asked Katya to hook her up with her source in order to ensure she had a steady supply.

"Ever since they released their first album Whack Job has been selling out its shows for months," she said. "Unless you've already got tickets, I doubt we can even get in."

Her mother chuckled and patted her knee. "These days, I do not think there is anywhere in New York that I cannot get into, whenever I please," she said. "While you were in Varna, I hired the best PR person money can buy. She has the pull of strings everywhere. All I need do is call, give her maybe two hours' notice, and magic happens."

Katya twisted the little bullet a half-turn, inserted it into a nostril and snorted hard. Once the powder hit her sinuses the drug was already working its way into her bloodstream even before she handed the little contraption back across. "So, call her. If we decide not to go, you might as well make this bitch earn her money anyway."

Milenka dug out her phone, had a brief exchange, and disconnected. "So, tell me. You say on the phone that you like this company best that has its own container ships."

Katya was starting to feel the wonder-dust eat at the edges of her weariness, making her less irritable. She shrugged. Almost ten hours in the air combined with a night where she'd gotten very little sleep were probably more than even a snootful of coke could handle for long, but for the moment she was suddenly up and perky. "The way I see it, Vasilev Limited's manufacturing capability for everything from patio tables and chairs to fold-out futons and recliners, combined with their shipping capacity, makes them a one-stop shop. Mr. Vasilev and his son, Giorgi, are a couple of pompous pricks, but their quality control is good, at least by Eastern European standards. They make a product comparable to any of the other higher-end stuff I looked at."

"Quality will be key," her mother said. "Amy has already created serious demand for the Brocking Chair brand. We do not want to mess with that. The new product will need to look every bit as good as what they are manufacturing here. This is important."

At maybe one-quarter the American manufactured price, Katya thought. She'd found it interesting when a shipping manager in Varna had informed her that it cost less to ship a sofa from the

Black Sea to the Port of Newark than it did to transport it by truck from New York to LA or Miami. Those new ULCS ships could carry upwards of 15,000 shipping containers, reducing the haulage cost for a single sofa when shipped with a few hundred others to just pennies a mile.

"Everywhere I went, I brought that quality expert dude that your uncle recommended along with me. He did close examinations of the products they made at every plant we visited. He thinks Vasilev's are better than most. Asshole CEO or not, I think that going with them is a no-brainer."

She watched her mother absorb all that and nod. The light of pure conniving nastiness she saw in her was so close to the one she saw in herself every time she looked in a mirror that she knew it probably should have scared her. Deep in the part of her that occasionally asked such questions, she wondered how long there would be room for two totally self-absorbed, heartless bitches to operate in the same sphere. She warned herself to be careful there, aware that in some species, mothers ate their young.

⊚⊚⊚

Jeff was more mystified than ever by the mechanics of female interaction when he arrived for his band's pre-Thanksgiving gig at Terminal 5 and was surprised to see that Patty and Amy had come there together, seeming to have formed some sort of bond. He'd been so busy trying to juggle time spent in his design studio with the demands of his band's ever-increasing popularity that it felt like he'd missed something that probably should have been obvious. Whack Job was scheduled to go into Ardent's Nashville studio to record a second album right after the first of the year, a venture that was currently requiring significant rehearsal time at their practice space in Brooklyn. Come February, it was expected that his new co-called "Brockstyle" pieces, recently added to the company's line, would win Amy a few more design awards. That additional notoriety would put even more strain on the production limits of their now-undersized factory, but with Patty gone to San

Diego and one fewer distraction, he figured he could still handle all the increased pressure headed his way.

His girlfriend and his partner were sitting together on a sofa in the green room talking to keys player, Rick Carlisle. Reacting to the quizzical look on Jeff's face, Patty perked up.

"Hey, hot-shot. Look who I managed to persuade out of her cave."

Amy looked over to flash him a weak smile. "She thinks I've wallowed in my misery long enough," she said. "That it's time for me to get back into circulation."

Jeff wondered just how much he'd managed to miss there. With Patty occasionally making appearances at the plant ever since she and Amy first met, he imagined they must have run into each other from time-to-time, but what was with this evident familiarity? At least so far as he was aware, they hadn't exchanged anything but a passing hello and maybe condolences over the tragedy befalling Amy's dad.

"When she told me she hasn't seen you guys play since some gig at Arlene's Grocery like over two years ago, I told her that was crazy," Patty said. "She needs to see how much better you've gotten since then."

Jeff guessed that Amy already had some notion of that. Their production floor assembly team regularly played Whack Job's breakout record as part of their everyday mix. At volume. He looked at his business partner again, struck by how much those recent turns in her personal life seemed to have sucked so much of the vitality from those incredible eyes. Not only had her half-sister conspired to brazenly wreck her marriage, her father presumably been murdered, and the business she'd worked so hard to build was now under attack from her step-mother. It was a lot to handle all at once and it was taking its toll.

In spite of his confusion over this new connection, he fed Amy a bright return smile. "I think it's great that you're here. We're debuting the new material for our next record. I'm eager to hear what you think of it."

"I just hope my sister doesn't show up," she said. "That would be so much like her."

Whack Job

So far as Jeff knew, Amy hadn't seen Katya since catching her on that security camera in her kitchen last summer. And ever since Milenka's recent power-play, she hadn't been out to her family's East Hampton house, either. "I seriously doubt she would," he said. "From what we hear from our producer at Ardent, your ex-husband is still super-pissed we used him as a stalking horse to get ourselves a better deal from them."

Amy's mood seemed to brighten at that. "One thing I learned in the brief time we were married? There's no honor in the record business. For all we know, his dad already had money invested in some other band with a sound similar to yours and wanted him to sign you just so they could bury you. He told me they pull that kind of shit all the time."

From across the room, Tanner Upton threw her a look of mock outrage. "Another band with a sound like ours doesn't exist," he scoffed. "Sure, there'll be a bunch of copycat shitheads before long, but right now there ain't nobody has our sound. Just wait 'til you hear what we got in store for you tonight, Mama. We're gonna knock your fucking socks off."

A member of the Terminal 5 security team poked his bullet head in past the green room door. "There's two ladies out front who say they're with the band, like that's a line I ain't heard before. They're being kinda insistent, saying they're your drummer's business partners or some shit. I figured I should clear it with you."

From her seat on the couch, Amy looked quickly at Jeff before addressing the man. "Tell them to fuck off," she said. And then she was suddenly on her feet. "Or better yet, let me."

TWENTY-FOUR

Katya hadn't seen Amy since being caught on camera in her half-sister's Amagansett kitchen and when she did now, it wasn't at all like the moment of triumph she'd imagined. Amy had always had plenty of spine in her, but to walk out onto that stage in front of two thousand people, grab a microphone, ask the house DJ to cut the music, and then point at her?

"That two-timing cunt right there fucked my husband!" she yelled into that mike, her voice amplified loud enough to fill the entire venue. "The one dressed like a Lincoln Tunnel hooker! And the best part of the story? She's my own fucking sister! Let's all let her know what we think of skanks who do shit like that!" And then she'd reached to hold that microphone out over the crowd.

It created a moment like none other in Katya's life. Hisses, boos and catcalls rang out all across the venue as curiosity seekers craned their necks to stare at her like she was a carnival side-show freak. And then, as that avalanche of invective rained down, she turned to look for her mother and saw her trying to melt away into the throng. A hand grabbed at her ass and she slapped at it in outrage.

"Her name is Katya Brock!" Amy screamed. "If you're married or have a boyfriend you want to keep, you might want to take a picture of her! Let's see how many hits we can get her on Instagram! Let's make her the most popular skank-ho in the state!"

Katya tried to flee in panic while a hundred cellphone flashes went off in her face.

"Katya Brock, people! Remember her name! 631-555-0087! Hit her up!"

More hands grabbed at Katya and at that point she lost it, screaming and flailing like a madwoman as she fought her way toward an exit sign.

✺✺✺

Whack Job was just prepping to hit the stage when Jeff first heard Amy's amplified voice, asking the DJ to cut the house music. He and Patty had looked at each other in surprise and then sprinted

Whack Job

down the hallway toward stage left and the bright lights, arriving just as she launched into her tirade while pointing Katya out to the crowd. She was dressed in another of those trademark outfits of hers, a quarter acre of cleavage bared and her hair up in a pile atop her head. And then, as Amy began hurling invective at her, he watched the woman's privileged little world suddenly turn to churned chaos, those words impacting like chum hitting shark-infested waters. They whipped the crowd surrounding her into a frenzy, people jumping up and down to get a better look. Some of those closer reached out to poke and prod her. Jeff wondered if this was what a stoning in a public square might look like, only with hundreds of cellphone cameras and data uplinks to thousands of additional viewers also in play.

Milenka had turned to flee in the face of it rather than make even the slightest attempt to shield her daughter. Once Katya started to shriek and flail as she fought her way toward an exit sign, he saw a look of vengeful triumph appear on Amy's face while she calmly replaced the microphone on its stand and turned to start his way.

"Holy shit!" Patty yelled at her. "You're such a badass!"

Jeff had only recently gotten accustomed to performing to crowds that big and he realized just how remarkable it was what Amy had just done. In no way did it bear any resemblance to his hiding behind a drum kit and having three other dudes up there with him to share the risk. A quarter-century of pent-up injustice had just blown the top off her outrage; erupting to spew molten invective over a half-sister who'd always made her feel like an outsider in her own family.

Patty hit her with a high-five. "How did that make you feel, girlfriend?" she yelled. "Fucking awesome, I bet!"

Amy's hands were shaking. There was a look of shocked surprise in her eyes, like she couldn't quite believe what she'd just done.

"Oh wow, what a rush!" she exclaimed.

The other members of the band had just emerged onstage to take up their positions. Jeff reached for the pair of drumsticks jammed into his back pocket, then looked back at Amy, seeing a completely different kind of strength there than he'd ever seen before. Not the determined and organized planner kind of strength, or even the committed visionary kind. This was the same kind you saw in a cornered animal that has just discovered it has sharp teeth and claws. Her step-mother might have come after her with an army of lawyers, determined to screw her and her dream over just because she believed that superior financial firepower entitled her to do anything she pleased, but if Jeff had been even a little bit worried about how they were going to confront an onslaught like that, he wasn't any more. From that moment on, if Milenka, Katya or anyone else wanted to try to stand in Amy's way, they'd better start shopping for body armor.

☺☺☺

The mechanics of precisely how Milenka intended to mess with them came to light on the Tuesday following the Thanksgiving weekend. Her lawyers had contacted Greg Logan in Chicago to ask for a meeting, requesting that both principals also be present. It would be held the day after a judge from New York State's 10th Judicial District was scheduled to rule on Milenka's petition to temporarily take stewardship of certain of her presumed-dead husband's financial assets. Because those interests were currently sailing rudderless and Milenka had a future stake in them, Logan could see no reasonable cause for a judge to refuse that request. He expected to see Milenka appointed trustee and advised Amy and Jeff to come to that meeting prepared for her to start throwing her new financial weight around. She'd already announced her intention to take a more active role in their company and this meeting was where she would likely start laying down the building blocks of her plan.

Amy had wandered down the mezzanine to Jeff's design studio to report on all that and found him hunched over his drafting table.

"I'm still trying to imagine just how she'll try to fuck us," she said. "Between the awesome job that Tamara and her staff are doing and all of those design awards we keep winning, every interior designer and important furniture retailer in the world knows who we are now. We're doing better than just servicing the debt on Dad's capital infusions. We've even started to pay down some of the principal. Nobody who's been in business for just over two years ever does that."

"Unless they're a Mexican drug cartel," Jeff said. "Not to

Whack Job

mention that we're busting the seams here and desperately need to expand for all the right reasons. And what does she know about furniture manufacture? Fuck-all would be my guess."

"Greg says the attorney she's hired is a total snake. He's pretty sure they have something diabolical up their sleeves. I just can't imagine what."

Jeff hadn't spoken two sentences to Milenka Brock ever since that fateful night in the East Hampton guest cottage. "I know they want both of us to be there, but I think you should handle this on your own," he said. "I have no interest in even being in the same room with the woman."

Amy smiled. "I hear you," she said. "And this isn't about you, anyway. It's a family power play and you're right. I should be the one to handle it."

"I can use the time to help Patty load the moving pod she's shipping west," he said. "I never realized how many books she has until we started packing them into boxes. Between them and her furniture and bed, I'm worried about everything fitting into that thing."

Rather than hire a mover, Patty had engaged one of those DIY companies that drop a smallish container at the curb and then pick it up to transport it to wherever you're destined.

Amy nodded toward the drawing before him. "How's work on your new table coming? You said you didn't like the first two versions but I thought the last one looked promising."

In addition to the two new chairs they planned to introduce into their product line that next season, they'd decided to expand the Brockstyle line to include more accent furniture featuring the same basic look. With so many prestigious awards now under their belts the whole design world was wondering what they would do next. Amy had never experienced that kind of pressure before, real or imagined, and the discomfort that came with playing the fraud in that realm was not just unsettling for her, but proving a distraction for Jeff as well. He'd lately been plagued by an unaccustomed self-consciousness that was resulting in a lot of over-thinking and second-guessing that had never been there before.

"I sort of like it but I'm still not thrilled," he said. "Matter of fact, I'm thinking about taking a few days off. I need to let my brain air out and then push the re-set button."

"Are you spending Christmas with your folks?" she asked.

He nodded. "And then maybe I'll head up to Stratton and do some skiing. See if I can even remember how. It's been forever."

That notion seemed to surprise her. "If I'd ever thought about it, I would have figured you for a snowboarder."

"No way. My parents were strictly old school. There's a little bunny slope right outside Pawling where they had me on skis when I was three."

"Do you even own pair now?"

"There should still be a pair of old K2s somewhere around my parents place. If not, there's a shop off the highway in Brewster where I can rent."

TWENTY-FIVE

Jeff stood with Patty on the sidewalk outside her East Williamsburg building on a cold Monday afternoon three days before Christmas and watched a long-haul trucker load all her worldly possessions onto the bed of his semi-tractor-trailer rig. Her plane to San Diego was scheduled to depart late the following morning, the same day that Brocking Chair's corporate attorney would arrive from Chicago to meet with Amy, her step-mother and her lawyers. Just that morning, a State Supreme Court judge had given Milenka interim control of her co-owned business interests until her missing husband's legal status could be resolved. While Amy dealt with her, Jeff planned to drive Patty to LaGuardia and then continue north for his own holiday.

After watching that semi truck drive off, they headed out on foot toward Testo for an early dinner. Jeff thought the occasion called for Champagne regardless of how bittersweet the moment was and once they were seated there, he ordered a bottle of Krug for the princely sum of six-hundred dollars. He and Amy had recently voted to up their annual salaries to $125,000, still well below the market price for talent of their proven skill-set. With the added money from his flourishing music career, he was now earning way more than he knew what to do with.

Their server poured their glasses full and Jeff raised his to Patty. "I know you've had a disappointing go of it these past couple of years, but it looks like smooth sailing from here on in," he said. "I'm happy for you."

She clicked glasses while wearing a mischievous grin. "It hasn't all been disappointing. In fact, this past year has been anything but. And I've got nobody but you to thank for that." She paused to take a sip and savor it. "Thanks for understanding who I am and not being another fucking weirdo. I hope you know there will always be a place in my life for you, no matter who else is in it, too. You've earned it."

He hadn't expected anything quite so sentimental and felt an ache in his heart. "And I hope that you know that's a door that swings both ways," he said. "If anyone else has a problem with that, they're not the right person for me. I hate possessiveness almost as much as you hate Ayn Rand."

She laughed. "That's another thing I love about you, Bub. You listen." She paused to collect her words, her eyes getting a far-off look in them for a moment and then coming back into focus while meeting his. "Which is something I want you to do again, right now."

This sounded serious.

"Amy and I have been talking a lot lately," she said. "A month or so ago I told her I know she's in love with you. I also said I happen to know that you're in love with her. And while I was at it, I told her I think it's time to drop the don't-shit-where-you-eat bullshit; that you two need to seal this deal before it becomes more of a hinderance than a help to you."

Jeff felt himself gape at her. "You told her that?"

It earned a solemn nod. "I also told her that while I've had a fabulous time with you over this past year, I've always known it was only until each of you could get your heads out of your butts. I said I think it's time for you to take all that romantic tension vibrating between you to the place where it's dying to go."

When Jeff opened his mouth to say that she seemed a lot more certain about all this than he was, she reached to touch his lips with a finger and shook her head.

"I'm not going to sit here and listen to you bullshit me," she said. "Any more than I let her. The woman is beautiful. You're tolerably cute. She's the exact yang to your yin. Your ambitions and life visions are so similar it's fucking scary. You wouldn't be shitting the nest, you'd be building one. And with you having each other's backs, there's no one in the world who can break you. Do you have any idea how amazing that is?"

He continued to gape at her, surprised that she would be saying this to him. "So, you're what? Giving me your blessing?"

"Fuck that. You don't need my blessing. You just need your own, and you're an idiot if you won't give it to yourself."

Some strange sense of release washed over him and he suddenly had to laugh. "Damn, I wish I'd been a fly on that wall. How did she react when you gave her this speech?"

"What could she say? That what I'd said wasn't true? I'm a woman. The first time she ever saw you and me together, I could see the pain in her eyes. And I've seen that same wish in her a dozen times since; that things could be different between you two than they are now."

Jeff murmured, "Jesus," and then wasted a bunch of good Champagne by taking too large a gulp. The sudden effervescent surge burned on its way down his throat while she reached across the table to grab his hand.

"You guys are going to be great together, Jeff. Think of this as my Christmas gift to you."

"I hope that doesn't mean you're not coming back with me to my place after this," he said.

"Where else do you think I'd want to sleep?" she asked. "I may have just set you free, but for one last time, we're gonna a least pretend that you're still all mine."

⊙⊙⊙

The next morning early, after loading a pair of Venus and David rockers fresh off the production line into the back of the new BMW X5 he'd recently leased, Jeff dropped Patty off at La Guardia for a tear-filled goodbye. Between then and stopping at that ski shop in Brewster to rent himself a pair of boots and skis—he'd learned from his mom that his old ones had since gone to Goodwill—he finally pulled off Route 22 into the Village of Pawling just after noon, the sun high in the winter sky. It had been a busy year for snowstorms in the foothills of the Berkshire Mountains where a fresh six inches of powder had fallen the previous night. Snowplows were out and most of the town's main streets were cleared.

Hungry, he decided to stop at everyone's favorite deli for a sandwich. While he was at it, he picked up a ball of their fresh mozzarella for his mother, regarded by many to be the best anywhere north of Arthur Avenue in the Bronx. He hadn't been up since Christmas a year ago and it felt strange to be home, even if exactly nothing ever seemed to change there. Yes, there'd been a flight of virtual workers from the city in the wake of a recent global pandemic but the core of the village itself hadn't grown by much. Its classic 19th Century main drag and quaint little train station still looked the same. Remnants of several recent Nor'easters were pushed into fifteen-foot-high piles in the parking lot of the old Pawling Rubber plant. Roadside berms all-but-blocked the gated entrance to Norman Vincent Peale's Foundation for Christian Living. The smell of oak wood smoke from fireplaces, a distinct characteristic of winter in the region, was heavy in the air.

His parent's place was located on a two-lane country road just north of town, situated on five acres, the family-owned cabinet shop standing 100 feet from his parent's house. Jeff's uncles, Rich and Tom, had houses on adjacent parcels, creating a sort of family compound. Jeff and his cousins had always had free range of all those houses as kids, running back-and-forth between them, often eating dinner at a table other than their own. The central social hub had always been the cabinet shop, where the adults had a big side room with beat-up old sofas, pool and foosball tables, a dart board, and one of those free-standing kegerator units always stocked with cold Budweiser. Most evenings after work and before supper Jeff's mother and his aunts more often than not found themselves out there with their men having a cocktail and lamenting about how the whole country was going to hell in a handbasket. They considered themselves to be patriots but didn't seem to quite understand the "freedom and justice for all" part of the Pledge of Allegiance. Jeff knew they'd seen that picture of his business partner on the cover of Vanity Fair, only because he'd sent his parents a copy. A year later he'd still gotten no reaction to it but knew that sooner or later he would. He couldn't wait for the subject to come up, knowing it was probably foolish to hope that his emerging status as a bona fide rock star might help steer them away from the touchier subject of women, especially those of color, running businesses.

Smoke curled from the chimney of the shop's pot-bellied stove as he parked next to a pair of Dutchess Cabinet Sprinter vans. A new Ford F-150 pick-up was parked alongside them still sporting its temporary plates. This led him to assume that somebody had bought

Whack Job

himself a Christmas present, probably his Uncle Rich, a man whose fondness for beer and pizza had seen him gain a hundred pounds in middle age and whose house was located farther away than easy walking distance for a fat man.

He'd just emerged from his wheels and was pulling up the collar of his jacket against the biting cold when his Uncle Tom emerged from the shop followed by his dad. Both were in shirtsleeves and had pint glasses of beer in their hands.

"What the fuck is that you're driving, Mr. Fancy Pants?" his Uncle Tom demanded. "Don't tell me that bullshit rock and roll you're playing paid for something like that."

Jeff nodded to them both. "Good to see you, too, Tom. Dad. I can't remember the last time I had a Bud, but right now one of them sounds pretty good to me."

Rather than step forward to embrace him, his dad wandered up to peer into the passenger side window of his rig. "Pussy's gotta love a rig like this," he said. "What's that you got in the back there? Looks like them naked statue chairs you're making."

Jeff's father was of the generation where many males believed a woman might actually be interested in fucking them because of the kind of car they drove. Heck, for all he knew, maybe some of the lower-evolved members of his own generation still thought that, too.

"Your Christmas presents," he said. "Sorry I couldn't find any Kid Rock or Toby Keith records for you and Uncle Rich, Tom."

"Sounds like you're still the same smart-ass," his Uncle Tom said.

"When you've got a personality as winning as mine, why change?" Jeff asked.

At that juncture his Uncle Rich emerged to join his two partners. "Nice car, faggot. They do call that a car, right. No man with any balls'd call it a truck."

Rich was his mother's oldest brother, the guy with whom he'd spent years on installation crews and the more ignorant and less likable of his two uncles.

"Call it whatever you want," he said. "As long as you do it inside. It's freezing out here."

"Sounds like the city's made your candy-ass soft," Rich growled.

"Nice boots, too, faggot."

Jeff was wearing a pair of British green-rubber Wellies he'd found in an Upper East Side thrift shop his second year at Parsons. Made for mud and muck in dreary English winter weather, they were heavily insulated and the most comfortable cold weather boots he'd ever worn.

Once inside the shop, he surveyed his surroundings to see how little had changed there, then headed toward the cozy warmth of that wood stove. His mom, along with his Aunts Bev and Leslie, were relaxing on those battered sofas around a platter piled high with Christmas cookies. Unlike his father and uncles, the three women leapt up to administer hugs and make comments about how much he'd grown—he hadn't—and how it looked like he hadn't been eating enough. His father grabbed an empty glass, filled it and handed it to him as his Uncle Rich stepped into his space, a look of curiosity on his face.

"So, tell me something, Jeffie. Why's that partner of yours winning all them design awards and you ain't winning none? I seen how good you are with that stuff. It's hard to imagine she could'a done all that good work herself and you ain't done nothing to contribute."

"Her name is Amy," Jeff replied. "And it's political. We're partners, but we both agreed it would be easier to make a mark in a crowded field if we had a woman fronting for us. It's something that seems to have proven true."

"She looks park gook."

Jeff stiffened. "Her mother is half-Vietnamese. You got a problem with that?" He took a sip of his beer. It was ice-cold and after that long drive in the dry heat of his car's interior, he was parched and it tasted wonderful.

"A man should get whatever credit he's due," his Uncle Tom said.

"Maybe in a perfect world," Jeff countered. "But that's not the one we're living in. The fact of the matter is that Amy did have some input on those chairs. And if the iF people in Germany only gave her the award for designing it, I'm okay with that. I'm a twenty-three-year-old kid with a company about to gross sixty million dollars in its second year of operation."

Whack Job

His Uncle Rich went wide-eyed and whistled. "No shit?"

Jeff nodded. "We've already outgrown sixty thousand square feet in Long Island City and are looking to expand. Having a woman as the face of our company is a huge part of our success. The world has had its knee on the necks of women since white men wrote the Bible. It's about time that changed."

His Uncle Rich looked first at his dad and then at his mom as he shook his head. "That's what you get for sending him to school in Faghatten," he said. "Him coming home talking pussy liberal bullcrap like that."

"They didn't send me," Jeff reminded him. "I saved up the money I made while listening to your bullshit and then went on my own."

His Aunt Leslie look hard at his Uncle Rich. "I think it's time for you to shush now, Richard," she said. Herself a bit of a low-flame liberal, Leslie worked as a nurse administrator at a big hospital in Poughkeepsie alongside personnel representing all colors of the human rainbow. Jeff knew she viewed her husband as an undeniably fabulous craftsman but an otherwise uncultivated ignoramus.

"So, tell us about Whack Job," his Aunt Bev prodded him. "My kids say you're super-hot right now. I've heard that record of yours at least fifty times and I can't believe that's you singing. Who knew you had a voice like that?"

Jeff took another sip of his beer and shrugged. "I sure didn't," he admitted. "I guess the more I tried different things, the more it just came out and then got better. I hardly sang at all in those bands I played with in high school."

His mother grimaced like she'd just bitten into a lemon. "Please God, don't remind me. Far as I'm concerned, all you ever did then was make noise. Some of that stuff you're doing now I actually kind of like."

"So, you're making good money, huh?" his Uncle Tom asked. Tom had played guitar in a number of local '80s bands, their audiences pretty much constrained to wedding venues and dilapidated Borsch Belt resorts across the Hudson River in the Catskill Mountains. Jeff remembered him from his childhood as being forty pounds skinnier, with a blond mullet that was outdated even back then.

"Yeah," he replied. "I am. Second week in January we're going back into the studio in Nashville to record our second album. I like the stuff we're doing now more than the songs we did on the first. From what our producer has heard of our demo tracks, he thinks this one could really set us apart."

"I could've been you if I hadn't gotten married and had kids," Tom said.

Jeff's Aunt Bev probably would have kicked him if she'd been within range. "You're so full of shit," she scolded. "You played cover tunes. Not a one of you in that band had a creative bone in your body." She turned to her nephew. "Don't listen to him, Jeffie. He's just jealous. Did you write any of them songs?"

"Our lead guitarist, Foster, does most of that," Jeff said. "We all make suggestions, but it's really his stuff. One of these days I might take a stab, though. If my furniture design gig ever gives me enough time to breathe." He stopped and turned to his mother. "I've got two of our Venus and David rockers in the back of my rig for you and Pop, Ma. I figure you can sit in them of an evening and squabble with each other in front of the fire."

"I can't wait," his mother said. "We're having a pork shoulder roast from one of them hogs the neighbors raise for supper tonight. One of your favorites."

Jeff's phone vibrated in his pocket as he was thinking about how good his mom's roast pork always was. He pulled it out to scan the screen. Amy. Undoubtedly to report on her meeting with Milenka and her step-mother's attorneys that afternoon.

"I've gotta get this," he said. "It's business." He drained the rest of his beer and belched softly before answering. "Hang on a sec," he said, and turned to his family. "This might take a minute. Why don't I meet up with you at the house once I'm done here."

TWENTY-SIX

Jeff climbed into his car and started the engine to get some warmth working rather than have that conversation out in the cold. He put Amy on speaker.

"Hey, partner. How'd it go?"

"Milenka is cutting off any additional expansion financing unless we agree to move our production to Varna."

Jeff sat confused, unable to imagine why. "Where's that?" he asked.

"Fucking Bulgaria. She sent Katya there three weeks ago to scout out a manufacturer. They've already opened preliminary negotiations with some company called Vasilev Limited."

Jeff's mental wheels were spinning like he'd hit black ice and was trying to get traction. "Who the fuck are they?" It was all he could think of to ask.

"To listen to her, they have a division that mostly manufactures patio furniture but also own a fleet of container ships. I Googled them. According to Forbes, they generate almost five billion a year in gross revenue, a lot of that through small-arms manufacture."

Jeff might be a designer and not a business guy, but he was learning that end quickly enough. "That's pretty big," he said. "But no fucking way we'll agree. It runs counter to our entire philosophy."

There was a momentary silence from the other end. When Amy spoke again she didn't sound anywhere near so sure of herself as he just had. "Greg tells me it will all boil down to whether or not she can break that control clause in our contract. If she can, we really don't have a choice. We can't go ahead with our own expansion plans if she cuts off the cash."

Jeff wasn't quite as willing to accept defeat as her tone suggested she might be. "Given our track record and the volume of our current orders, it should be pretty easy to find that money somewhere else, right?" he asked.

"You'd think. But Greg tells me that as long as we've got Milenka's legal cloud hanging over our heads, other financing will be really hard to come by."

Jeff hadn't had enough time to process everything she'd just hit him with but he could see her point. "I may have some ideas there, but now's probably not the time to talk about them," he said. "You sound really down right now, but don't be. We're gonna get through this and we aren't moving our manufacturing to Eastern fucking Europe." He paused to look out at the landscape surrounding his childhood home, the snow on rooftops and clinging to the branches of barren trees. He flashed on memories of loading cabinets into those vans and heading out with his Uncle Rich to do installations; memories of endless Rush Limbaugh broadcasts and the idiot crap that too often came out of Rich's mouth. He loved his family but wasn't sure how long he could take his uncle's ignorant banter. New York City had made him less willing to tolerate that stuff anymore.

"I just realized I've never asked you if you ski," he said.

"My family has a house in Aspen," she replied. "Of course, I ski. When I was younger, my dad used to take me to Switzerland for a week in Zermatt, just the two of us. Milenka and Katya hate the snow and would go to our place in Tulum instead."

Once again Jeff was confronted by just how different their two worlds were. She came from people who had houses in East Hampton, Aspen, Tulum and God knew where else. His parents had one, and he was staring at the sum total of their holdings. Property that had been in his father's family for two hundred years, somehow remaining in their possession through a dozen major financial downturns and the Great Depression. He knew for a fact that money didn't grow on any of these winter-barren trees while in Amy's world, those money trees seemed to grow in orchards that never lost their leaves.

He then said something that he hadn't planned on saying. "I think, as soon as you've had Christmas with your mom, you should come skiing with me. From what I just heard in your voice, it sounds like you could use the break, too."

His suggestion met with silence at first, and then, "The way you said that, you actually sounded like you meant it."

He continued to stare out at the winter landscape, his gaze travelling to the chimney over the shop and the smoke curling from it as he thought about what an ignorant fuck like his Vietnam-vet Uncle Rich would think of Amy. Would he even be able to see beyond her background and realize how smart and beautiful she was? Or was he just so blinded by the prejudices engendered through his life experiences that those things could never even occur to him?

"I am serious," he said. "It's time for us to have some fun. All you and I have done together for the past two years is work our asses off. We can probably have better conversations about Milenka and what strategy we want to adopt in a more relaxed atmosphere than at the plant."

"How are you since dropping Patty off?" she asked. "Are you okay?"

"It hasn't really sunk in yet. It's not like I didn't know it was coming and I'm not quite Cro-Magnon enough to claim it's not gonna affect me. I know I'll miss her."

"Good," she said. "You should. She's amazing."

"You coming skiing?"

"I don't know. It's tempting. I need to think about it."

"If you take the train to Pawling, we could drive straight up together."

"What? You don't want me to meet your parents?"

He grunted at the thought. "Didn't I just mention something about us both needing to relax," he asked. "My family wouldn't be part of the winning formula I have in mind."

⊚⊚⊚

Amy had been curious about the world Jeff came from ever since first meeting him. He'd certainly seen most of hers in all its crazy dysfunction and she could only imagine how disparate their two worlds were. Once she disconnected from that call, she had serious cause to reflect on how unflappable he'd always seemed and wondered what had spawned that. Was it something one or both of his parents had instilled or was it just part of his nature? She also wondered if his upbringing had anything to do with the kind of luck he always seemed to attract. The man was like a good fortune magnet. He'd needed an outlet for his prodigious creative talent and he'd found her. He'd needed a sustainable means of blowing off steam and had found those guys in Whack Job. Somewhat improbably, his singing and Foster Bragg's song-writing and guitar work had managed to help turn them all into rock stars. He'd needed companionship rather than a meaningless string of one-night-stands and had found not just any woman, but one as cool and grounded as Patty Conlon. He was confident and charming without being at all full of himself. Where had all of that come from? Pawling fucking New York? She'd been through the area any number of times. It was quaint enough, she supposed, but not so unique as to explain a Jeff Land.

Her meeting with Milenka and the feeling of sudden helplessness that it had produced was still gnawing at her as she made her day's fourth cup of coffee rather than pour herself a big glass of wine. It was like she still needed to fuel her rage but with a focus behind it that could help her find an actual solution to her dilemma. Her step-mother and half-sister were conspiring to destroy the only real dream she'd ever had, and right then she was asking herself if the simple realization of it was just too much to ask of the world.

Cup in hand, she wandered into her living room and stood contemplating her spectacular view while thinking about how her partner had just reacted to her news. Yes, he'd only just said goodbye to his girlfriend and arrived home to visit his redneck family and had to be distracted by all that, but he'd still seemed so impossibly cool about the whole prospect of seeing two years of hard work stolen from him. He'd told her that she needed to take a deep breath and take a break, and she knew he was probably right. Their operation in Long Island City would be all but mothballed over the traditional dead week between Christmas and New Year's anyway. A decade ago, her mom had remarried and while she didn't feel the same about her new step-father as she did about Milenka, she wasn't all that fond of him, either. He'd never actually said anything overt about it, but she knew that he was uncomfortable with how psychologically fragile her beautiful Vietnamese mother was. What he did like was all the money she'd walked away with in the wake of her divorce, and the kind of lifestyle it afforded him, and so he just played at being charming. A day with them at Christmas was about all that Amy could stomach, so what was she going to do with the rest of her week? Sit home and stew or accept Jeff's invitation?

Whack Job

She turned away from the view to cross the room to her big entry closet. Toward the back, past several pieces of empty luggage, she found her skis, poles and boots along with several pairs of ski pants and ski jackets on hangers. The last time she'd hit the slopes would be three years ago, January. She knew she would be rusty, but how much more out of practice could she be than he was?

One sure problem would be accommodation. This was high season in Vermont and New Hampshire. Hotels in most of the decent ski resorts in the region would have sold-out months ago. And for all she knew, Jeff hadn't even thought about that. Once he got to Stratton and found no room at the inn, he'd probably be happy to go the Mary and Joseph route and sleep in the back of his SUV. That not being an option for her, she retrieved her wallet and called the concierge number on the back of her Centurion card. Fifteen minutes later, an accommodating woman on the other end had managed to find a two-bedroom suite at a 5-star resort hotel in Stratton where they'd just had a cancellation. She booked it for four nights. Regardless of whether either she or Jeff came up with any good ideas regarding how they might stave off Milenka and save their company, they could at least blow off a little steam. It looked like she was going skiing.

TWENTY-SEVEN

Katya was naked in the spa adjacent to the swimming pool drinking Tito's on the rocks when her mother emerged from the house to join her, steam rising from the surface of the churning water and dissipating into the star-filled and frigid December night sky. Milenka had been in the city all day meeting with her lawyers and Katya's half-sister. Her bearing as she strode across the stone terrace seemed triumphant rather than road-weary and as she slipped out of her robe and slid into the water opposite her, Katya scanned the contours of her mother's body. It was impossible not to admit how remarkable it was that any woman twenty-three years older could have managed to maintain herself like that. While her mother had resisted the temptation to embrace the kind of augmentation procedure that had produced the goods Katya now flaunted shamelessly at every possible opportunity, even at forty-six her body seemed to somehow defy gravity. It was no doubt aided by all those years of Jazzercise, Zumba, Pilates, yoga and training with light weights. She had elegant, long-fingered hands and narrow, sculpted feet, wide shoulders, and rounded hips that offset a tiny waist. Katya had witnessed men undress her mother with their eyes ever since she was a little girl and knew how it had helped shape her own desires. As far back as she could remember she'd always wanted men to look at her in that same hungry way and still needed to be the belle of every ball she ever attended.

"So?" she asked. "That look on your face says a lot, but I want you give it to me blow-by-blow."

"The lawyer she brings with her from Chicago is good," Milenka replied. "But this is New York State. The partners at our firm all go to law school with half the judges on the State Supreme Court. Our strategy is to strike the non-interference clause from the contract your father signs with her and her partner. For our dispute the premise is simple. Is based on the pre-nup I signed back before you were born. I claim now that your father had no right to agree to this clause in Amy's contract. Not without getting my permission first."

"I still don't understand how that could be," Katya said. "I know that once he's declared dead, the interest in some of his assets revert to you, but Brock International is more than just those."

"When he divorced Amy's mother, he does a lot of shuffling and re-financing to buy her out. For one big cash settlement. To pay it, he must create a separate merchant banking fund. In it is many Brock assets. This fund still exists and contains more than one billion dollars of company assets and another hundred million in cash. Guess where it is my money comes from if he is dead or decides to divorce me."

Katya was fairly adept at connecting a simple line of dots, even while moderately drunk. "There."

Her mother nodded. "And guess where the fifty million dollars in capital he has invested in Brocking Chair has come from."

"You're making this too easy."

"No, your silly father did. He is so busy with his eye on the big picture he does not stop to think this through. If he was still alive, he could maybe even sue his legal team for malpractice for not protecting Amy. I most surely will not. Once this clause we break, your sister and Jeff Land will have no choice but do whatever it is we tell them to do."

No wonder she was gloating. She'd just all but taken control of a hot new furniture company that was the current darling of the international design market. Katya, like her mother, was pretty sure that market didn't give a rat's ass about where the furniture was actually being made. The designs themselves, the prestigious international prizes they'd won, and the quality of how the individual pieces were built were all that really mattered.

"So, how did Amy react when you told her this?" she asked. "I'm guessing she shit a brick."

"She tells me that she will work with me over her dead body. And when she says this, I remind her that she is not the only designer in the world; that if she wants to fight me, she and her rock-star partner will find themselves locked out of their own factory, with me in control of the brand they create. I do not think the furniture world is any different from fashion world. At all major labels, head designers they come and go. Is the name that people buy."

Katya wasn't about to say it to her mother's face, not when she'd just come back from the field of battle with her enemy's head on a pike, but she wondered how much truth there was in the assumption she'd just made. Milenka had a history of impulsive behavior that compared pretty favorably with her own and Katya was all too painfully aware of how many times she'd failed to do her homework before making certain moves. The trip she'd just been sent on to Bulgaria and the time Milenka had since spent with her legal team were both decent indicators that she was using more than just a petty desire for revenge to engineer this hostile takeover, but before she went and pulled any plugs, Katya hoped she remembered to take the baby out of the bath water.

"So, what's our next move?" she asked.

"We sit here and we wait," her mother said. "The lawyers they tell me it will take maybe one month to push my petition through the court. Already Amy's attorney has assured us that they will appeal any decision that goes against them. This could drag on until summer, but meanwhile? Amy's hands will be tied, too."

"Can't they just continue rolling out new product designs?" Katya asked. "There's nothing to prevent that, is there?"

Her mother shrugged her expressive shoulders before sinking down into the water until it touched her chin. "Their current orders, they are backed up now. Until I throw this monkey wrench into their works they have a big expansion planned. With no more capital, this cannot happen. After we drive this last nail into their coffin, they are operating on life support."

☙❧☙

When Amy called Jeff on Christmas Eve to tell him she'd managed to find them a suite in the nicest hotel in Stratton and had booked it for four days, check-in on the afternoon of the 26th, he'd just finished eating a huge dinner attended by a majority of his extended family; two aunts, two uncles, eight cousins and six of their spouses, his mom, dad, married older sister and brother-in-law. That year his Uncle Tom had pen-raised six wild turkeys from eggs he'd discovered while helping a neighbor mow hay. Fed mostly on cracked corn, the meat from them tasted more like veal than turkey, which to Jeff wasn't a bad thing. His Aunt Leslie was always in charge of any roasting and invariably tended to dry out the usual store-bought Butterballs by over-cooking them. These birds had turned out moist and succulent.

"Wow, that's fantastic," he told Amy. "I figured we'd find a motel somewhere farther away and just drive in every day. That's what we did when I was in high school."

He heard her laugh. "And probably slept ten-to-a-room. You're a grown-up now, partner. And because my bitch of a step-mother might be about to steal a company you've sweated your balls off to build, this is my treat. It's the least I figure I can do."

"Nobody's stolen anything," he said. "Not yet. And between now and when I pick you up at the train, I want you to stop worrying about that and try to enjoy your Christmas."

"Have you heard from Patty?"

"Only that the sublet the university helped her find is in some place called La Jolla Shores and close enough to the beach that she can walk. That, and today it was seventy degrees."

"Tough duty. My heart bleeds."

"She knew we'd be talking and asked me to say hi."

"Did you tell her that we're going skiing?"

"How could I? You only just told me. But I did tell her I'd asked you and was hoping you'd say yes. She said she was hoping so, too."

There was a momentary silence from down the line and then she asked, "How much snow you got up there?"

"Shit tons. It's been a good year." He had a schedule out that he'd picked up at the train station that morning. "I see a train leaving Scarsdale at eleven-forty that gets you into Pawling at twelve-fifty. There's a nice little restaurant here in town where we can have lunch and then drive up."

"Damn, partner," she said. "I'm almost getting excited about this."

"Almost? I mean, I realize it's not Zermatt or Aspen, but Stratton's got a half-dozen double black diamond runs and a bump run that's world class."

"I've skied it," she said. "Those moguls kicked my ass. I hope you're as good as you make it sound like you are. I get a little competitive once I'm buckled into a pair of bindings."

He laughed. "But you're so fucking mellow and laid back otherwise, right? See you day after tomorrow. Feel free to bring your A-game, and Merry Christmas."

Jeff had stepped into the empty study off his parent's living room to take Amy's call and once he disconnected, he looked up to see his Uncle Rich standing in the doorway staring at him, his belt buckle and the top button of his pants undone, a bottle of Heineken in one hand.

"Who you talking to, lover boy?" Rich sneered. "Girlfriend?"

"My business partner, not that it's any of your business."

"Gook poont was never my thing even when I was in stationed in Korea," Rich said, "but that bitch looks tasty. You had yourself a slice of that yet?"

Without even thinking, Jeff took a quick step forward to shove his uncle hard in the chest with both hands. One moment Rich was standing there leering at him and the next he was on his ass with a look of surprise on his face. His bottle hit the floor even harder than he did, shattering and sending glass and its contents in all directions. Jeff loomed over him, seeing nothing but red.

"You need to learn to watch your mouth, fat man. I've been listening to that shit coming out of it for way too long. It fucking ends right here."

Everyone in the dining room and kitchen had heard the bottle shatter and come running, his parents, aunts, and Uncle Tom now staring at the scene in wide-eyed wonder.

"What the hell's going on?" Jeff's dad demanded.

"Uncle Rich just stepped on his dick, tripped, and fell," Jeff said. "Somebody help his fat ass up. I'll go get a mop."

TWENTY-EIGHT

Two days in Scarsdale had been one too many for Amy to spend in the presence of her mother and step-father's awkward stabs at making nice. She was ready to climb the walls of her mother's house come Boxing Day. The pair of them had always seemed to feel obliged to host their little combined family for this annual event but her step-father never ceased to give off the vibe that his life had been rudely interrupted. Things might have been a little less uncomfortable if he could sustain a decent conversation or was in some other quirky way interesting. But instead he was a typical hale-and-hearty, golf and tennis playing empty suit who thought charm came with perfectly-coiffed hair, starched shirts, and razor-sharp creases in his jeans.

The lump-sum payout her mother had received in her divorce from Amy's dad had made her rich beyond most any mortal's imagining. It had also never seemed like quite enough to make up for the double gut-kick she'd received while being exiled to California to deal with her post-partum depression. Not only had Bert Brock taken up with a much younger woman who'd worked for him, but he'd also managed to get her pregnant. No matter how hard Amy's mother had tried to bury that hurt it was something that she'd never been able to completely deal with. And Christmas always seemed to bring out the worst of that inner conflict in her. She might live in a ten-thousand square foot house in Scarsdale, have a country-club-acceptable husband, and drive an electric Porsche Taycan that went from zero to sixty in less time than it took to hiccup, but since Amy's birth, none of her Christmases would ever be as happy as she'd once hoped they all might be.

It was years since Amy had last ridden upsate on a commuter train and the trip on the Metro North from Scarsdale to Pawling—dragging along skis, boots, poles and luggage—had felt like something of an adventure. As her train wended its way up through Westchester County the snow-covered landscape became more rural with every mile. By the time she reached Brewster in Putnam County to change trains, a kind of peaceful calm that she hadn't felt in a very long time had come over her. The city, the plant, her problems with lawyers and Milenka all felt like they were a million miles away. She reflected on her awkwardly inept father trying so hard to make his emotional inadequacies magically disappear on those trips they'd taken to ski Switzerland together and how, for at least a few days a year, they almost had. Those memories and all of the fresh snow surrounding her now made her miss him more than she realized she could, and recognize that she still hadn't properly grieved him. Even though a year-and-a-half had passed since his disappearance, up until then it had all seemed so strange and surreal to her, like he was just away on an extended business trip.

Her journey from Brewster to the rural village of Pawling was made aboard a smaller two-car train that reminded Amy of a trolley from an old cartoon. She spotted a steep but not particularly tall hillside with several groomed runs and an actual ski lift between the towns of Patterson and Pawling, guessing it was the slope that Jeff had described from his childhood; the place where he'd first learned to ski. She thought that for a kid, having a place like that only a quick car ride from home must have been epic. Maybe not like growing up in Park City or Aspen, but snow was snow and slopes were slopes and as a young skier close access to them was everything.

There were plenty of fellow travelers heading north the day after Christmas and the platform outside the station in Pawling was crowded with people waiting to meet them. She spotted Jeff in the middle of that throng as she disembarked, talking amiably to a couple who looked like contemporaries. She waved and saw a smile break out as he excused himself and hurried to help her with her gear.

"Kore 93s. Dope-ass skis," he said. He grabbed them and thumbed one of her edges. "Feels like you had them sharpened before you put them away."

"You never know when you might get a call from your business partner, desperate to be delivered from the bosom of his family. Gotta be prepared."

"You a former a Boy Scout?"

She deployed the telescoping handle of her suitcase as he grabbed up her boots and poles. "They wouldn't let me join," she said. "At eleven, I might have been in the middle of my ugly duckling phase but I still had too much girl in me." She followed him, picking her way carefully across the icy walkway as he led her to his car.

"That restaurant I mentioned is right across the street," he said. "Damn, it's good to see you."

She felt herself smiling openly at that. It was good to see him, too. "You sound like you had at least as much fun with your family as I did with mine. Why is Christmas so warm and wussy in all those holiday movies? In real life mine have always sucked."

"I bet you didn't knock one of your uncles on his butt for being an asshole," he said. "Or get called a faggot for what kind of car you drive."

She laughed. "Nobody ever got called a faggot for driving a Turbo Carrera, but ouch. That bad, huh?"

He triggered his rear tailgate and leaned in to nestle her skis next to a pair of Blizzard Bonafide 97s, a ski generally rated expert. He had said something to her about bringing her A-game.

"My Uncle Rich has had it coming for years. He was the guy I always had to do installations with. Rush Limbaugh talk radio. Thinks fucking Sean Hannity is the smartest man on the planet. I figured I'd filled out enough over the past couple years, it was worth taking a shot."

"I don't see any black eyes or broken bones."

He retracted the tow handle on her suitcase and hoisted it aboard like it was a block of balsa wood and not full of fifty pounds of crap, half of which she wouldn't need. She could only imagine that his uncle might have met his match.

"The fat fuck has gotten so big he couldn't even get back up off the floor without help. That was after Christmas dinner and before dessert. Needless to say, I skipped my mom's apple pie."

"And did what instead?" she asked.

He straightened to point to a tavern across the divided main boulevard. "I called a couple buddies from high school. Met them for drinks and played pool and darts until they closed."

"And then what? Drove home drunk?"

He laughed. "Believe it or not, I'm getting smarter with age. I brought my sleeping bag and slept in my car."

"Damn. It must have been freezing."

He smiled again while running the tailgate back down and tugged the wool cap he was wearing tighter over his ears. "Not as chilly as the atmosphere at home. Trust me. C'mon, let's eat."

☉☉☉

Jeff couldn't put his finger on what it was and he wasn't sure he even wanted to try very hard to define it. Something felt different between him and Amy than it had back in the city just the week before. For whatever reason, there was a kind of familiar ease there that had never existed before. Maybe he'd always felt she had the upper hand in their business dealings because she was the one with the rich daddy who'd put up the money for them to get started, but now she didn't have that anymore. And since he'd taken up with Patty, most of the sexual tension once existing between them had since dissipated. Whatever it was, she seemed totally at ease and was even chatty during the lunch they shared and then throughout the three-hour drive north to Stratton. She found music agreeable to both of them on Sirius XM, talked about what a fabulous skier her father had been and her most recent exchange with that liaison she'd been dealing with from the State Department. They stopped to pee and grab coffee at the I-90 interchange near Stockbridge where Amy peeled out of her jacket. Now reclined in her seat, she held her cup in both hands.

"He told me the CIA has people all over that region," she said. "Some of them actual Arab natives working inside the various fundamentalist Muslim factions. Not just in Yemen, but in the Emirates and Saudi Arabia and North Africa, too. He says they worked overtime listening for any word of what might have happened to him for the first few months after he disappeared. As carefully as they could at any rate, without risking exposure. And they ran into a total wall of silence."

"Do they think that's because nobody wants to admit to anything, or because nobody knows?" Jeff asked.

"Good question," she said. "Apparently, all of the Saudi royals involved in what was essentially an attempted coup were quickly identified, rounded up, and delivered to the same fate that met the crown prince, which has made it impossible for American intelligence to interrogate any of them. All of the Yemeni Houthis involved have fled to Iran and gone into deep hiding for obvious reasons. He seemed to imply that we have people working inside Iran, too, but they aren't willing to risk exposure while looking for clues about the fate of one American businessman."

Jeff continued to drive with his eyes ahead on the road. All around them the naked deciduous forests that cloaked the landscape further south had given way to a mixture of leafless trees and thick stands of pine and hemlock, heavy with snow.

"That sounds like they've given up," he said.

"It definitely feels like that," she agreed. "I think they believe the early theory that daddy's body and the rest of the crown prince's were chained to concrete blocks and dumped somewhere in the gulf. It's only over these past few days that it feels like I've started to accept that, too."

"I know you and your dad had your issues, just like I have with mine," he said. "But I can still imagine how that must make you feel."

She shifted in her seat to stare out at the landscape unfolding before them. "Surprisingly alone," she murmured. "And a lot more fragile than I've wanted to admit I am for a really long time. It's hard to admit what kind of a security blanket just his existence always was. And now I don't have that anymore, which frankly is scary as hell."

"You're a fairly formidable force, even without him," Jeff said.

She snorted with derision at that. "Yeah, right. It feels like the only smart thing I've done is find you. I've got an out-of-whack shit filter when it comes to choosing romantic partners. I've got some decent organizational skills but no measurable design acumen. I was just lucky enough to be the daughter of a man with eight billion dollars, which does tend to help grease life's skids a little bit."

Jeff had a look of sadness on his face as he slowly shook his head. "You've got a lot more going for you than that, partner. I'm not gonna elaborate on what those things are right now because we still need you lean and hungry."

"What the fuck is that supposed to mean?"

He laughed suddenly while shaking his head. "You might want to watch some videos of those interviews you've done over the past two years. At first you might only see the same woman I met over Guinness and shots of Green Spot two years ago. But focus on the face and watch the intensity there. Then tell me you aren't someone who could sell refrigerators to fucking Eskimos."

"I believe they're referred to as Innuits now."

"Whatever. You know what I'm saying. You've got a power of presence that's unique. I saw it that first night I met you in the fabrication shop at Parsons. It kinda rocked me."

She looked over at him, eyebrows raised. "Only kind of?"

"Fuck you. You know what I'm saying. My believing in what you might be able to pull off was more than enough to get me to put my ego in a drawer and let you play the star of our show. Not because I thought you deserved it, but because I knew you were the one who had to be for us to succeed the way we have."

She took a sip of her coffee and sat with her eyes closed for a moment. "It's worked pretty well, hasn't it," she said.

"Fucking-A-right it has. You and me together are a kind of magic formula that comes along once in a lifetime."

"I think that what Milenka is trying to do could mean that party's over," she said.

He'd been thinking about that a lot over the past few days and hadn't yet come up with any solution to their dilemma . "I don't really know," he said. "But what I do know? I'll be fucked if I'll produce another design for that bitch. We've got people, right in New York, who have proven they can deliver the highest quality products possible and we've proven we can still be profitable while paying them a decent wage. I'd rather just take my ball and go home before I let Milenka Brock fuck all those people over."

She drank more of her coffee and turned to stare at his profile. "I expect we'll have plenty of time over the next few days to talk about all of this," she said. "I haven't landed on anything solid either, but I'm working on a few ideas. Something tells me that

Whack Job

before we drive back out of here, we may not have come up with a solution to Milenka, but we'll have come up with some good ideas about where to start."

TWENTY-NINE

Katya had been thinking a lot about what her mother had said to her in the hot-tub Christmas Eve. In light of those words she'd been trying to figure a way to insinuate herself into orchestrating her half-sister Amy's demise without needing to exert too much effort. As much as she was loath to admit it, the seduction of Amy's business partner had been a failure while the seduction of Amy's husband had been a little bit too successful. Not that the latter event had seemed to affect her sister all that much. By all reports, she actually seemed relieved to be rid of Jason, just like she'd always seemed relieved whenever she dumped any other medium-to-long-term boyfriend she'd ever had. For Katya, it sort of ruined the satisfaction of having wrecked her sister's marriage. And what continued to bug her in the face of all that was how Amy's business partnership had survived all that turmoil and even seemed to be flourishing.

Torn between heading south to the family's house in Tulum for some warm weather or trying to find something amusing to do in the city, Katya had lounged around the East Hampton house all Boxing Day drinking mimosas and watching an endless string of Hallmark and Lifetime Channel Christmas movies, predicting each cornball plot twist three moves ahead. Her mother had gone to lunch with Brock International's Chief Operating Officer, Financial Officer, and Corporate Counsel in her new capacity as keeper of the Bert Brock merchant banking fund purse strings and returned home just in time to provide Katya with some much-needed distraction. Milenka mixed herself a Gibson at the bar in the TV room and moved to join her on the sofa.

"You say in your last text that you want to talk," she said. "Is now good? I know how complex these movies are. I do not want to ruin your concentration."

Katya reached for the remote to pause a pretty brunette with too much collagen in her lips and a rugged Soap Actor-type in a wool hat and plaid lumberjack coat with their faces just inches apart, freezing them onscreen in a soulful gaze. By her calculation, this was the third of five times they wouldn't kiss before they eventually did.

Whack Job

"Now's good," she said. "I'm not sure how yet, but I've decided I want in. I want to help you steal my bitch sister's company from her."

Her mother contemplated her over the rim of her martini glass. "This sounds to me like you have just asked me for a job," she said. "Me, who still tries to forget how much bitching you do when I ask you to take the trip to Bulgaria for me."

"That was different," Katya argued. "You know how much I hate your family and Sofia."

Milenka took a sip and smiled. "And just where else do you think you can be of help in this?" she asked. "I am needing boots on the ground in Varna. Worn by someone I can trust. You are my direct family. Kosta Kevalenko might try to screw over an outsider but he will not fuck with you. Not with me now in control of a billion Brock dollars. But still, we will need someone to watch his every move, at least at the start."

Katya hauled herself off the sofa to cross and grab more Champagne and OJ out of the mini-fridge. She hadn't eaten anything since breakfast and done nothing but drink since. To steady herself she caught the edge of the bar, realizing she needed to go a little slower to avoid falling on her face.

"Your family hates me because I'm only half Bulgarian," she complained.

"My family loves money," Milenka countered. "And now their prodigal daughter has buckets of it. You just watch how they kiss your zaden now, Baby Girl. You are the emissary I have sent already once. Even before we get worked out the legal details, we must get our ducks there in a row. You are the best person I can think of to do this."

"So, what's in it for me?" Katya asked. "Once daddy's declared dead, I'll have three times as much money as you. To get me to agree to move to fucking Varna, I need more incentive than just helping you screw Amy over."

Milenka chuckled and patted the cushion alongside her. "That is the little mercenary Mommy has taught so well. Come sit before you fall down."

Katya added a disproportionate amount of Champagne to

the thimble-full of orange juice in the bottom of her glass and recrossed the room to resume her seat.

"The problem with all that money you inherit is you cannot touch it until you are thirty. Today you are just twenty-three," her mother said. "And yes, you can decide to sit here until then and rely on hand-outs from me, but would you not rather have access to some real money much earlier than that?"

Regardless of how drunk she was, Katya felt herself starting to get cagey. "What are you suggesting?"

"You help me to get the production of Brocking Chair up and going in Varna and I cut you in for half of my share. After service for the debt, amortized relocation and set-up cost, that will be five million in the first year. This I base on projections from current orders alone. I will pay you this because I do not need this extra money so much as I need satisfaction."

Five million dollars a year of her own money didn't completely sober Katya but it did help sharpen the fuzzy edges of her perceptions a bit. "How long?" she asked. "Would I need to commit."

◉◉◉

It was dark by the time Jeff and Amy checked into their hotel suite in Stratton. Both were tired from their respective Christmases and neither was hungry after the late lunch they'd had in Pawling. Rather than search out a restaurant, they elected to hit the resort's semi-outdoor fire pit lounge instead, order hors d' oeuvres, and share a bottle of wine. Once they were settled under lap rugs in a pair of chairs near the fire, Amy faced him and lifted her glass.

"Are you okay with this arrangement?" she asked. "This week in particular and on such short notice, that suite was the best I could do."

They'd gone democratic and flipped for rooms, her winning the one with the balcony overlooking the brightly lit ski mountain. Each had its own bath and king-size bed. The living room was spacious and equipped with a gas-log fireplace.

"It's perfect," he said. "When I look at all these people I can't believe you managed to get even that."

"Before we get into full-relaxation mode there's something I need to talk to you about," she said. "I didn't really want to bring it up before you were sitting down without a steering wheel in your hand. At least from my point of view it's not ideal but I may have come up with a way to thwart Milenka's attack. And I need you to listen to me all the way through before you say anything."

From just the look he saw on her face, Jeff was seized with a sudden sense of foreboding even as he nodded his agreement. "Okaaaay," he said.

"It would mean the end of Brocking Chair, but not necessarily the end of our enterprise."

He wanted to ask how but had agreed to keep his mouth shut.

"We decided, and you agreed, to let me take credit for your designs because I thought we'd have a much better chance of success if they came from an ambitious young woman," she said.

One who was also articulate, attractive, and extremely rich, he thought, but sure.

"But now that those designs are out in the public eye and have won all those awards, they have their own set of bona fides," she continued. "I don't think it's as important now that a woman created them. In fact, I think that if we want to survive Milenka and keep making furniture, it's time I admit to the world that they aren't really mine."

As Jeff started to open his mouth to say something, she held up a hand to cut him off.

"I'm not finished. We'd need to do this right. Go to the same woman who wrote that cover article for Vanity Fair, offer her an exclusive, and tell her the whole story; how I found you as a Parson's undergrad and convinced you to make a deal with the devil just to advance my own ambitions. You agreed to go along because fame wasn't as important to you as having actual control over how your designs were manufactured and where they were made. That, and getting to see them make the kind of splash that they have. I tell her about Milenka's attack and how she's trying to steal the company from me out of spite when it really isn't just my company at all. I tell her you're the same Jeff Land who plays drums for Whack Job and critics say has a voice that will tear your heart out. A story like that will be a bigger deal than anything she printed the first time. I'll go down in flames but Milenka will go down in even hotter flames and Jeff Land, rock star design genius, will rise phoenix-like from the ashes. You'll be huge."

Jeff took too big a slug of his wine and closed his eyes, head swimming. "Whoa," he murmured. "Why do I believe you're fucking serious about this?"

"I've been wracking my brain over the past three days and it's the only sure-fire strategy I can think of," she said. "I think I can probably get my mom to float us the next ten mil we need to get us into a bigger factory."

He opened his eyes again at that. "Us? You were just talking about falling on your sword for me."

"That doesn't mean I can't help put Humpty back together again. I like to think I've gotten pretty good at this whole product launch and promotion thing. That, and overseeing our day-to-day operations. Nothing would stop me from still being your business partner and doing all of that."

"But meanwhile, Milenka still takes control of Brocking Chair and can continue to manufacture the pieces we already have in our product line, right? We'd be starting from scratch again."

He saw a caginess sneak into her expression that he hadn't seen a moment ago.

"Not necessarily," she said. "I spent an hour this morning talking to Greg Logan about this and he reminded me of something. I don't know if you remember, but back when we started down this road he had us apply for design patents for all of our products."

Jeff had some recollection of that. Greg had explained that without patent protection other companies could produce knock-off versions, cut quality corners, and pump them into the marketplace for any amount of money they wanted to charge for them.

"Okaaay," he said. "But then wouldn't Milenka still control those patents?"

Amy smiled while reaching for the bottle to pour them more wine. "That's just the thing. Greg tells me that we, as in you and I, control those patents because we are the entity that owns them. And as long as we're still in control of the company we have the right to license anyone we want to produce them. Worded correctly, that agreement could even prevent Brocking Chair from producing them if we assign exclusive rights to someone else."

"Why couldn't we just sell them?" Jeff asked.

"Greg says we'd have to do that at actual market value or Milenka could sue us for fraud. This way she'll be taking control of an empty shell without anything to manufacture."

Jeff took a deep breath, looking around at that throng of revelers crowding the lounge, everyone dressed in cutting-edge after-ski wear while he wore jeans, his green Wellies, and a heavy Aran sweater he'd found at his favorite Upper East Side thrift store. Those people all lived a galaxy removed from where he sat at that moment. "Can we lease our whole plant to that other entity, too?" he asked.

Amy clicked her glass with his. "Now you're getting my drift, Prodigy-guy. As long as we write those contracts and get them signed and sealed before Milenka can break the clause in our agreement with dad, Greg says we'll be good to go."

"Wait a sec. Did I just get upgraded from boy to guy?"

She continued to smile, the flames from that pit dancing reflected in those incredible green eyes. They'd been missing that light when he'd greeted her outside the train station that afternoon, but had since caught fire again.

"Yeah, I think you just did," she said.

THIRTY

Even though they'd worked practically shoulder-to-shoulder for two years and she'd once gone so far as to suggest he might want to temporarily move into her place in SoHo, the time that Amy spent with Jeff their first night and day in Stratton felt much more intimate to her than any of those other interactions with him had been. After their session by the fire pit in the hotel lounge and the talk they had there, she retired to her room emotionally spent. Eager to get an early jump on breakfast and a whole day of skiing, she'd hit the hay at ten o'clock.

The next morning she was mightily surprised when Jeff proved to be an even better skier than he'd claimed to be. Even after a three-year layoff she was still much better than just pretty good and she spent all day wearing herself slick just trying to keep up with him. She'd had too many days on the slopes ruined by friends who just didn't have the skill to make skiing with them any fun, but once Jeff dropped out of a lift chair he did everything balls-to-the-wall. Not only an awesome technician, he was also a total blast. Part of it might have owed to the fact that Stratton was his go-to mountain and he knew it like the back of his hand. But even more of the fun stemmed from how he'd challenged her to take that tiny little extra risk, to dig in her edges at just a slightly steeper angle and accelerate out of every turn with inertia similar to being shot from a cannon. As sessions went, it was as exhilarating as any she'd ever had.

That evening she'd used the concierge service connected to her Centurion card again to get them a reservation at one of the nicest restaurants in Stratton Village. The place was jammed and service was understandably slow, but neither of them cared. They had an excellent bottle of wine—Jeff bowing to her greater expertise in that realm and asking her to choose—and a nice dinner once it eventually arrived.

They were walking back to where he'd parked his car when Amy brought up something that had been at the back her mind ever since she'd first spotted him in that crowd at the Pawling train station yesterday.

"Other than telling me that she landed safely in San Diego and has a great sublet near the beach, you haven't talked at all about how you're feeling since putting Patty on that plane," she said. "I know it's been less than a week, but how are you doing?"

She'd expected to see some measure of pain in his eyes when he looked over at her but there was none. Maybe just a hint of sadness.

"Patty and I weren't ever the kind of item you seem to assume we were," he said. "For sure, we were more than just friends, but we never saw each other as soul mates. We both really like each other and dug the conversations we could have. But it's not like either of us was ever smitten." He paused to think about what he'd just said, the golden glow of holiday lights wrapping every light standard on that main drag soft on his face. Then he nodded like he was satisfied with the truth of it. "More than any age gap, there's always been an awareness of how we're on such totally different life paths," he continued. "That's probably been the biggest factor for why things between us have always stayed so uncomplicated."

What he'd just said might have seemed cavalier and even insensitive coming from many men but for some reason, coming from him it didn't. At least not in that current context. It felt to Amy like he was just stating simple facts.

"Considering the kind of romantic meat-grinder I've been through lately, that sounds almost refreshing," she said.

He reached to take her gloved hand and thread it through the crook of his arm. "You know what she said to me before she left? She told me that she thought you and I were meant for each other and that we need to get on with it."

She found herself chuckling at that. "Believe it or not, she said pretty much the same thing to me," she said. "We had lunch right after she found out the job in San Diego had come through. A lot was said that day."

She had no idea what she was doing right then, walking down the middle of a sidewalk in Stratton Village, the street and storefronts decorated like in one of those stupid Christmas movies, and feeling the proximate warmth of this amazing man who felt like a mixture of kid brother, creative genius, reckless rock & roll bad-boy, and trusted partner all rolled into one confusing package. A guy who was four years younger than her but a thousand years older in his cool and irritatingly pragmatic mind. One who never seemed to question who she was or what her motivations were and who had always treated her like an equal.

She opened her mouth to say something but before she could, he raised a gloved index finger to his lips. The same twinkle of intrigue she'd seen in his eyes earlier when he'd lifted his wine glass to her over dinner was there again. The effect it had on her was maddening.

"One thing I discovered the first day I met Patty is that, when it comes to human behavior, she always seems to be right. I think it's a Cultural Anthropologist thing," he said.

"And you think what she said about us is right?" she asked.

"I think that night you grabbed my bare ass and I got my first whiff of you, I might have gone with you to a coal-walking ceremony if you'd asked me," he said. "It was probably the eyes."

Unable to help herself, she broke into a broad smile. "It seems like I pretty much did. How are your feet?"

"Not as cold as they were back when you said you thought I should move into your place for a while. More warm and toasty now."

She laughed. "And that's a good sign, no?"

"That, and the fact that we ski really fucking well together. When we get back to our suite, I think we should have room service send up a bottle of Champagne and celebrate all that."

☉☉☉

By the time the Champagne was gone and Jeff found himself lying exhausted with Amy's beautiful ass spooned hard up against his spent member, Stratton Mountain lit brightly outside the balcony off her room, many things left unspoken for the past two years had been spoken, sometimes in words and sometimes not. For the first time in his life, he'd made love to a woman with whom he believed he might actually be in love. And while his sexual experiences were broad for a man of just twenty-three, his familiarity with that other realm was not. And what a difference seemed to exist between those two worlds. Never in his life had he ever found himself so absolutely lost in another human being, so much so that for an ecstatic, indeterminate stretch of time he'd become as much Amy as he was Jeff and had felt that same sense of communion flowing back through her to him. She'd glowed. She'd become the most beautiful thing he'd ever touched. He'd ached with the pure joy of it and for the first time in his life he believed he might have seen God.

The two of them slept like the dead and woke to the early morning with sun streaming in from low over the Green Mountain peaks to the East. Jeff found Amy watching him when he opened his eyes and saw something akin to wonder there.

"Morning," he murmured. "How long you been awake?"

"Ten minutes? I've been splitting my time since, thinking about how awesome last night was and coffee."

He reached out a hand beneath the bedclothes, running it slowly across the contours of a thigh, hip and down into the valley of her waist. "Yep. You're really real and not some amazing dream I just had." He felt his penis stir. "What are your energy levels like right now?" he asked.

"If you're asking if I want to fuck again, yes please. You're not just a design genius. It turns out you're a magician in the sack, too. But I should probably take a shower and get a caffeine infusion first if you want me at my best."

He hooked her waist with that hand to drag her closer. "If you want to wash away all that good shit I'm smelling right now, something tells me you seriously undervalue the power of pheromones. And screw the coffee."

THIRTY-ONE

They didn't make it back onto the slopes until early afternoon after consuming a languorously slow and relaxed room-service breakfast and numerous cups of coffee. A four-inch layer of new powder had arrived overnight and once again, the skiing was excellent. That evening they opted to wander out for burgers and beer at a crowded bar in the village rather than do another upscale dinner. There, they'd lucked into a table by a crackling hearth. Once his bacon-cheeseburger was ravenously consumed, Jeff picked at his French fries a moment before bringing up a subject still very much on his mind.

"I've been thinking about one part of your latest survival strategy that I don't think I can agree with," he said. "For us to succeed in a new venture, it isn't necessary for you to tell the world that those designs are actually mine instead of yours. I think there's another way of attacking Milenka without you needing to commit Hari-kari."

Amy looked back at him, her expression confused. "What other way?" she asked. "I can't see one."

"Instead of trying to pull an end-around, we attack her head-on. Find a writer like the one who wrote that article for Vanity Fair and tell them our whole story, only in this version shade the design-credit truth only a little bit. You can admit that those concepts are actually a collaborative effort between you and me and we chose to go public with just you in the spotlight because contemporary society doesn't have an interest in championing anything created by a straight white male anymore. On my side, I can say that Whack Job's big break-out is already putting me in the limelight and I don't want to blur those lines and steal any of your thunder in the process. We could spin it as a post-postmodernist power couple story. Two kids who met while studying design at Parsons who've hatched the New-American dream. A dream that's now under attack from someone with interest in nothing but grubbing for money."

Amy sat staring at him for a long moment before finally opening her mouth to speak. "That was quite the speech," she said.

"Do you think we could actually pull something like that off?"

"I'm the fucking lead singer for Whack Job. You're the winner of a handful of prestigious international design awards. In the eyes of the world, we're both sort of celebrities now. Will Vanity Fair want to do a story like that? Fucking-A they will. With a picture of the two of us standing together on our production floor, with more pictures of Milenka, your father and an aerial shot of that monstrosity of a house in East Hampton to accompany a story about a jealous step-mother engaging in a bitter campaign to steal her step-daughter's dream? All of it against her tragically dead billionaire husband's will? That's fairytale shit. Their readership will want to crucify her."

Amy drained her beer and signaled their server for another round. "I'm afraid you've watched too many movies like Erin Brockovich and Spotlight," she said. "When your adversary has a billion dollars backing her play, the outcome you're hoping for usually doesn't happen like that. Not in the real world. My dad didn't get where he did by rolling over when he got a little bad press. And Milenka? She learned from the master. Her lawyers will try to squash us like a couple of pesky bugs."

Jeff agreed that Milenka would try to do exactly that. "But a judge will read that article and then have to make a very public call about whether to strike down that clause in our contract or not. A judge who has to worry about his political future and whether or not he can get re-elected."

"But what if he does it anyway?" she asked. "Are we willing to risk everything on one roll of the dice?"

Jeff had thought of that, too. "I don't think we have to," he said. "We still go ahead with those design patent licensing contracts and keep them in our back pockets, along with the possibility of you falling on your sword. If we lose the first round in court and exhaust every avenue of appeal, we can always bite the bullet and play your trump card."

She smiled. "So, my public humiliation in the eyes of the design world is our trump card, huh?"

"One I seriously doubt we'll ever need to play," he said. Why didn't he feel more confident just now as he said it than he had while mapping that strategy out in his head?

"Have you come up with a brand name for this new entity we'll need to create?" she asked. "The one we're going to license everything to?"

"How about Brockland?" he asked. "I noticed last night how much you seem to like being on top."

◎◎◎

Katya was still trying to square how much she wanted to help her mother screw over her half-sister with the idea of moving to a dirty port city on the Black Sea while they set her mother's plan in motion. At least legally, they wouldn't have the green light to go ahead with her scheme until a State Supreme Court judge ruled in their favor, but Milenka had already purchased examples of those Venus and David chairs and every newer Brocking Chair product currently being offered and since air-freighted them to Vasilev Industries to be disassembled, assessed, and precisely duplicated in one of their factories. Meanwhile, her legal team was advising that it would probably take them a month to procure a court date with a sympathetic judge. More delay might be involved if Amy decided to take any unfavorable ruling against her to the State Court of Appeals. By the time that last hurdle was finally crossed, Milenka had planned it that Kosta Vasilev would jump directly into production and start shipping orders.

Katya had just returned from lunch with several of her old high school friends when her mother found her in the parlor, pouring peach schnaps into a cocktail shaker.

"What is this you are making?"

"Sex on the Beach. Want one?"

"How many is that for you?"

Katya shook and poured, then took a tentative sip to make sure she'd achieved the correct balance of orange and cranberry juice. "Three in town. This will be my fourth."

"It is only three o'clock."

"But it's also the week between Christmas and New Year's

and if I was in Tulum like I should be, I'd probably be on my fifth or sixth by now. Instead, I'm planning what I need to pack for a trip to fucking Varna. Gimme a break, Mother."

Milenka was smart enough to change the subject before her challenge escalated and turned into something nasty. She knew all too well that Katya could still decide to dig in her heels, refuse to go, and put her whole diabolical scheme in jeopardy. "My Uncle Olek he tells me he manages to find you a nice apartment on the Black Sea. Two bedrooms, two-bathrooms on eighth floor, with Jacuzzi tub and sauna. On the beach in district with the best nightclubs and bars."

"Too bad I'm not into Bulgarian men and think most of the rich girls I've met there are bitches," Katya grumbled. "I know you're trying to sugar-coat this trip but please don't. I'm doing this for the same reason you are. I want to see Amy fall on her fucking face."

There were few times in her life when Katya had actually stopped for a moment and asked herself why she hated her half-sister so much as she did, for any reason other than that Milenka had planted that seed from the first moment she'd latched onto her tit. Throughout her childhood, her mother's loathing had become ingrained in her as well, Milenka never failing to mention some lavish gift her father had bestowed on her sister and thereby cultivating a jealousy that had eaten into Katya's soul like battery acid. But now, whenever she paused to ask herself what was really wrong with Amy, a deep sense of jealousy always surfaced to block any rational perspective she might otherwise have. In the face of it there were too many things she knew deep-down that she could never bring close enough to the surface to ever give them proper scrutiny. Amy had been a better student all the way through school, probably because she was just plain smarter. She was seven inches taller and had legs and a butt every bit as good as her own. And even though men everywhere seemed to find Katya in all her splendid voluptuousness plenty appealing, she knew that if Amy ever chose to try as hard as she did, she might well be her equal in that department, too. It made her want to scratch the bitch's eyes out.

"I am only trying to help you make the best of this," Milenka said. "When we are up and running, this extra five million dollars you get every year will make the sacrifice you make now much easier to swallow." The promise of those sizable paydays was at least as much motivation for Katya as her jealous hatred. The seven years that stretched between then and when she would turn thirty seemed like an eternity to her.

"Try to keep your eyes on the prize, Baby Girl. Believe me, it is the strategy that helped me through the twenty-three years I spend married to your father. With any luck, your ship will come in much sooner than mine finally did."

THIRTY-TWO

The author of that first *Vanity Fair* cover article about new women entrepreneurs currently making a splash in the American business world loved the Hera, jealous mother of Greek mythology, aspect of Amy and Jeff's story even more than she liked their ambition to bring back a dying tradition of quality American manufacturing. She was also a big fan of Whack Job and Jeff's vocals in particular. The notion that he and Amy were a sort of contemporary version of Charles and Ray Eames, the couple responsible for the creation of some iconic furniture from the mid-Twentieth Century, didn't hurt her enthusiasm for their story, either.

Milenka Brock's lawyers had within just that past week introduced their petition to the New York State Supreme Court when that new article appeared in *Vanity Fair's* February issue. A photograph of Amy and Jeff was featured on the magazine's cover over one of the juiciest tag lines either of them had ever read:

Bitter Grows the Jealous Seed: How an Evil Step-Mother Has Conspired to Steal the Made-in-America Dream of Heiress Amy Brock and Whack Job Lead-Singer, Jeff Land.

As expose's went, the impact of the article was everything they'd hoped for and then some. People across America who had never heard of Brocking Chair suddenly wanted something they made. Orders, especially for those Venus and David chairs, went through the roof. And while it shouldn't have affected any legal decision handed down by a supposedly neutral judge hearing Milenka Brock's petition, the language of his denial made it apparent that it had. He or at least one of his clerks seemed to have been significantly swayed by it.

Meanwhile, Greg Logan had pressed ahead to ensure that all of their design patent applications were up to date and Amy and Jeff had begun looking in earnest for an expansion site somewhere in the New York metro-area.

The evening that the judge handed down his verdict they headed for Carolibbean to celebrate. With the cork popped on a bottle of Champagne and their glasses full, Amy raised hers in toast.

"Damn, Prodigy Guy. You don't know what a relief this is."

Jeff grinned. "Actually, I think I do. Not that we don't still have a shit-ton of work to do. I'm sorry that so much of it will fall into your lap."

Whack Job's second album had been released to good reviews two weeks earlier and Ardent had announced the dates of their first limited-performance national tour in the face of heavy streaming demand, starting with an appearance at the South-By-Southwest festival in Austin in mid-March. From there they would fly to the west coast to play San Diego, Los Angeles, San Francisco and Seattle before moving on to Denver, Chicago, Boston, Atlanta and finally, Nashville. All-in-all, Jeff would be gone from New York for two weeks, an inconvenient amount of time when they desperately needed to find a new factory location and start building it out, the old one now bursting at its seams.

"We've still got another few weeks to find a building," Amy said. "Once we do, I can handle the lease stuff and get our production team working on implementing the plan you've already put together."

Her mother had agreed to float them a bridge loan of twenty million dollars; enough to get them over that next financial hump. Jeff had followed those negotiations, in which Amy's financial-planner step-father had proven himself a proprietary dick by initially claiming he was trying to protect his wife's welfare by contending the loan was too risky.

"How badly did the asshole get us on the interest?" he asked.

"Five percent over prime, which is about what you'd get on a used car loan with sketchy credit. That should give us plenty of incentive to pay it off as fast as possible. At least I got him to agree to no pre-payment penalties if we do."

"After this tour, I should have a nice chunk of my own to throw into the kitty," he said. "What are we carrying in accounts receivables right now?"

"Due in the next thirty days? Close to ten million. But we'll need a big chunk of that for salaries and other operating expenses. Still, with orders coming in the way they are right now, it looks like we can count on some seriously decent cash-flow for the foreseeable future."

Whack Job

Jeff touched his glass to hers for a second time before he drank. "I wonder where Milenka is right now. I only can guess how she must be feeling."

"I guarantee she's having a cow. Greg is asking the court to subpoena the books of daddy's merchant banking fund for the time since she assumed stewardship of it."

Still not a business guy, Jeff understood very little of how the financial mechanics of anything so large as a billion-dollar merchant banking fund actually worked. "What could they show?" he asked.

"We'll see. Four months ago she was stupid enough to tell me she planned to take control of Brocking Chair and move our production somewhere offshore. I know the fund's controller. He tells me she's used funds from it to foot the bill for Katya to visit Sofia and Varna on so-called company business. She made her first trip there in November. Milenka's family has strong political ties in Bulgaria, so I imagine she's been working them to get whatever she needs."

"So, what? She spent funds on pure spec without board approval?" Jeff asked.

Amy nodded. "Which means she could be in serious hot water." She wore one of her smug, knowing expressions now. "None of the staff at the East Hampton house likes her any more than I do. I talked to Hector, the family driver. He tells me that he drove Katya and two suitcases to Gabreski Airport in West Hampton just after the first of the year and put her on a private jet. Nobody at the house has seen her since."

"Wow. So, if Milenka sent Katya to Bulgaria again to help lay the nuts-and-bolts groundwork for this, that can only mean she figured it was already a done-deal."

"And probably spent God-only-knows how much to get the ball rolling over there. I'm not sure how far they can get without our manufacturing specs, but I imagine they could still secure the necessary space and start hiring key people."

"They wouldn't need the specs," Jeff said. "All they'd have to do is get their hands on all our offerings and have their engineers tear them apart. How do you think the Chinese knocked-off the AK-47? I'm pretty sure the Russians didn't send them the blueprints."

She sat back in her chair to stare at him. "So, they could already be setting up manufacturing?"

He shrugged. "Why not? There's nothing to stop them. And if she's misappropriated resources to finance it, that could mean big trouble for her. I assume that's why you want the fund's financials, right?"

"Yep," she agreed. "I can't get her removed as the interim trustee based on a couple of plane rides and some hotel bills, but if she's already spent a lot of money in start-up costs for a project she doesn't have any legal control over? Greg says that as one of daddy's primary heirs, I can sue her for fraud."

◉◉◉

"What do you mean, tell them to stop?" Katya demanded. It was one in the morning in Varna. Her mother was calling her at six PM from New York and while it was late, Katya had snorted copious amounts of coke and was still wide awake after a night of heavy debauchery. The center midfielder from a visiting Italian professional soccer team was currently passed out on the sofa in her living room.

"I mean just what I have said," her mother replied. "Thank your Uncle Olek for the nice apartment, pack your bags and hurry back here. There is a kettle of hot water on the boil."

Having just done another bump, Katya went wide-eyed with comprehension as that additional coke hit her bloodstream, everything suddenly coming clear. "Oh, Jesus, mother. The judge denied your petition."

"Is not over yet," Milenka growled. "I will be fucked if this bitch beats me. Is setback, yes, but only temporary."

Personally, as much as Katya had always wanted to win every fight she chose to pick with her sister, she also knew that there were some where she had the right weapons to bring to bear and some where she simply didn't. With the exception of having had some moderate fun hunting for various morsels of tasty man-meat in the local dance clubs and bars, she'd felt totally out of her depth in Varna. After all, what the hell did she know about furniture manufacture or manufacturing any kind for that matter? Her expertise lay more in the realm of sowing discord and chaos. And now here she was, buzzed half out of her gourd, learning that she'd been on a wild goose chase and was about to suffer some serious embarrassment in the eyes of her mother's family.

"Temporary setback?" she demanded. "What recourse do you think you have? You made a risky call and blew it. I'm pretty sure the trustees of daddy's banking fund aren't going to be happy about the six million you just blew here on bribes. Not without anything to show for it but egg on your face."

"I have not blown anything," her mother insisted. "We must only put this on pause. We can still manufacture knock-offs and make deals with Wayfair and Overstock to flood the market with them."

The crash-course in furniture manufacturing that Katya had just undergone hadn't been a total waste. Presented with a huge amount of information over that past month, she'd managed to absorb maybe ten percent of it. And one thing that she had learned was something about copyright and design patent law.

"You're smoking crack, mother," she snapped. "Flood what market? We might be able to unload some product to the very few Third World countries that don't respect international copyright law, but you can't ship anything to either Europe, America, or most of Asia. Customs in those places would send them all to the nearest scrapyard."

She heard a lot of empty silence at the other end of the call. "Copyrights," her mother eventually said. "What is this nonsense? These are not industrial cranes or bottling machines we talk about. They are fucking chairs."

"And as long as Amy and her partner own the design patents to them, they're the only ones who can legally manufacture them, or license them someone else to do it. It was one of the first things Kosta Vasilev had his people check on. None of those patents has been granted yet, but all of them are pending, which pretty much means the same thing."

There was more dead silence and in it Katya realized just

how half-cocked her mother had actually gone off. "Oh, wow," she murmured. "You really don't know anything about any of this, do you?"

THIRTY-THREE

Milenka Brock's lawyers sought to block Greg Logan's access to those merchant banking fund financials but the shitstorm created by that Vanity Fair expose' seemed to have forced the hand of the State Supreme Court judge hearing the case. In light of what had been written there, he seemed almost as eager as Amy and Jeff to see what malfeasance those records might reveal and ordered them turned over the week that Jeff travelled with Whack Job to Austin to headline at the SXSW festival. Jeff got the call from Amy regarding them while unpacking in his hotel room right after check-in.

"You been swarmed by groupies yet?"

"Not exactly swarmed. We missed the record the Beatles set at Kennedy Airport by maybe ten thousand. But the woman working the front desk was really nice. She gave me a complimentary New York Times print edition."

He heard her chuckle. "Sounds like you've managed to miss yet another of history's gravy trains, white boy. Timing is everything."

"Don't I know it," he said. "I wish you could be here with me, Aim. The food scene in this town is legendary. Our PR person from Ardent got us a table tonight at Franklin Barbeque. During this festival that's like getting a personal audience with the pope. Serious VIP shit."

"Okay, now I am jealous," Amy said. "I've had Aaron Franklin's cookbook for years."

Jeff walked to his window, a cup of lobby coffee in hand, to stare out at the dome of the Texas State Capitol building. The street and sidewalks below were packed with festival goers, the atmosphere alive with anticipation. "I bet you didn't call to talk about smoked brisket," he ventured. "What's up?"

"Those forensic accountants Greg hired just sent him their preliminary report. Since November, Milenka has been elbow-deep in the cookie jar. She's funneled almost ten million in cash into a secret project in Bulgaria and they've traced some of that money to an apartment rented for Katya in Varna, along with some pretty outrageous expenses she's managed to run up while she's there. The rest was paid to executives at a company called Vasilev Industries. You've probably seen some of their shipping containers around the city. Among other things like light armaments, I'm told they also manufacture patio furniture."

Jeff had to marvel at the balls on Milenka Brock. "Sounds like somebody put the cart way before the horse," he said.

"Probably because in her world she's always gotten her way. I doubt she could even imagine she might not succeed at this."

"And all because she and Katya hate how much your dad doted on you. That's kinda fucked-up." Jeff thought about his own dust-up at home over Christmas and wondered if the truly functional family was some sort of Norman Rockwell myth. He couldn't think of anyone he knew who'd had what he might call a normal upbringing, with two rational parents and well-loved and nurtured siblings who all got along. If something like that had ever been a typical part of the social fabric, it appeared to have long-since rotted away.

"So, what next?" he asked.

"I've called for a meeting of the fund's Board of Directors. If they won't force Milenka out and she refuses to step down from her current role, I'm suing them all for fraud."

"Where's Katya now?"

"She could be back in Amagansett and fucking Jason for all I know. The woman is like a bad penny. Not to change the subject, but how does it feel, getting ready to headline at the biggest music festival in America?"

"Pretty much like every other day at the office," he said. "Only my girlfriend isn't here and I kinda miss her."

"Kinda?"

"I only landed two hours ago. Gimme another half a day to really start pining."

She laughed outright at that. "Just remember what Paul Newman used to say," she said.

"And what was that?"

"Why go out for hamburger when you can have steak at home?"

◉◉◉

Whack Job

Katya and her mother had been in an oddly combative place ever since her return from Varna. Faced with their failure to steal Brocking Chair and the new stream of revenue they'd planned on to support their extravagant tastes, and then that banking fund being hit with a subpoena demanding they turn over their financial records for the last two quarters, Milenka was starting to do something that Katya had never seen her do in her entire life. Panic. According to her, if they didn't change some of their most fundamental behaviors, they were in danger of actually going broke.

Rather than air their laundry in public, Milenka had requested the cook prepare them a simple lunch and serve it in the guest cottage. She'd then dismissed him and the rest of the staff for the rest of the afternoon. Katya wasn't fond of barely seared Ahi tuna but she ate it just to avoid exacerbating her mother's already foul mood.

"You're going to need to explain this to me in more detail," she said. "Because right now I don't understand what it is you're trying to tell me." She paused to gesture with her fork at their surroundings. The automatic storm shutters covering the big windows facing the Atlantic were run up and the room was flooded with late-winter sunshine. In the distance the ocean sparkled like a blanket of blue velvet sprinkled with diamonds. The carpets and every fixture and stick of furniture in the surrounding rooms had cost a king's ransom and this was just the guest cottage on a fifty-acre East Hampton estate. "Daddy was worth over eight billion dollars. How could we possibly be in danger of going broke?"

"Do you have any idea what the household expense is every year here?" Milenka asked. "The housekeeper, maids, cook, driver, and gardeners, then property taxes, utilities and maintenance? More than five million dollars. Add to this the fees for the apartment in the city, the taxes and upkeep on the Aspen, Palm Beach, and Tumum houses and they are close to eight million. Until your father is declared dead, which can take years, the only money I have is the ten million I am paid for my steward role."

Katya was starting to see the bigger picture. "And after what Amy's accountants have just uncovered, you stand a good chance of losing their vote of confidence. You're afraid they'll force you out."

"Amy has threatened to sue them for control if they do not," Milenka said. "It does not really matter how the Board votes if I lose that."

It wasn't often that Katya was pressed to think with anything approaching nimbleness, at least not in matters more complex than where to find a next bump of coke, and she just wasn't very good at it. "What about daddy's fifty-percent share of Amy's net profits?" she asked. "Aren't you still entitled to those?"

Milenka closed her eyes and slowly shook her head, the edges of her impatience showing. "For now, they are still income for his fund and not mine. Until he is legally dead, they go into trust along with all other income it might accrue. You and me? We will still get our annual allowances for clothing, entertainment and travel, but those are just pin money. Your father paid the household expenses out of his own capital and right now, I do not have access to any of that."

Not blessed with a particularly long attention span, Katya was growing impatient with the direction all this seemed to be heading. "So, what is it that you expect from me?" she asked. "I went to Bulgaria and kissed your family's ass before you even did your due diligence. You're so fucking impulsive, mother."

Katya had no time to duck when her mother suddenly swung at her. She took the full impact as the heel of Milenka's hand caught her flush on the bridge of her nose and felt something give just an instant before blood began to pour down the front of her blouse. When she grabbed at her face in panic, trying to stanch the flow, it leaked from between her fingers.

"You fucking bitch!" she screamed. "You broke my nose! Oh, my God! Call an ambulance!"

THIRTY-FOUR

Jeff had been back from his national tour for a month. Spring had sprung in New York and three weeks earlier he and Amy had signed a lease on a 120,000 square foot single-story industrial building in the Brooklyn Navy Yard. It was a deal sweetened by NYCIDA Industrial Program tax breaks, the NYC Industrial Development Fund, and some Made at the Yard campaign incentives, all created by the City of New York in recent years to encourage a Renaissance in local light manufacturing. America had fallen in love with those Venus and David chairs in particular and orders were up more than triple after that write-up in Vanity Fair. The smaller plant in Long Island City was still cranking out product as fast as it could.

While trying to imagine how the transition from the old plant to the new one was going to play out, Jeff had done a lot of thinking about his and Amy's relationship and how his living situation would be affected. When they'd first started down their current romantic road they were both still jealous of their own personal space. They'd agreed that spending a few nights a week apart, with him in his digs at the plant and her in her SoHo loft, would be a wise means of feeling their way into this being-a-couple thing. Less pressure with more obvious periods designated as times for either work or play. But in the past month those worries had since taken a back-seat to the realization that they genuinely enjoyed spending almost all of their time together, whether working or amusing themselves with lots of sex and exploring each other's quirks. It was with those concerns on his mind that he brought up the subject of their immediate future together while helping prepare dinner one night in early April. Lately, Amy had decided that they were eating out and poorly too often and had launched a healthy cook-at-home campaign. To Jeff's delighted surprise, she'd proven herself a better-than-decent amateur chef especially in the realms of various Asian cuisines, with some really good instincts for how those flavors should go together. In the interest of being useful, he'd turned himself into an adequate sous chef, which mostly meant taking orders from her in the kitchen, stepping and fetching, slicing and dicing, and washing a lot of pots and pans.

"I was looking at the layout plans for our offices in the new place again this afternoon," he said. His current assignment was peeling and cutting butternut squash into one-inch cubes. Lest he lose a finger, he was endeavoring to maintain at least half his focus on the task at hand as he spoke. "I'm wondering what you think about me building another living space there."

Amy paused to glance over at him while softening chopped shallots and garlic in a skillet, wooden spoon in hand. "If, in your pathetically passive-aggressive way, you're asking me what I think about us cohabitating, why not just ask me straight-out?"

Unsure about whether or not he should feel chagrined, he just nodded. "I don't know about you, but for the record, I've noticed I hardly spend any nights at the plant anymore."

"More like none. And you might recall that it was me who once-upon-a-time suggested you could turn my painting studio into a space of your own here. I know that circumstances were different then, but…"

"Is that a yellow light or green?"

She pointed with her spoon. "Keep chopping, scullery boy. If we turn it into a secondary studio for you, we might get a little work out of you while you're free-loading around here. You could still keep your main studio there. If nothing else, it might make a good place for you to hide from any real work during the day."

"I'm thinking about quitting the band," he said.

That one stopped her. To avoid burning her sauté she turned off the flame beneath her pan and turned to face him, spoon hand on her hip. "Why? You love the band."

"That was true when we were less well-known and playing mostly smaller gigs around the city," he said. "I was having a blast back then, but this rock star bullshit? It might sound like an enviable status in theory but the reality is turning out to not really be my bag. For our whole last tour, I mostly found myself missing what you and I do together here and didn't really enjoy the crowds and the hype at all. Tanner and Rick thrive on that shit, but I think even Foster isn't all that crazy about it. He's a bigger introvert than he lets on."

"But your singing," she protested. "It's gotten so good. They wouldn't be the same band without you."

"I've been thinking that if they want, we can probably work out some sort of deal. I could still go into the studio with them and record, and then for their live gigs they could audition two other dudes. One who plays drums and one who can sing."

"You think they might agree to something like that?"

He shrugged. "I'm pretty sure Foster would. Live bands hardly ever sound as good as they do in the studio. These days a lot of them are making money just releasing studio albums and collecting streaming royalties."

"You need to be really sure about this," she cautioned. "I think that you being the star of that show helps balance out your letting me be the star at Brocking Chair."

He finished cubing the squash and used the blade of his knife to scrape it into a stainless-steel bowl. "I don't have any misgivings about what show I'm the star of, babe. You keep treating me the way you do and I don't really give a fuck about much else. I know who I am. I don't need some rock critic's bullshit approval or screaming fans throwing their panties at me to confirm that."

Amy set the spoon down and reached into an overhead cupboard for a bottle of Midleton Irish whiskey and two hi-ball glasses. "A lot just got said there, Prodigy-guy. I think this might call for a drink. How about we wait until we finish with dinner and I scream and throw my panties at you afterward?"

⊙⊙⊙

On the first Tuesday in April, the Board of Directors of Bert Brock's merchant banking fund met and voted to not only strip Milenka of her financial stewardship but also to sue her in civil court for fraud and the recovery of that $10 million she'd spent with misappropriated funds. The Brock property in East Hampton was hit with its annual Suffolk County tax bill later that same week. American Express wrote to inform Milenka that access to all funds charged to either her or Katya's unpaid Centurion black cards had been revoked. The utilities bills for the East Hampton property and the condo in

Trump Tower were overdue and Milenka couldn't make payroll for the house staff or their driver. Because it was less costly to maintain the guest cottage than the main residence, she and Katya both moved into it, taking all of the liquor from the several bars in the big house with them. They were currently running up the balances on the dozen lesser credit cards they owned between them and were still unable to completely rein in their spendthrift ways.

That evening they'd dined out at one of their favorite restaurants in East Hampton village while comparing notes on the direness of their straits.

"I know you still must to have money stashed somewhere," Katya said. "Once we max out our remaining cards, how much longer will that be able to carry us?"

Milenka's eyes narrowed as she stared back at her over the rim of her fourth Gibson. "Carry us? I do not expect to carry you much farther at all, Baby Girl. You are adult now, even if you cannot manage to act like one. How do they call it? Your gravy train? It has just pulled out of the station. It is time for the reality check. When is the last time Jason called you?"

Katya made a face of disgust. "You're kidding, right? In his eyes I'm nothing but a pair of tits."

Milenka smirked. "Given how you dress to feature them, I thought that was all you were in your eyes, too."

Katya scowled while toying with the stem of her Cosmo glass. They'd both had two drinks before dinner and afterwards had ordered two more. It didn't feel like they were near being finished but with a driver no longer in their employ she needed to consider how they were going to get home. Via either Lyft or Uber she supposed. "If you want to continue eating like this and to live with a roof over your head, you need to answer when he calls," her mother continued. "You resent that your body is all he cares about? How does that make him different than any of the other men you have slept with? If I am where you are now, I might see if I can get him to marry me. Men like him are basic. They think the wallet will buy them anything they want. So, make him buy you."

That earned her an impatient, sneering sigh. "I doubt he

and Amy are even divorced yet. And besides, I'm not Jewish."

"Amy converts."

"And how many times do you think his mother will let him get away with that little charade?"

"In seven years you will be worth three billion dollars at least. Jason and his family love money. They will just need to wait a little longer for you to get yours than Amy will, hers. If you hate to live with him, I will help when your father he is declared dead and I get my money."

"Knowing that I'll be good to pay you back, right?" It came out as a sneer.

"We can worry about this later, Baby Girl. I do not know about you, but I have not lived in a house with no electricity. It does not sound like fun. How goes the saying? Desperate times are for desperate measures?"

"I think it's call for," Katya said. "But close enough."

☉☉☉

With construction in the new Navy Yard plant well underway and the old facility still operating at full capacity, money from Brocking Chair accounts receivables was starting to pour in like someone had opened the floodgates. When Amy got a call from her divorce attorney informing her that Jason was suddenly interested in speeding up the process there, she didn't need to wonder what night be up with him. Clearly, he had another woman on his hook. Because she had started Brocking Chair before she was married, her divorce attorney had deemed her interest in the company to be wholly hers, regardless of the fact that New York was an equitable distribution of marital property state. That is what they had been fighting over for the past year-and-a-half, her attorney arguing that unlike the Amagansett house or anything else they'd purchased together as a couple, her company assets had never been comingled. Jason's team had disputed that point and included her co-ownership of her company and nearly a dozen design patents as part of his claim.

She wandered down the mezzanine walkway after taking that

call to find Jeff perched on a stool at the drawing board in his studio. Most contemporary designers had abandoned rendering their initial ideas by hand, opting to do everything digitally, but Jeff was still old school. He loved to draw, contending that his imagination just worked more expansively when he had a pencil in his hand and that he couldn't imagine ever abandoning that first, hand-sketched phase of his process.

"Hey, babe. I just got an interesting call from my divorce gal." Amy flopped onto one of his new Brockstyle 'Air Cloud' loveseats located against the wall perpendicular to where he worked. He had a smudge of pencil lead on his nose when he glanced over. That made her smile.

"What's up there?" he asked.

"Good question. All of a sudden Jason wants to settle. And to get that done he's willing to give up any claims he thinks he has on my Brocking Chair assets and pay me the five hundred grand in equity I put into the Amagansett house."

Jeff set his pencil down and swiveled to face her. "Isn't that everything you asked for in the first place?"

She nodded. "Pretty much. I'm fairly sure the only reason he'd be making an offer like that is so he can be free to marry someone else. I wonder who the lucky girl is this time?"

"I bet our producer at Ardent could find out. Theirs is a small world."

Jeff had worked out a deal with the guys in the band where he would continue to record with them and play out locally but no longer on tour. Twice that past month he'd done pop-up gigs with them at Arlene's to try out new material before a live audience, but had otherwise all-but walked away from the limelight. At least so far as Amy could tell, he seemed completely content with that decision and she frankly loved it. They'd become a couple of low-key SoHo homebodies when they weren't at the plant.

"I don't really care," she said. "But if I know his mother, I doubt it's another shiksa."

"What ever happened to him and Katya?" he asked.

"Like I give a shit? Wipe your nose, you've got pencil lead

on it. I'm still friendly with Agnes, daddy's old executive assistant at Brock, and she tells me that Milenka is in arrears for the East Hampton house property taxes. It gets more interesting considering that he used assets from his merchant banking fund as collateral when he bought that property."

"What's that mean?" he asked.

"It means that the fund is on the hook to pay those taxes if she can't and because they're involved in that fraud lawsuit against her, they might have to evict her and find someone else willing to lease it. If Katya is still living there, that eviction would apply to her, too."

Jeff slid off his stool and reached for his empty coffee mug. "You might want to warn any married friends you have that she's on the loose out there somewhere. Want a coffee?"

Amy rose to wander out with him toward the break-room. "I could take out an ad in the local paper," she said. "Like the county does to warn people of rabid animals in the area."

⊙⊙⊙

They read about the betrothal of Jason Wuthrich to Katya Brock in the Style section of the Sunday New York Times three weeks later. It was a lazy mid-summer weekend morning and they were sprawled on one of the sofas in Amy's loft, reading the paper together, when she held up the article compete with a photograph of the happy couple.

"Wow, I wonder who wrote this," she said. "There's no mention at all of how that skank first fucked him while he was still married to her sister."

Jeff took the page from her to peruse the write-up. In the picture, the happy couple were on a big boat somewhere tropical, her in a sarong and bikini top and him in a Hawaiian shirt, both beaming with umbrella drinks in their hands. "I wonder if there's a clause in her pre-nup that requires her to feature those things in every picture taken of her," he said.

"Interesting how they managed to Photoshop out the fangs," Amy said.

Chuckling, he passed the Style section back to her. "Is there anything actually interesting in there?" he asked. "Like a new chair design or something?"

THIRTY-FIVE

It had been a terrifying and harrowing two-year journey for Bert Brock if ultimately an enlightening one. Close to its end he had begged U.S. State Department officials in Mogadishu, Somalia to keep a lid on the news of his survival until he could return to the quiet safety of his home in New York with his new Ba'Alawiyya Sunni Imam.

After being taken captive while in the company of Saudi Crown Prince Ahmad ibn Abdullah on the fourteenth fairway of the InterContinental Palms Golf Course in central Riyadh, Bert had been forced to witness the other man's beheading in the service bay of a commercial garage and was then smuggled overland the 815 miles to the Yemeni capital city of Saana. There, he'd been held captive for six months of political re-education before he and his new Imam were transported by Somalian pirates across the Gulf of Adan and Arabian Sea to Mogadishu. For the next year-and-a-half he'd studied Sufism at the Somali capital city's Fakr Ad-Din mosque.

Made aware of Bert's survival and sworn to secrecy, the COO of Brock International had flown there in a corporate Gulfstream G-5 jet to collect him and the Imam from the Adan Adde International Airport on the 16th of July, flying with him directly to Gabreski Airport in Westhampton. There, Bert and his Imam were collected by private limousine and transported to his East Hampton house. As they rode, the Imam seemed impressed by the summer lushness of eastern Long Island.

"So, this is where you have lived these many years before our fates brought us together," the Imam said.

"Yes, Imam sahib," Bert replied. "I think you will be very pleased with the lodgings I can offer to you and your pupils at our new madrasa. The property touches the sea." Several thousand hours of intensive study of the Koran and the Arabic language had affected Bert's speech patterns, causing him to speak with more formality and to choose his words with greater precision.

"I expect that our appearance here today will come as something of a shock to this wife and daughter you have spoken of. I know that you foresee difficulty in making them understand the changes that you have undergone. All I can recommend are firmness and patience. Of course, if they refuse to follow you, your laws in America are different than those in my country and they cannot be made to comply with the tenets of your new faith. If they do not, you must divorce this wife. Such is our law."

As he had done countless times over the several weeks since he began preparing for his return to America, Bert thought about Milenka again now. He considered how she had acted for the two decades prior to his abduction, and how unlikely any capitulation on her part actually was. An icicle had a better chance of surviving hell.

"It is fortunate that I can afford to take care of them in a style to which they have become accustomed, or at least within reason," he said. "It would be best if my daughter could be persuaded to marry and to channel some of her more selfish energy into the raising of children. She has a wildness in her of which I am certain you would not approve."

The Imam nodded. "A willful daughter must be brought to heel," he said. "This is what I mean by firmness. You, yourself, have confessed to a certain permissiveness and excessive indulgence that has not served this young woman well. Perhaps you will find a means of sending her to our mosque in Mogadishu for the same re-education you undertook yourself."

Fat chance of that, Bert thought. It would make more sense to just pay Milenka what their pre-nup stipulated and then write her off as a lost cause. Katya, he had no idea what to do with.

☉☉☉

Jason's mother, Rebecca, was more of a stickler regarding the traditions of her Reformed Jewish faith, at least so far as Milenka could tell, while her first husband, Abe, was a pussy hound first, a free-booting capitalist second, and a Jew a distant third. When it had come to choosing a profession that fit his particular personality like a glove, she couldn't imagine anything that might have suited him better than the record business. In it, honesty and honor—unless it was among thieves like him—were just two more words in the dictionary. As soon as he learned that his son had managed to get himself engaged to yet another heir to the Brock International fortune, this one with a much sexier and less brittle mother, he'd packed his bag and flown East to get better acquainted first hand. That was almost two months ago. This current visit was the fifth he'd made to Eastern Long Island since.

On his first trip it had taken Milenka Brock less than two days to sink her hooks; a simple matter of tossing a pussy hound the right hunk of hot, ripe meat; an act of desperation in which she took no particular pride. All men of his ilk were incapable of saying no to a taste-treat like her and under current circumstances, her having to screw the fat fuck a half-dozen times a month hadn't been too steep a price to pay for getting her lights turned back on, property taxes brought up to date, and one housekeeper, her cook, and driver brought back into her employ. Of course, part of that price was the added illusion that she actually enjoyed fucking him and would most likely continue to do so. Once Bert was eventually declared dead, she would have her hands on money of her own again and Abe Wuthrich would become no more than an unfortunate memory.

She was upstairs getting ready for dinner out, Abe downstairs fixing them drinks, when he called up to her.

"Are you expecting anyone? A black Caddy Escalade just pulled into the driveway."

"No," she yelled back. "I wonder how they got the gate code?" She'd just finished fastening the clasp on a delicate little gold neck chain with the single word 'cunt' suspended from it in tiny gold script. It was a recent gift from Abe, who preferred women with foul mouths who liked to talk dirty to him in the sack.

"The fucking gate's prob'ly on the fritz," he hollered. "It's two towel heads in turbans and robes. Don't worry. I'll get rid of 'em. Hustle it up, Sugar Tits. Our reservation's in twenty minutes."

Milenka adjusted her decolletage to better nestled that little gold necklace. The restaurant wait staff would either be appalled or get a kick out of it. That was generally how every experience played out whenever she rolled with Abe.

◉◉◉

The front door to Bert's house was answered not by the housekeeper or another member of his domestic staff but by a fat, deeply-tanned short guy with a shaved head, a ridiculous soul-patch growing beneath his lower lip, and dressed in a tailored beige suit. Bert thought he recognized him but wasn't sure. Wasn't he that horrible record producer cretin who had fathered Amy's husband?

"I beg your pardon, but aren't you Abe Wuthrich?" he asked.

"Better question? Who the fuck are you, Ahmed? And who's this other goat-fucker? I think you got the wrong house."

"That is not possible," Bert replied. Though it had been a while, he felt some of the corporate titan flowing back into his veins. "This house belongs to me. Twenty years ago, I paid thirty-seven million dollars for it."

He watched the rude fat man do the math and saw puzzlement in his eyes.

"I think you gotta be mistaken, pal. This house used to belong to Bert Brock, only it belongs to his widow now 'cuz that asshole is dead."

It was then that Bert heard Milenka's voice for the first time. "Who is it, baby?" It sounded like she was descending the stairs from the second floor.

"You are the one who is mistaken, sir," Bert said. "I am Bertrand Brock, and I am not even close to being dead."

The interloping infidel's eyes narrowed for only an instant before widening to register sudden misgiving. Bert imagined that the eight-inch beard, the turban and the white disdasha robe had been a lot for the buffoon to work his way through.

And then Milenka, turned out like a hotel bar hooker in spike heels and a short, skin-tight dress with a plunging neckline, appeared to stand behind the fat guy and stare open-mouthed at him.

"Hello, Milenka," he said. "You were going out? Perhaps you should cancel your plans and wish your crude friend here a pleasant evening. My Imam and I are thirsty after a long trip. Could you please be kind enough to fetch us a pitcher of water and two glasses? No ice, thank you. We'll meet you in the sunroom. It would appear that we have much to talk about."

◉◉◉

Amy and Jeff were in bed when her phone rang at ten-thirty that evening. Once she rolled over and saw father's name on the caller I.D., she gasped and sat suddenly upright, a look of wide-eyed astonishment on her face as she answered.

"Daddy?" she exclaimed. "Oh, my God! You're alive!"

THIRTY-SIX

"He's at the house in East Hampton," Amy told Jeff. "With his Imam, he says. Whatever that is. He wants me to come out in the morning; says we have a lot to discuss. I don't know where he's been or what happened to him but he talks kind of weird now."

"Weird how?" Jeff was still scrambling to process what he'd just heard and what it might mean. If Bert Brock was alive, everything that Milenka had tried to do to them and their company was likely to come to light. It was highly unlikely that he'd look in favor on the fact that one of his daughters had seduced the other's husband and after forcing an ugly divorce, was now getting ready to marry him. Jeff had only met Bert Brock that one time and didn't know him well enough to predict with any accuracy what his reaction to news like that might be, but he was willing to wager it would likely be explosive.

"His voice is softer and his speech is, I don't know, more formal, I guess. Like he just came back from two years in a monastery."

"You just said he's with his Imam. That's the Muslim version of a guy like a priest or rabbi. Oh, wow. Did he say where he's been all this time?"

She shook her head. "He said he'd tell me everything at breakfast. This is freaking me out, Jeff. I think I need you to come with me."

Jeff didn't know whether to be surprised by that or not. After the night when Milenka had jumped him in the Guest Cottage, Amy had always preferred to deal with her dad in East Hampton one-on-one. "Did he say where your step-mother will be during this reunion?" It was asked with clear trepidation in his voice.

"That's one of the few things he did mention. He told me she's been banished—his exact words—and that he's divorcing her."

Because no mention of helicopters or cars and drivers had been made, Jeff and Amy got up at the crack of dawn to beat Sunday morning beach traffic. It was one of those sultry East Coast July mornings where the overnight temperature hadn't dropped but a handful of degrees from the previous day's high. To make their drive into the unknown more enjoyable, Amy ran the Cabrio's convertible top down and harnessed her hair in one of her trademark bandanas. Jeff had recently decided he was looking a little too much like Kurt Cobain and had his dirty-blond locks shorn short. It was interesting to feel how the wind massaged his scalp like gentle fingers while Amy piloted them at speeds often well in excess of the limit.

"You drive like a maniac," he hollered at her.

"I wouldn't if there was anyone else on the road," she shouted back. "One of the benefits of getting up at four-thirty to drive to East Hampton. Even the cops are asleep."

Once they left the Long Island Expressway at the intersection with State Route 25 to start south towards Riverhead at a more sedate speed, Amy removed her right driving glove and reached over to take Jeff's hand.

"I've got no idea what we're heading into here," she said, "but I have the feeling we should probably fasten our seat belts."

He grunted a laugh. "I buckled mine eighty miles ago. But I know what you mean. And I've been thinking. The State Department has to have known your dad was alive for days now. So why is this the first you're hearing about it? Why wasn't there something on the news?"

"I can think of only one reason for that," she replied. "He didn't want it to be in the news. That's just how much weight he can throw around when he wants to. Don't forget he was playing golf with the next king of Saudi Arabia when he was kidnapped. People in his world breathe a different kind of air."

"If he just sneaked back into the country with no fanfare, what do you think his game is? That he's worried ibn Abdullah's enemies might be his enemies, too?"

Amy shook her head without thinking much about that one. "If that was the case, he'd already be dead. It's not like his kidnappers didn't happen to have a sword handy. I think something else happened."

Jeff hadn't attended Amy's wedding and the only trip he'd ever made to East Hampton had occurred at a time of year when there were no leaves on the trees. Now, the verdant green they encountered shielded from view more than half of what he'd been able to see back then. During that all-too-memorable limo ride that he and Amy had shared back to the city after his first visit, the bigger houses he'd been able to see then were now all but hidden by trees and shrubs in full foliage. The huge main house of the Brock estate wasn't visible at all from the main gate when they arrived.

Amy punched the code into the keypad and looked over at Jeff while they waited for those gates to slowly swing wide.

"I have no idea what goes down next, but I'm really glad you're here with me," she said. "I have this strange feeling that my whole world is about to tilt on its axis."

"Take a deep breath," he said. "Ever since you told me he intends to divorce Milenka I've been thinking nothing but positive thoughts about all this."

They rolled up a driveway that carved a sweeping turn through thick woods to emerge into the bright light of the rising sun. In the middle of a wide stretch of lawn they spied a pair of figures on their knees, facing east and bent forward, their foreheads touching the ground.

"What the fuck?" Amy murmured.

"He said he'd brought his Imam back with him, so maybe he's actually serious about this shit."

Fighting the glare on the windscreen glass, Amy peered hard as they continued to roll forward. "Oh, my God, Jeff. He's got a beard. And he's wearing a fucking turban. Tell me I'm not seeing things."

He smiled and shrugged. "You're not seeing things."

Out of respect for whatever her father and his Imam were up to, they held back, parking and exiting the car as quietly as they could and disappearing around the house to the pool terrace. As soon as they'd pulled up chairs at one of the tables, the housekeeper emerged from the sunroom to ask if they wanted coffee.

"We'd love some," Amy replied. "It looks like dad's not ready to see us yet. We had to leave early to beat traffic."

The housekeeper nodded, the look in her eye philosophical, like there was nothing in that world that could surprise her anymore. "They brung these little rugs with them. Prob'ly to keep from getting grass stains on them white robes. Lordy, I didn't recognize your daddy first-off with all that hair on his face and that turban. Seems he's gone off and joined the A-rabs."

So it would appear, Jeff thought. And he wondered what exactly that might mean. Would Bert Brock still be capable of running Brock International or did being a Muslim even matter in that regard? Arabs ran some of the biggest companies in the world and look at what a guy like Sheik Maktoum had done to Dubai and the United Arab Emirates. They didn't all just drive around in gold-plated Ferraris and live high off their oil proceeds. Some were looking forward into a world with a much-diminished demand for fossil fuels. They were anticipating the end of that gravy train and getting other big things done to compensate for when that day came.

They were on their second cups of coffee and talking about pressing matters in their own business when Amy's dad and his Imam, a short, weathered man of indeterminate age with fierce almost black eyes, eventually put in an appearance.

"You must forgive us for not greeting you on your arrival," Bert said. "We'd only just begun our morning prayers." He extended his right hand to Amy and leaned to kiss her lightly on the cheek. "You look well, my daughter. This is my Imam, Saleh."

The Imam didn't offer his hand but instead kept both clasped at his waist and bowed slightly. "A pleasure, daughter of Bertrand," he said.

Amy turned quickly to indicate Jeff. "We aren't married, but Jeff and I are partners now," she said. "And by that I don't mean just in business. We live together."

Jeff felt her father scrutinize him, those deep blue eyes taking in the sneakers, cargo shorts, the Hawaiian shirt with palm trees and outrigger canoes on it, and then his face. He nodded, maybe a slight hint of amusement twitching the corners of his mouth. It was hard to tell with all that beard.

"You've cut your hair," he said. "It makes you look less like a boy and more like a man. Is this the new fashion for rock musicians?"

"I've backed away from that world a little, Sir," Jeff replied. "With our company growing the way it has, it was hard to maintain my focus on both."

"And you have chosen my daughter's enterprise over your own desires?"

"It's both our enterprise," Amy interjected. "And it's a decision he came to on his own."

Jeff was still trying to get a handle on this new version of Bert Brock; how he spoke and how he now looked directly into his eyes with such penetrating frankness. The old one had been almost dismissive and definitely patronizing. He'd likely only given him any attention at all because he was such an important component of his little girl's dreams.

"Was it ever lucrative, this music you played?"

"More than I ever imagined it would be," Jeff replied. "And to some extent it still is, sir. I don't perform live anymore but I still record with the band, singing and playing drums. My voice has a certain quality that they can't seem to find anywhere else." He saw the Imam perk up at the word drums. In some Muslim sects they were an important part of their ceremony and culture. Maybe he'd unknowingly scored some points there. "Mainly, I'm more content to stay home with your daughter and work on growing our dream together."

Brock turned his gaze on Amy again. "And how is that going?" he asked.

"You mean in spite of the fact that Milenka and Katya have done everything they could to steal it from us?" she asked.

This strange manifestation of Amy's father now got a saddened look in his eyes. "I heard of this just yesterday," he said. "Our COO came to Mogadishu to accompany me home. He briefed me on what has been happening in my absence. Last night when I arrived here, I found your step-mother in the company of your odious former father-in-law. According to the customs of my religion she is no longer my wife. I'm sure that a court with no respect for the laws of Islam or even Judeo-Christian morals will try to make that tearing asunder a bit more difficult for me, but in time I will prevail there as well. It was through the housekeeper that I learned last night of the sordid details of Katya's behavior and your divorce. And for what she has done to you, she will be disowned."

Jeff thought about Amy's comment about the earth being

about to tilt on its axis. So far as he could tell, it just had. Thank God beheading and stoning were illegal in America.

The housekeeper emerged to ask her father if he was ready for her to start preparing breakfast. He said yes, but warned that any sort of pork product was no longer in his diet. He then refocused his attention on Amy.

"Nearly two years ago, after I was forced to witness the execution of the Crown Prince, I was introduced to other ways of life that I had never before considered. The Yemeni men who worked in concert with several disaffected members of the Saudi royal family to abduct the prince left me in Saana with Imam Saleh as a reward for his efforts in trying to moderate the Yemeni conflict between the Sunnis and the militant Houthi Shia there. He is a member of the Ba 'Alawiyya Sufi sect; a kinder and more gentle interpretation of the Prophet Mohammed's teachings. In them, women are more included in their religious lives and they believe, as I also do now, that everything created by man is but an illusion. If you have never read the poet Rumi, I encourage you to do so. He is perhaps the most famous voice of Sufism. His writings are beautiful." He'd turned his eyes to include Jeff in this exchange. "I've brought Imam Saleh here to America to found a Sufi school in East Hampton on this property. I will also live here under his tutelage. You will be welcome to visit any time you wish."

Holy shit, Jeff thought. The man had either gone totally off his rocker or had a rare religious epiphany. And one way or the other, it looked like a lot of things at Brock International were about to change. He could tell that Amy was just as stunned as he was. It was then her turn to surprise him when she spoke next.

"I've read Rumi, Dad. And I agree with you that there's a unique kind of beauty in his words and what he's trying to say to us as people. You probably don't remember this, but back when I was twenty-two, between my graduation in Chicago and my moving here to start school at Parsons, I spent a month in a meditation camp run by a Sufi master in the mountains of northern New Mexico. I'd just broken up with my college boyfriend and was a total mess. I needed to spend time trying to find myself again. The time

I spent at that retreat was the most intense period of self-discovery I've ever undergone."

Jeff was too busy registering his own surprise to notice whether her father was displaying any as well. "You went to a Sufi camp in New Mexico?"

She smiled back at him. "They taught me how to sit in one place with my head empty of outside thoughts for so long that the walls actually started to move and physical things became immaterial. We had these drum circles that lasted for hours on end. Everything but the rhythm of the beat was obliterated from my consciousness."

Jeff was watching the Imam out of the corner of his eye as Amy spoke. A very slight but serene smile had appeared on his stoic face. Then the Imam said, "If you would like to experience those things again, you should come to our school." He turned to Jeff. "You too, man who plays drums. It will open your heart to a new way of seeing this world."

THIRTY-SEVEN

"What difference does it make if he's divorcing you?" Jason Wuthrich asked Milenka. "You've been married to him like, what? Twenty-four years, right?"

"It means that he isn't dead and that billion dollars in his merchant banking fund won't be mine," his prospective mother-in-law replied. "It means I signed a pre-nup that entitles me to ten million measly dollars if he chooses to divorce me before he dies."

Jason's fiancé, Katya, was seated in a chair across the table, a look of sheer panic in her previously glazed-over eyes. She'd been pounding Moscow Mules all afternoon. "He's also threatening to disown me!" she whimpered.

"I assure you, he didn't just threaten," Milenka said. "Somebody told him everything about what happened here two summers ago; that you're the one responsible for Amy and Jason's break-up."

Katya looked plaintively at Jason. "Tell her," she demanded. "Tell her what you told me. That Amy doesn't fuck worth a shit and you would have split with her eventually, anyway."

Jason had his record-producer-deals-with-a-difficult-diva hat on now as he reached to pat the air in a calming gesture. "I said she doesn't fuck like you do, babe. That's not quite the same thing." Damn, the idea of her no longer being the heir to a few billion bucks was coming as a serious blow. The notion of actually marrying her might no longer be on his table, but for the moment the idea of continuing to get blow-jobs from anyone with a set-up as fabulous as hers was enough for him to keep her on the hook, at least for the short haul. "But we need to get back to basics here," he said. He returned to Milenka. "It sounds like you're expecting me to let you stay here until you can get back on your feet. And you expect me to do that, even though my step-mother and the rest of my family knows you've been fucking my father?"

Since she'd arrived there in the middle of last night, Milenka had started to make it a habit of looking panic-stricken. "How do they know this?" she demanded.

"My dad's made like what? Six trips out here over the past

six months and stayed four or five days at a pop? Add to that the fact that you haven't been exactly discreet in how you've carried on. People in their circle visit friends out here all the time."

"That does not prove anything," Milenka protested.

"It doesn't have to. A private detective could do that easily enough. You think my step-mother has never heard of one? All she does is watch Netflix and read Nora Roberts and Mary Higgins Clark novels all day."

Abe Wuthrich had flown back to L.A. in his company jet shortly after meeting some bizarre new version of Bert Brock at Milenka's East Hampton house last night. Milenka had shown up in Amagansett in an Uber four hours later, drunk.

"So, where am I supposed to go?" she asked.

"What's wrong with your apartment in the city? If you're lucky, you'll meet our lunatic ex-prez in the elevator. I'm sure he'd be happy to party with you."

For the first time since he'd asked her to marry him, Jason saw Katya's hackles go up. "Don't talk to my mother that way," she snapped. And then she turned to Milenka. "We'll go over to the house so you can get some of your things and then you can stay here however long it takes. If you want to head into the city instead, I might go with you, just to give this asshole time to figure out what his priorities are." She glared at Jason as she said it. "Maybe he'll spend more of it at the gym and less eating junk food and ice cream while I'm gone. Quick before he ends up looking just like his fat-ass dad."

☉☉☉

Bert Brock had described more of his new dream to Amy and Jeff in the conversation that ensued between them throughout that day; how in the interest of helping a people who had no oil and had been torn by starvation and strife while being violently oppressed by their more fortunate neighbors for the better part of a century, he wanted to turn the Yemeni capital of Saana into an environmental technology mecca. To do that, he planned to dedicate his entire share of Brocking Chair net profits to building a technical university there where people could work to develop alternative energy strategies that would eventually help put their more aggressive neighbors out of business. And meanwhile, he planned to use much of his own money to build huge, bio-sustainable aquaponic farms, solar and wind-powered desalination plants, and passive atmospheric moisture converters to provide the water and food needed to help the people of Yemen become not just self-sufficient but also to thrive.

Sunset was fast approaching when Amy and Jeff eventually said their goodbyes and started back toward the city. Jeff took a deep breath and pushed it out in a whoosh as they sat idling before the big gates, waiting for them to open again.

"Damn. That was one hell of a day," he said. "I'm not sure if your dad is crazy or a born-again holy man… or if there's really any difference."

"He's definitely been through some changes," Amy said. "That's not the same dude who left here two years ago. But you know? Even though some of this new wackiness kinda scares me, I've got to admit I like this new version a lot more than I did the old one."

Jeff didn't have as much to compare it with, but from things she'd told him he was pretty sure he liked this edition better, too. "He sure was intense," he said. "I'm glad you decided to pull the plug when you did. There's only so much of that bigger picture my brain can absorb in one sitting."

"Oh, me, too. And you know, just because we managed to make our escape doesn't mean we have to drive back to the city right now. On a Sunday at this hour in July, the L.I.E. will be a parking lot. I say we find a nice quiet place to have dinner and a glass of wine. After everything dad just laid on us, I can guarantee the conversation won't be boring."

Jeff reached over stroke her bare thigh. "Is it ever?" he asked.

She fed him a look with an almost evil twinkle in her remarkable green eyes. "Want to make it even more interesting?" she asked.

"Uh oh. What are you thinking?"

"There are still some things I need to get from the Amagansett house. Jason e-mailed me last week saying Katya was going to throw them in the garbage if I didn't come get them, soon."

"Why can't they just ship them?"

"They could, but considering all that's happened since last night, and that it's just three miles away, don't you think it might be more fun to drop by and grab them now?"

"You're pretty sure your step-mother will be there, aren't you?"

"Yep. And I'm also pretty sure we'll want to see their faces when the two of us pull into their driveway."

Whack Job

ABOUT THE AUTHOR

Pete O'Brien is an old white guy who resides somewhere in the state of California, where the mostly sunny weather helps bolster his mostly sunny disposition. In recent years it has been explained to him that he is no longer allowed to employ an entire litany of once oft-used words or to "appropriate" characters of any gender experience outside his own. This sometimes seems unreasonable and even unjust to him and so his writing often soldiers into those forbidden realms, forever in pursuit of truth and an authenticity of voice.

Visit him at:
www.peteobrienauthor.com and follow him on Facebook at Pete O'Brien Author and Instagram at @peteobrienauthor

For more Impolitic Press offerings
please visit www.impoliticpress.com

Made in the USA
Las Vegas, NV
27 January 2024